The Satanic Bridegroom

a novel

Joe Gola

ISBN 978-0-9904616-1-6

The following is a work of fiction. Any resemblance to real persons, living, dead or otherwise, is purely coincidental.

Printed in the United States of America on acid-free paper.

Many thanks go out to all those who have offered their help and encouragement along the way, particularly my parents, my wife Lisa, and my son Charlie. Special thanks go to Scott Shapiro, who has been a booster from way back. Very special thanks go to Chris Tannhauser, whose unholy exhortations and lendings of blighted eldritch volumes were instrumental in the revelation of the fell events contained herein.

http://golarama.com

Text edition 1.04

for Frageau

Contents

Foreword

Greetings, seeker!

Enthusiasts of the spectral and bizarre have long been aware of *The Satanic Bridegroom*, the novella written in the early 1920s by Alexander Stirgil. A fine example of the so-called "weird fiction" of the last century, the story has been featured in numerous collections and anthologies over the years, including our own *Tales of the Crepuscule*, first published in 1961 and still in print today. Though perhaps not as well-known as such beloved classics of the genre as *The Coachman in Black* and *Lord Vapor*, *Bridegroom* retains a strong cult following, and curates of the outré continue to pass the story down to new initiates with no signs of slowing or cease.

At least part of the tale's fascination can be attributed to the fact that its history is as strange as its contents. *Bridegroom* is the only known work by Stirgil, an Englishman residing in what was then known as the British Honduras, now Belize. His early life was interesting if somewhat unaccomplished; born in Belize City in 1883 and educated at Cambridge University, Stirgil was sporadically involved in both his family's timber concern and the elite circles of British Honduras society, but otherwise had the reputation of an idler and libertine. He never married or was even engaged, though according to his elder brother, Charles, there were rumors of a prolonged affair with the wife of a family friend while in his twenties. The sole evidence of ambition in those early years seems to have consisted of an unsuccessful attempt to finance the staging of the Offenbach opera *Les contes d'Hoffmann* in Belize City in 1910, a daring production which was to feature an actual wood-and-metal automaton in the role of Olympia.

In the Spring of 1920 Stirgil suffered a catastrophic mental breakdown for reasons which were entirely mysterious; though famously an eccentric, there was no known precipitating cause or prior distress. It was said that Alexander quit his house and took up residence in the branches of a large mangrove tree at the outskirts of town, and that he refused to speak to or even acknowledge former friends and associates. Within a matter of weeks his brother Charles had had him institutionalized, and Alexander spent the better part of a year in a sanitarium. According to his caretakers he suffered from disassociation and delusional paranoia, and it was noted that he had a particular horror for cellars, wells, sewers, and every other kind of underground cavity. His attendants reportedly had to go to great lengths to avoid taking him past staircases leading to the basement level of the asylum, as he would panic and sometimes even attempt to leap out of windows in fear. It was said that on one occasion the patient even tried to hang himself because he had been transferred to a cell which had a noisy warren of rats living in the flooring beneath.

Upon his release in 1921 Alexander Stirgil departed Belize City and reportedly adopted the life of a banana farmer along the Monkey River. Very little information about this period of his life is known today, but Charles Stirgil wrote of a visit to Alexander's plantation in the spring of 1924; he described his brother as stable but impoverished and strange, and he noted that he had taken in a local woman of mixed blood as a mistress. He also reported that Alexander slept armed and alone in a makeshift cupola erected on the roof of his house with nothing

The Satanic Bridegroom

inside but a few blankets and boxes of ammunition. It would be the last he would ever see of his brother; in October of the same year Alexander Stirgil died from an embolism of the brain at the age of forty-one. He was buried alongside his parents in a cemetery on the outskirts of Belize City, his brother to follow him thirty-two years later.

The story does not end there, however. Though Alexander had broken off contact with his society connections following his mental collapse, discovered in his effects after his death was a package inscribed with the name of one Reggie Warwicker, a fellow Belize City socialite known for having vague literary aspirations. The package was delivered, and inside was discovered an untitled manuscript with no explanation or instructions of any kind. Impressed by its strange quality, Warwicker submitted it to the British literary magazine *Satyr Spring* as a kind of posthumous tribute to his late friend. The piece was accepted and was published serially between July 1926 and January 1927 under the fanciful title, "The Satanic Bridegroom," the name chosen by the editor. The novella became an instant success, and it was said to have even gained the notice of occultist luminaries Aleister Crowley and Frederick Leigh Gardner. It was quickly translated into German and published in the pages of *Prana*, where it met with an even more enthusiastic reception than in England. There was even talk of a film version to be directed by the famed Paul Wegener.

It was generally acknowledged that part of the story's odd charm was that it was written in the first person, with Stirgil himself featured as the narrator. However, at that time there was of course no thought that the novella was anything other than a work of fiction, and the more outlandish details of the story were assumed to be some kind of chronicle or consequence of the author's mental breakdown. In particular, the character of "Helen Pulver" was generally supposed to be nothing more than an imaginative romanticist's dream of elusive love. Reggie Warwicker insisted that he did in fact once meet Stirgil traveling out of the city with a young American woman fitting her description, but this was considered to be a tall tale designed to increase the novella's already considerable mystique.

The span of a lifetime passed, and like any other lifetime the story's fame saw its heyday, lulls, comebacks and decline. Fascination with the otherworldly and occult paled and was replaced by the horror film with its twitching zombies and dark bloody basements. Through it all, however, there yet remained keepers of the flame, loyal fans and enthusiasts of weird fiction who passed down dog-eared anthologies to newer, younger devotees to spread the word in turn.

Then, in 2010, a peculiar discovery was made. A young graduate student of literature named Michael Sexton unexpectedly inherited a stack of diaries written by his great-uncle, a successful if somewhat solitary businessman who had spent his early career as a sugar importer in the Caribbean. He found the stories and style of his relation's life appealing, and so in between his own studies he set about working his way through the dusty journals to learn what he could of the earlier generations and days gone by. However, when he reached the account of his uncle's time spent in Cuba in early 1920, he discovered something rather odd: some of the individuals being described had an eerily familiar ring to them; meanwhile, the story that was unfolding was so strange, so inexplicably mysterious, that it seemed as though it could have only come from the pages of some volume of weird fiction.

It was then that the realization hit him with full force: though the names differed, the people he was reading about were the characters from another story—or rather, the characters from another story were being described in his uncle's diaries as though they were real people who had lived ninety years in the past.

Public records were quickly consulted, and it was soon confirmed that the names given in Peter M. Sexton's journals were those of actual individuals—individuals who were not only alive in 1920, but who had traveled to the Caribbean in that year and there met some mysterious fate which altered their lives forever. Even more astonishing, the events related by Sexton would seem to have predated the action in Stirgil's novella by only a few weeks, thus providing a kind of seamless introduction to the story.

Such incredible serendipity must surely be considered unique in the annals of literature, but there is something more: the fact that "Helen Pulver," "Mordecai Seagrave," "Irene Karas," and "Percival Lamb" had walking, breathing counterparts who had trod the real earth that we live in confronts us with an unsettling and perhaps terrifying thought, namely that Alexander Stirgil's *The Satanic Bridegroom* might not be a work of fiction, but rather one of *reportage*.

Presented here for the first time is the complete story— the "true" alongside the "invented." No edits or changes of any kind have been made, except that we have replaced the names given in Peter Sexton's diary with the more familiar pseudonyms provided by Stirgil. At the surviving families' requests, we withhold the real identities of the individuals involved, who are in any case all long deceased. We gratefully thank Mr. Michael Sexton for providing us with his great-uncle's manuscript, and we leave it to the reader to draw his or her own conclusions.

I dedicate this volume to the friends of the occult and the celebrants of the bizarre—those fearless travelers who know all too well that the middle ground between fact and fiction is a broad, twilit country, one full of phantoms and madness, where compasses fail to point and the maps are drawn by a hand that has never been seen. There is more above and beneath this world than is currently known, and it is held together by mystery, and love, and death.

Fiat lux!

Markus K. Owlglass
New Haven, 2013

From the Diaries of Peter M. Sexton

Santiago de Cuba, 1920

Wednesday, March 10

Through my open window I feel the wind that blows across the city night. The gauze curtains flutter crosswise as the breeze wheels round, rushing to the east, carrying with it the stench of the bay. Then it turns again, combing the mountain for scents of leaves and grass. There is arguing in the streets below, and a dog, and somewhere a guitar, and a girl's laughter, bright and hard like chimes. Tonight I feel far from home, farther than ever before, and the sky is new and strange. The stars hang down over the city just a stone's throw away; I look at them and they seem to be the lights of a vanguard fleet from elsewhere, hovering, the travelers silent and unseen, watching from the bows.

Before me is the carved mahogany plain of this writing-desk, my raft, my asylum, my retreat. Everything of importance is here: my pen, my pocket watch, the handbook of the Company, my photograph of Mother, the Bible, coins, rubber bands, glass decanter of rainwater, a lime, this little diary. The desk is heavy and well-made, and of a pleasing size; even the very sound of it, when I rap it with a knuckle, is comforting and deep, the knock of a friend on a chamber door. I rap it again and the dollars ring, Mrs. Liberty and the man with the golden moustache.

Here too, stacked with care, are my volumes of Long-fellow, his translation of the poet Dante and the tales of the other worlds. I had carried them here with me to Cuba in hopes of bettering myself and finally reaching Paradise, but, weary of Purgatory, I keep finding myself turning back to the Inferno. Who can resist peeping at the terrors of that great pit, with its rivers of boiling blood, its midnight cities, the titans in chains, and, at the nadir, the furious bat-winged beast? While wandering among the roster of devils and torments this evening I stumbled across a passage that struck the heart of me, namely that level of Hell where the cheap and greedy roll great weights before them and eternally clash with their neighbors. How much like my life today! I visit the offices of would-be sugar barons and watch scurrying inkstained clerks collide in the halls while hulking red-faced managers scream. Strange correspondences! Cuba today is mad with greed, of that there is no doubt, and if the Fourth Chasm were to be found anywhere on surface Earth surely it must be here. And what part do I play in that? What share of the blame is mine?

Young men in the street now, drunken, crooning, singsong Spanish, a rallentando of Os. From above I only see a brace of straw boaters golden in the lamplight, like a string of coins. The silhouette of the dark Cuban daughter across the way looks down from her bedroom window, fingers touching the glass, but they are already gone.

Ah, so I have strayed from the point, and just as the light of thought threatened to shine on my own affairs. How wriggly we are! No, I will say it: some share of the blame is mine, to be sure. Yes: I am here with the rest. The money beckons. And yet: a man has to make his way in the world and improve his station. He who does not move forward is falling behind; that is what my father said. Dante too is a pragmatic poet, and is forgiving of the man of business, I think. Fortune he describes as a blind and blissful agent in the Divine Machine:

> That she might change at times the empty treasures
> From race to race, from one blood to another,
> Beyond resistance of all human wisdom.

The Satanic Bridegroom

Therefore one people triumphs, and another
Languishes, in pursuance of her judgment
Which hidden is, as in the grass a serpent.

Here, though, is my own small thought to add to Dante's: beyond the fear of the pit there is something else which argues against greed, something which tears away at us in this life, for just as the chiefest sorrow of damnation is to be denied the presence of God, the sorrow of greed is to be denied the presence of thankfulness.

And what am I thankful for? Tonight I am thankful to be in my room, here at my desk, neither sickly full nor tipsy-weary. I had to beg off from yet another dinner with Hal C— of Cuban-American and his noisy flabfaced chummie from United Fruit. I could not take another night of excess for the sake of excess, third-rate champagne poured into the slops like sauce, cigars lit and thrown away. I knew too that they would look on me askance if I once more parted ways with them at the doorstep of their final destination, that place in the alley with the orange-shaded lamps and the vacant, slatternly girls.

No, tonight I dined here in the boarding house instead, or rather I should say I endeavored to dine, for the meal was rough going and an uphill climb. The maid Ayana was effecting a kind of revenge against me for something that had happened this morning: she had come into my room early to undertake some chore while I still lay in bed, and I had scolded her and pushed her back out into the hall like a sack of laundry; after all, she hardly knows what sort of character I might be, and if nothing else there would have been a world of trouble for her if Doña Calvo y López had caught her in my quarters at that hour. So, for doing her the grave disservice of ejecting her from the bedroom of a half-clothed unmarried traveling man, my evening meal of pork chop had been grilled into a crispy bootsole, and it was only for my incisors and youthful vigor that I was able to make headway against my own dinner. Don Peppo, who had become accustomed to receiving the secondbest cut of meat at mealtimes, gave me puzzled and chuckling glances, and he was no doubt wondering how I had fallen so far from favor with the hired help.

And so it was in precisely this awkward state, with my mouth full of dry, intractable pig leather, that something rather extraordinary happened: here in the depths of the Caribbean I heard English being spoken in the adjoining room. A surprise, to be sure! I was at the one moment both delighted by the familiar cadence and on alert for business rivals, but before I could decide on the right attitude of welcome or aloofness an exultant Doña Calvo y López whirled into the room with two young ladies in tow. The Don and I hastily stood in greeting, he silent because of his lack of English and I because of the impenetrable bolus in my mouth, and the Doña hastily introduced her two new American boarders, Miss Pulver and Miss Karas; such was her excitement that she failed to mention that I too was a citizen of the great country to the north. The newcomers politely returned our bows and sat down at the opposite end of the table while Ayana produced place settings and a meal. Our hostess then breezed back out to attend to their rooms, and Don Peppo and I were left alone with the females.

The two young ladies I judged to be in their early twenties, though both had the practiced poise of older women. Their appearance I assumed to be fashionable, if only because it was slightly outrageous: they both wore tube-like sheaths that missed the ankles by several inches and showed off pearl-colored stockings with serpentine archaeopteryx embroidery climbing up into the darkness. Miss Pulver's blonde hair was fixed into rigid, improbable waves, crafted as if by a sculptor's adze, while Miss Karas's black hair was slightly longer and somehow less precise, straying this way and that as it saw fit. Their eyebrows had been all but removed and then reapplied with paint, for reasons which were as unknown and mysterious to me as the comings and goings of Venus and the tides.

Miss Pulver is a beauty, of that there is no question. Her face has an endearing sweetness to it, each element so finely drawn, and beneath the surface I could see gentleness and liveliness mixed in the proportions most pleasing to gentlemen, as sweetness with the salt, each element tiresome without the other but together more than the sum of the parts. Her eyes moved here and there, attending, distant, now hidden beneath lashes, now running and bright. I could see, however, that her mind was worried by some difficulty that weighed upon her, for her brows were knitted and her two white hands were restless, roughly choking her napkin or slowly breaking the back of a spoon.

Miss Karas is the mathematical opposite of Miss Pulver; where Miss Pulver's cheeks are pink and plump, Miss Karas's face is pale and angular. She keeps her mouth tightly closed to hide flat, ungainly teeth which seem too big for her mouth, and, in contrast to the lively eyes of her friend, Miss Karas's eyes seem to slide away from the room, always evasive. Her face has a serious, almost mannish cast, though I would not say that it was unattractive—just unusual. Her voice is flat, artless and matter-of-fact, her speech dry and almost clownishly candid, but somehow I liked her for this, as one might find an awkward child more endearing than a clever one who has already tamed her masters.

I could not help but notice that Miss Pulver had a ring of engagement on her finger, though no accompanying wedding band, whereas Miss Karas was unencumbered by that sort of jewelry.

I had every intention of introducing myself as a fellow countryman the moment that my mouth was cleared of Ayana's cooking, but, apparently assuming that no one could understand them, the two young women suddenly began speaking openly together as they ate, and I was so amazed by the strangeness of their conversation that I held my tongue so that they would continue and I could puzzle out what it was that they were talking about. It was wrong of me, to be sure—I admit it and regret it—but it was purely unpremeditated, for I truly was as if dumbstruck by the very oddness of it all. I will try to set it down as best as I recall it, though I will say that it is easier to remember sense than nonsense, and I may have not perfectly retained some of the more baffling utterances.

It was Miss Karas who had broken the silence: "This underwater city folderol, oh, I can't understand it, Helen. Why would he make up such a story? Surely he must be mad. He ran amok, killed them, drowned them, oh, I don't know. Why on Earth aren't they questioning him further? Isn't it clear that he has *done* something?" She rubbed a spot on the tablecloth with her finger. "There must be money involved in it somehow, that's all it is, the usual baseness."

"Well, which is it, money or the other?" asked Miss Pulver with an edge in her voice (which, I must interject, I found quite musical and pleasant, even in this moment of crossness).

"Oh, I don't know. Both. Or one caused by the other."

Miss Pulver addressed this with cool logic. "First of all, his crew is corroborating his story to a man, and while I don't rule out the possibility that they are all working together for some purpose, even so, in a group of ten or twelve people there will always be one who is greedier than the rest, or one who has more of a conscience, or one who is simply too dim-witted to keep the story straight; it would be a solid miracle if ten men all lied in perfect concert, even for a good purpose. So, I find that far-fetched, to be frank. Second, if he had …"—here she glanced over to see if we were listening, and I hid behind a sip of water—"… you know … *murdered* the others, why bring back Mordecai? Surely he might come to his senses and tell what really happened."

"Poor Mordecai," said Miss Karas. "Poor Seagrave."

Miss Pulver swallowed thickly and blinked, and two teardrops fell from her lashes onto the table before her. "I just don't understand it. It just can't be." At this point there was a loud, honking sob from her quarter, which sent a previously oblivious Don Peppo rummaging through his pockets. I dumbfoundedly proffered a mostly clean hand-kerchief, but the young woman instead accepted a rather tattered one from Ayana, who began fussing over her in Spanish and who even went so far as to stroke the shining blonde hair which was clearly fascinating her. If Miss Pulver minded this imposition, she did not show it, and after collecting herself opened a little purse that had been sitting on her lap and extricated a compact mirror. In the course of digging this item out (I will make no jokes about women and their overloaded handbags) she removed and set aside an unusual object the likes of which I had never seen before.

"Ah, is that it?" asked Miss Karas in something akin to awe, and she took it up and held it in front of her. It was a thick black cylinder, perhaps four inches long and an inch and a half crosswise in diameter; it seemed to be made of stone, though some parts shone like glass, and there was a thick, flat loop on the end, almost like a handle. Beyond this it was devoid of any adornment except for a line or scoring that circled it a half inch from the end opposite the loop. Don Peppo gasped in admiration; he produced a pair of spectacles, leaned across the table, examined it briefly, and then pronounced the word "*obsidiana*" with satisfaction, nodding to each of us in turn. "*De un volcán,*" he added to Miss Karas dramatically. When she gave him a puzzled look he put his finger to his chin, looked at the ceiling, and then performed an elaborate flapping pantomime of an eruption with his hands. "*Un volcán.*"

"Ah," said Miss Karas. "A volcano."

"*Volcano,*" beamed Don Peppo. He repeated the performance for Ayana, who chuckled and frowned at him. Miss Karas then handed the object to Ayana for her examination. Ayana hefted it and looked at every side, then held it at arm's length and studied it with a cocked eyebrow, as if she were uncertain whether it was a thing of any worth. She held it to her breastbone like a pendant, thought for a second, looked at it again, and returned it to Miss Karas with a polite smile. Miss Karas handed it back to Miss Pulver, who put it on the table and regarded it sullenly.

"Do they have volcanoes underwater?" asked Miss Pulver.

"Of course they do, stupid, where do you think Bora Bora came from?"

"Witch," said Pulver. She casually reached under the table and, it would seem, pinched Miss Karas, as the latter squeaked and bounced upon the chair and then glowered at the water jug in silence.

It was at that point that a hired wagon arrived with the young women's traveling cases, and they skipped out to supervise the transfer of their belongings. Weary, bewildered, and gustatorially compromised, I chose that moment to excuse myself and retreat to my room. I lay on my couch listening to the laden tramp of feet up the stairs and wondered about underwater cities; before my mind's eye I saw the face of Helen Pulver, young and bright, and her dark, strange friend. Even now I hear the padding of their feet as they move to and fro, and muffled words like ocean waves float down from above. I feel underwater and alone.

But enough of that. This country is restless, and loitering is forbidden.

Thursday, March 11

Lying in bed last night my thoughts circled around the events of the evening, and I wondered about my new housemates and why two young American women would be in south Cuba talking of madness and murder. My first thought was that Miss Pulver must be the sweetheart of some officer at the American naval base in Guantánamo Bay, but if that were the case, why was she not there instead of here? It was all quite curious. Images of her face and her tears hovered before me until my own weary world closed in and I disappeared into nothing.

The mind works in strange ways, I think, for upon waking this morning I found myself recalling a newspaper article that I had glanced through a couple of days prior; at the time I had been distracted by business affairs and so gave it very little of my attention, but in this morning's idle moments it struck me as being important—capturing my imagination, as it were. It concerned an ill-fated underwater expedition carried out via submarine, and, according to the article, a portion of the scientific team had inexplicably gone missing. How it was that a number of people could disappear while confined to the insides of a sealed underwater vessel was rather a mystery, and as I recall the news item was generating a fair amount of excitement and interest among the local population. I myself would have certainly been intrigued by the affair had it not been for the soaring sugar prices and upcoming political election, which were demanding my attention in a rather more pressing way.

As I dressed myself I let my imagination wander the doomed bathysphere, picturing the smooth metal egg diving into the gloom, until my reveries were disturbed by strange sudden noises from above my head. There were heavy footfalls and thumpings which seemed to adhere to no pattern of ordinary human activity; now it was as if there were a footrace, then a heavy rhythmic squeaking of the floorboards, and next a heavy slam that shook dust from the moldings. And then further sounds of an even more unfathomable purpose.

It was, of course, our new house-mates—the American ladies occupying the third floor—and as I stood listening to the cacophony in amazement it suddenly struck me that these two separate mysteries, the ladies' presence and the underwater disaster, must be somehow related. Had they not mentioned an undersea city and disappearances? Suddenly everything made sense, or at the very least everything became a bit more connected, which had to be some kind of improvement. I descended the stairs feeling that there was an eerie sense of portent in the air.

Ayana had some thankfully edible eggs and leftover pork ready for breakfast, and when I asked her about the early-morning noises from the feminine quarter of the house she informed me with a certain thrilled wonderment that the ladies were engaged in an exercise regimen designed to promote health and beauty. Without a word of warning the girl then began demonstrating one of the purportedly salubrious techniques, raising her arms over her head and swinging up and down at the waist like some kind of pinwheel or out-of-control oil derrick. The display actually somewhat alarming, and I began to feel anxious that the lady of the house would enter the room and be scandalized by the frenetic carryings-on; it was all well and good for wealthy guests to behave like lunatics, but the servants were expected to maintain a certain reserve and decorum. When Ayana began puffing like a bullfrog and performing back-bends I gulped down my coffee and bolted out the door.

I had a luncheon scheduled with the agent Valdes today, and we were to meet in a café near the Plaza de la Libertad, also known as the Plaza of Mars, where men in grave moustaches walked alone or in pairs, oblivious to the radiating blue of the sky, the high white zeppelin clouds casting no shadow. The day was fine and still, the time moving by with typical Caribbean slow fecundity, as though anything could happen but only at its own pace. My skin prickled.

Señor Valdes turned out to be a lean, middle-aged man with a creased brown face and dark, expressive eyes. Though the meeting had been arranged with much apparent enthusiasm by both sides, something must have changed in the intervening time, for as we talked I began to feel that the tide was inexorably turning against me; my attempts to broach the subject of the Cieloverde plantation were met with bluff and digression, and Valdes seemed more inclined to discuss the qualities of the coffee and the waitstaff—the former acceptable, the latter in doubt. Unsure if I were truly being rebuffed or if it were just my companion's nature to be slow to come to the point, I made a stronger push towards the matter at hand, advancing to the very edge of what was permissible to force him to either step forward or back away. As I waited for a response, Valdes looked across the plaza, then back to the table. Time halted. Then he caught sight of the dubious waiter, frowned and signaled him over. An elaborate order was made, a plate of shellfish that was to be seasoned in a very particular way and then garnished with plantains and stewed papaya slices arranged in a interweaving loop at the periphery of the plate, the fruit in an over-under arrangement in the clockwise direction. As the thin, pockmarked steward retreated to the kitchen, Valdes touched his nose gravely and informed me that he would be watching to see how closely the old man would be able to reproduce that for which was asked, for upon this task the very gratuity hung in the balance, so to speak.

The message was clear. It was as though I had been performing on stage and the backdrop had suddenly fallen to the ground, the footlights abruptly snapped off to reveal a darkness of empty seats. An unseen stagehand advanced from the wings and whispered into my ear in a stony workman's voice that not only was the play over, but that the tickets had never been sold.

I sat in stunned silence for a moment, and then I shrugged and made conversation. What else could I do? My companion seemed relieved and became a bit more expansive, perhaps by way of apology. In spite of my professional disappointment, I found myself rather liking the man; he had a warm, busy intelligence to him, and beneath his severe exterior I thought I glimpsed a foxy kind of wit about him. It suddenly occurred to me to broach the subject of the mysterious newspaper article that I had half-read earlier this week, and it turned out that Señor Valdes was an authority on the topic. What follows is the gist of the incident that he related to me.

It had all started some years ago. During the war, the Americans had begun to take an understandable interest in hydrography and the mapping of their surrounding waters, in particular the Caribbean, home not only to their naval base here on Cuba but also to the strategically important

The Satanic Bridegroom

canal in Panama and their new submarine base in Coco Solo. One noteworthy item they had discovered in the course of their watery inquiries was an undersea ridgeline running straight as an arrow from the southwestern tip of Cuba all the way to Belize City, and to demonstrate this terrain Señor Valdes hastily arranged a map composed of silverware and salt cellars, with a creased napkin standing for the ridge. He pointed to a particular point halfway between the soup spoon of the Cuban coast and a jumble of lime seeds representing the Caymans, for it was at precisely this location on the ridge that a promontory was discovered—an underwater mountain or failed island, depending on one's point of view—with the peak of this rocky, miles-wide reef being only some thirty feet below the surface. Even more curious, peculiar animal specimens were seen in the vicinity—unheard-of octopi and new crustaceans—and so the biological department of a *famoso* American university organized a diving expedition to collect specimens. What they discovered was ... *something else*, though no one in Cuba knew what exactly that something else might have been. What *was* known was that another expedition had been undertaken this very month, funded by that same American University, or rather by some of its more well-connected trustees. However, this time around the expedition was not undertaken by divers but rather by an underwater vehicle. What was also known was that the American scientists involved were not biologists but rather experts in human archaea. Had they found the ruins of an ancient civilization, sunken into the sea after some antediluvian earthquake had crumbled its foundations? Perhaps fabled Atlantis itself? Señor Valdes performed a theatrical Latin-American shrug. It seemed the expedition had only found

23

disaster, for—and here Señor Valdes leaned in close and whispered for dramatic effect—*three of the four scientists did not return*, and the one who had made it back was brought to a private hospital in Santiago in some kind of cataleptic state and had not spoken a word to anyone in the five days since. The police had interrogated the submarine crew (though the question of jurisdiction was of course somewhat fuzzy and complicated by the wealth and position of the expedition's backers) but no arrests had been made.

At this point the waiter returned with the platter of mussels, which my companion began examining with the care of an engineer, sniffing shells and checking the undersides of plantains. It was deemed unsatisfactory, and the waiter was informed of the many divergences from his original instructions, but in the end Señor Valdes chose to suffer the inadequate luncheon rather than waste hope on a second attempt, which of course might go just as poorly as the first. The waiter was dismissed, and for his many faults was left with a tip that was merely extravagant instead of princely, after Valdes had demolished the plate with blithe and well-mannered ferocity.

I left the restaurant and wandered the streets in a funk, playing hide and seek with the bay and worming away from the thoughts of defeat and the voyage by sea that would send me home. I lost myself in the white pillars and red clay roofs spilling down to the shore, the slopes and steps, the thin dark faces in doorways, the drays and trolleys, the starched young ladies behind their ironwork gates, sudden lovely dictators with Spanish faces. It was a boon to be lost, a roaming stranger in the wild and beautiful city, a kind of freedom known only in the dreamiest moments of childhood, when we wandered into the meadows and trees looking for arrowheads, hardly speaking, every stick a sword, every deer trail an outlaw highway. I stopped to watch a gang of boys climb a pair of trees; they saw my gaze, warned me to go on my way, told me that they were pirates waiting in ambuscade for a rival band of buccaneers. I asked them if they went to church on Sundays, and grudgingly they admitted that they did. I gave them the coins in my pockets and went on my way. For what is a pirate without treasure?

Later, as I crossed the thoroughfare and rounded a standing streetcar, a colossal square building with an imposing façade caught my eye. It seemed to have an air of ill luck about it, for no idlers sat on the broad steps leading up through the arches, and those who moved in and out scurried like shades. As I looked over its yellowing cornice and eerie blank-eyed windows I realized that this was the very hospital to which Señor Valdes had said that the young American archaeologist had been brought. The unlucky hero of the ill-starred expedition that had baffled Cuba was just behind those walls, perhaps only a few staircases away.

My skin tingled again. Dreamy thoughts of adventure still clung to me like smoke, and it suddenly occurred to me that I could go inside the hospital and try to learn more about the young man, to see if it was in fact the Mordecai Seagrave that the two young ladies had mentioned the night prior. As an American I could pose as a relative of the cataleptic, and I might find out some little piece of information about his condition. Perhaps I might even encounter the winsome Miss Pulver.

I hesitated a moment more and then strode forward. My mind was a blank; I did not know precisely what I was about, but I went on nonetheless. At the desk I informed a young woman that I was there to see a cousin, Mr. Mordecai Seagrave, all the while feigning a hesitating, apologetic Spanish, as if I were recalling the words from a very great distance, and I pitched my voice to the somber sad church-tones of one who calls at a sickbed. I knew not what to expect, and readied myself for rebuff, but the woman only looked at me with a moment of reciprocated solemnity and then skittered off her chair through the crisscrossing functionaries to an office in the rear. Like an elastic ball she bounced out again, this time with a small, bald, professional man in a doctor's white gown. With extreme courtesy Dr. Segurredad shook my hand and steered me by the arm to the great bustling hallway in the rear.

We walked through a doorway maze of beds and inva-lids, the doctor all the while informing me of the patient's condition in overconfident, incomprehensible English, extrapolating on his technical terms by making odd gestures with his free hand, now fluttering like a caught bird, now moving across an invisible flatness, now still with fingers curled to thumb in quiet. There were shrugs and lip-pursings and brief appeals to the ceiling or what hung above, and then finally he opened a door into a sunlit room and gestured inside. Red rays poured in from the west, and facing the windows was a single bed in which a young man lay. The doctor remained in the doorway as I stepped forward and then withdrew.

The patient was a well-proportioned and handsome young man with a broad, clear face, thick dark hair, and irregular patches of beard growing in tufts along his lip, jowls and chin. Looking at his form as it lay beneath the sheet I could see that his primary vocation must be book-

The Satanic Bridegroom

study and the warehouse of the mind, but that he also had some little bit of athleticism to him as well, perhaps as a rower or a stalwart of some New England track and field team. Nevertheless, he lay slack and still in an odd position, like a rag doll that had rolled off a table onto the floor; his face was tilted away from me to his right while his left arm was thrown back away from him across the bright yellow coverlet. I could see that his eyes were open but that the gaze was as blank as snow, staring off at something which was not there or perhaps anywhere. The lids were unblinking but now and then closed and opened slowly, deliberately, like a lizard on a stone. So this was Mordecai Seagrave.

I watched him for some time, lying still, unheeding, and then I clasped my hands before me and silently asked Christ to help the young man. Quaint as it may seem to some in this modern age, I do believe in the power of intercessory prayer; I have seen some minor miracles in my life, and my mother and grandparents have related as many or more to me from their own times. It requires only a certain sincerity, a concentration of caring and good will, and just this in itself I find to be a worthwhile exercise—a stretching of the empathetic muscles, one might say. Were the prayers to flitter off and be trapped in eaves and trees like shining paper kites, never reaching the ears of God on high, still they would have a purpose and usefulness in the world, for I would be a better man for them. This much I believe.

When I looked down again Seagrave was staring at me, and I started. Had his senses returned? My voice seemed stuck in my throat, and I could not speak. He was clearly looking *at me*, but not as one man looks at another, but rather as an animal might look at a patch of peeling paint or a shadow upon the wall—blank, incurious, beyond. Then he

27

turned away, back to the west and the setting sun, and closed his eyes, slowly, and then opened them again.

It occurred to me then that I had rather much to do, still terribly much to do, and so I departed, eager to leave the inmates to their dinners and to be free to pursue my own.

Friday, March 12

Today I was told a tale so very fantastical I can only try to set it down exactly as I heard it. Thoughts of belief or disbelief I reserve for later.

This morning I found myself at the city library, scanning the American papers for any news regarding the upcoming election, and it occurred to me that I could try to find the article that I had read concerning the expedition of the young gentleman that I visited the night before. With a little help from a wan and sickly librarian I found the correct paper, and I picked apart the story for any new information, but there was very little that I did not already know—scientific expedition, three men lost, one man hospitalized. Then, just as I was about to fold the paper closed and set it aside, I had a moment of electric recognition which nearly made me jump out of my chair. Printed in the paper alongside the story were photographs of the submarine docked in the harbor, and also of the submarine's captain, an ex-American naval officer named Adamski. The picture showed a broad-chested man with dark, sunken eyes, close-cropped hair and a wide handlebars moustache. I realized with a start that I had seen this man in the flesh only the day prior: when I had left the hospital at sundown, I had spotted him loitering outside. His face had struck me because he had looked intense and restless, watching those who entered and exited, and momentarily he fixed me with his stare. Upon his features I could see a kind of gruff manliness grappling with anxiety, as though he were not sure if it were a prudent moment to be afraid, but then he backed away behind a column and began scanning the street again.

Suddenly now this person began to interest me a great deal. No doubt it would be only natural for him to be concerned about young Seagrave's health, but what purpose did lurking around the hospital gates serve? Did he wish to ambush someone going in, perhaps an agent for the backers of the expedition? Was it a question of money? Or was he trying to ambush someone *coming out*, a doctor, or young Seagrave himself? Does he have something to hide? Or, maybe, something to reveal?

Since my successful infiltration into the mental hospital last night I had been fancying myself as something of an amateur adventurer, and so no sooner had I the thought to visit the harbor than I was striding off downhill to the waterfront. I had never seen a submarine before, and if it had not been towed back to wherever it had come from it might yet be down there, bobbing in the bay. Perhaps Captain Adamski would be there with it, and who knew what sort of fascinating secrets were ready to be shared with a sympathetic yet unrelated party such as myself? Little did I know what was in store for me.

The expedition turned out to be an uncomfortably long one; the water's edge is a warren of sheds, piers and plankways, some areas with no apparent access to the land lubber, others guarded by sun-scarred men sipping at old-fashioned pipes through pursed and toothless mouths, a gallonsworth of spittle suddenly crossing your path in a looping squirt as you passed. One white-haired sailor grabbed a pinch of my jacket and demanded to know the country of its manufacture, what specie of ovine supplied the material, what the process for the dyeing. He thought little of me when I had difficulty supplying the answers, and another fire-hose blast of saliva was shot over the rail into the water, dropping itself cleanly into the gap between a young Cuban laddie heaving by in a scull and a bobbing cormorant dreaming of home.

Fed up after what seemed like hours of pounding boardwalk I finally did the sensible thing and gave an urchin a penny to tell me where the *submarino* was. He lit off like a monkey with a fire on its tail, his dirty simian feet clambering up and over every obstacle in his path, and I had to bolt like a fool to keep pace with the little monster. He called back to me, *aquí aquí!* and I imagine it must have been a sight of no small hilarity for the sea dogs watching me, the young man in his fancy jacket and hat leaping across the docks and railings to keep pace with a spry little gutter boy who'd never interfered with clean linen in his life. In no time we picked up more children, all screaming and chasing my leader in a wide flying wedge, and it was a great jolly footrace in the salt air like nothing anyone had ever seen; we were cursed and cheered, with chips of wood and pegs and even empty rum bottles thrown after us in great arcing heaves from afar, but these hitting no one, for in their wake I had acquired some of the exemption from harm that belongs to children and drunks and the very very foolish.

When I could run no more, we were there, and the children lined the rope at the water's edge and looked down on the great metal slug below. At first I could only collapse onto a coil of rope and try to catch my breath, the children obscuring the view like a screen, but after a few moments of gawking they boiled off, holding their noses and looking for new sport. Indeed there was an unfortunate funk or about the place, notable even for the waterfront.

In time I was able to stand again, and I looked down to where the machine was berthed about twenty feet below. What I saw was a gray shadow shaped like an elongated lozenge, with a little fez of a cap in the middle and then a long pole or mast on top of that. There were also awkward-looking metal-and-glass boxes affixed on either side of the deck near where the hat was, and by the coloration I judged that these were recent additions to the machine, perhaps sensitive apparatuses designed for scientific exploration.

After a few minutes of study I came to the realization that it was almost a kind of necessity that the exterior surfaces of submarines be somewhat uninteresting, as this one most certainly was, for they had to be fashioned to avoid both interference from watery turbulence and attention from enemy vessels. This dullness did not deter the more nautically inclined onlookers, however, for there were yet a few enthusiasts who gaped at the thing, despite the fact that the ship had certainly been tied up here for some days now and was not showing any signs of gradually becoming more fascinating.

In time an older gentleman of the seafaring variety took notice of my attention to the ship and struck up a polyglot conversation with me about the marvels of modern engineering—men encased in metal scooting beneath the waves, liquid armored moles, deadly, like the blind gunpowder in the bullet casing, ready and waiting to spark the movement that spits the torpedo out to its final awful flowering. Here the suntanned man made an explosion with his mouth and threw up his hands like a wave. How long before we would have giant undersea cities, encased in metal, lit with electric light, powered by who knows what kind of fuel bubbling away down there, unknown and untapped? Great swaths of soggy sea coal, perhaps? Or how about teams of yoked sperm whales turning millwheels and plowing up the sea bed for crabs and fresh young oysterfruit? There was enough room down there for civilizations to live, all the room in the world, no more bumping elbows with the other countries, each in its own bubble, an end to war (he spat), a new frontier, the next human era. We had already proved that we couldn't get along with each other, that it only took the shortest of shoves to tumble us out of civility and into barbarism, so now it was time for the P.C. age—Post-Christ—and instead we would worship Neptune, the great crushing father that presses in at the bubble and divides us from our enemies. From the cross to the trident: it was the dawning of the Age of Aquarium.

I must confess that I did not much care for that kind of sacrilegious talk, but then again I suspected that there might be dark-hour U-boat memories that weighed upon the sailor's soul and discolored his thinking, and so I did not protest, but only felt a strange, sad empathy for him. By way of extricating myself from his grasp I asked, as innocently as I knew how, where the captain of the ship would be? Certainly it would be instructive to make the acquaintance of a man of such daring and accomplishment. With a touch to his nose the fellow winked and said that since his return from the undersea kingdom the famous Capital Adamski was often seen patronizing a particular cantina out on the road to Siboney, not too rough but not too polite either, and that he had been steadily drinking his fees, perhaps to relieve the sorrow of being back on dry land and out in the open air again.

I thanked him for the information and discourse and took my leave. Meanwhile, however, I had finally realized what had created the terrible stench that I had been smelling all the while; as my eyes adjusted to the dimness of the shadow in which the boat lay, I began to perceive that the submarine was encrusted with strange, ugly creatures, coral and barnacles striping it like rainbow cancers; on every place where feet would not tread the surface was rough and rotten with sea-parasites, and I wondered how it was that a metal ship that was surely still a part of the American Navy only some short time ago had fallen into decrepitude so quickly.

I had no appointments this afternoon so I returned to my room, changed into cooler clothes, and then found a cab to take me up into the hills beyond the city to the east. As the horse climbed, concrete and ironwork gave way to towering palms and shacks of planks and straw, the Sierra Maestras a bluish haze before us like petrifying thunderheads falling to crush the land. I looked at our fellow travelers on the road as we passed and watched as shoes thinned out and disappeared and pant cuffs disintegrated upwards towards the knees. The faces somehow became more alive, however, some sly and laughing and others wary and aggrieved, though still as if searching for an excuse to forgive. One middle-aged man silently threw me a guava as we passed, and this gesture affected me oddly; the tension of the past few weeks and the looming shadow of failure suddenly broke like a wave, collapsing in on itself and scattering into foam. I bit into the fruit and it was sour, but good; I stood up in the cab, ready to throw the man a coin or at least a wave, but he had disappeared.

I had been on this road once before, for upon arriving in Santiago Don Z— had taken me by automobile to San Juan

The Satanic Bridegroom

Hill, considering it symbolic of the good relations between our nations and a sure-fire point of interest for any American familiar with the youthful adventures of the late President Roosevelt. What my guide didn't know beforehand was that there was a celebration taking place that day, and the road was blocked by young women in white dresses who were singing and climbing the hill in a file. We decamped the car and fell in with a couple of stragglers, and they informed us that the procession was in honor of Ms. Katherine Tingley, the famous theosophist who had founded the Raja Yoga school for girls here in Santiago, of which the ladies who marched before us were former students. Our winsome interlocutors explained to us that in addition to science and dancing they were instructed in practical occultism and the Bhagavad Gita, and would frequently spend hours absorbed in mental meditation like Nepalese lamas snoring away on mountaintops. As one of the girls handed me flowers and straightened my necktie, the setting sun firing the delicate brown down on her arm to gold, it occurred to me that never in my life had I seen so much female beauty gathered in one place, and even those with snub noses or pock marks marring their complexions had a kind of inner shine that I found arresting.

No beauties in white gowns were on the road today, however. There was only emptiness, dust and flies, and then there appeared around a bend a large, rambling wooden building with sagging walls; a faded sign identified it as "El Club Huracán," quotation marks included. Negroes in straw hats squatted against the walls while on the porch a group of men played at dominoes and smoked cigars.

I instructed the driver to wait—*quizás una hora o cinco minutos, no sé*—and stepped up the porch and into the cantina. Inside it was like a cave; lowered blinds strained the sunlight to slivers while the heavy air and tobacco smoke ambushed and diffused it. The walls were mostly bare, the failing plaster only occasionally accented by a picture torn from a magazine, but behind the bar hung an elaborate painting of a band of shirtless men with machetes charging a wooden palisade. Like soldiers, the men in the Huracán had established redoubts of their own, one group holding the high ground of the bar while others circled tables or defended nooks. A heavyset barkeep and two women leaned against what was handy and stared at their feet, waiting. Off to the right a solitary man occupied a wide swath of territory, the other patrons at a distance like the edges of a fan; his back was to me but his fair skin and a curled point of moustache jutting beyond a cheek suggested that I had found the person for whom I searched.

I was by now fully enjoying my new role as the daring adventurer, and so I walked up to the bar and loudly ordered a glass of rum, and this in my best American accent. From the corner of my eye I thought I saw the round head off by the wall snap to attention; I took the drink and carried it back towards a table near him and tried to look as unpurposeful as possible. The man watched me with undisguised interest, and at any moment I expected him to speak, but there was nothing, and by the time I had sat down at my table he was again looking down into his drink. Unsure of what to do, I took a sip of the rum and waited. It was sweet, spicy stuff—familiar, almost like I was tasting some essence of the dirt, some tang of local sweat and air, like I was drinking Cuba itself. The alcohol burned through, however, and my eyes watered as I tried to keep from coughing. I sat still, thinking, and the captain—for surely it was he—sat still as well, waiting. Finally I hit upon an idea.

"Excuse me sir, but your face seems very familiar to me, do we perhaps know each other?"

The captain rolled his eyes in my direction, the rest of his body rigid. "Well, mister sir, how do you imagine that we would know each other?" He had a broad chest and the words rumbled out like distant thunder.

"Or perhaps, yes, perhaps it's just that I've seen your face before. A picture, maybe? Is it possible … are you not the famous submarine captain? Are you not just back from a daring scientific expedition? I apologize for being forward, but it sounded like a fascinating story and I simply had to find out if you were the same man."

"I've been in the water a bit," he said, biting into a lime. "You … American. What brings you to Cuba, mister sir?"

I gave him my name. "Business," I said.

"Oh? What is it then? You're a rum smuggler? Sugar man? Tobacco man? Or … some other kind of man?" Here he finally fixed me with his eyes, which drilled into my own with a sudden sharpness.

"Sugar man," I said, which was close enough to the truth. I mentioned the company's name, and his posture relaxed somewhat.

"Well, everybody likes sugar, little tiny babies, and …"—he sucked lime juice off his thumb—"… sweet old ladies, yes they all like sugar. So you're a sugar man. I guess I'm a sailing man. Sit down here with me, then, have some of this sugar." He held out his bottle, and as I sat down at his table he replaced the tiny sip that I had previously removed from my glass. "And speaking of little old ladies.…"

"*Hola, cariño*," came a lathe of a voice, and one of the women from the bar slid a chair next to Captain Adamski and placed her chin on his shoulder. "*¿Quién es el guapo?*" There was a loud scrape and then a chair was next to me as well, the other woman on top of it. I glanced at her; she was about my age, with a face that looked hard though not hateful. There was something catlike in her eyes that unnerved me, but she stared away at some distant corner, graciously granting me an opportunity to look over the skin bared at her bosom, had I wished to take it. Her companion was older and more frightening in countenance, her face a lean doll's mask of pancake makeup and rouge, but she kept up a clownish pantomime of the coquette that softened the terrifying edge of her appearance.

"*Pregúntale. Señor Azúcar.*"

"*Señor Azúcar!*" the women chimed gleefully, and, despite a certain distaste apparent in his face, Captain Adamski filled up the two additional tumblers that had appeared out of nothing. The woman next to me leaned closer, smiling and pressing a knee against my leg. I shifted away. She gave a tiny shrug but stayed close, elbow on table and chin in her hand. Adamski looked at me. "Everybody likes sugar." He downed his drink and poured himself another.

"So, tell me, Captain—may I call you Captain?—what is it like traveling *under* the sea?" I held up my glass in a toast and sipped off a quarter inch of liquor.

The captain shrugged, nearly tossing the older lady perched on his shoulder off her chair. "It's...."

"*Ay, están hablando en inglés. ¡Que aburrido!*" She opened a pinchbeck cigarette case and set about trying to choose which one to smoke.

The Satanic Bridegroom

"... I say, it's—the devil with these sluts, they drink like fish—it's a strange life to be sure. Well, for part of it it's just like being on any other ship, for you know most times you're on top of the water, except of course the crew lose some acquaintance with sun and air and develop what you might call a *stoop*," he winked and tried to pinch his lady's cheek, a maneuver which she dodged with the facility of long practice. "It's not ever so roomy inside the vessel, you see, and one needs to learn a great toleration of one's shipmates, or else go a little mad. Sometimes, both. But then again submariners are like brothers ... closer, really ... like brothers who chose to stay in the womb maybe three or four extra years, with just that many extra moons of pardon me and excuse me and if you would be so kind, brother dear. Here, poke that one's belly, see if she has room for two! You can call her Vionaika, by the way, should you choose to call her anything. *Sí, estoy hablando de ti, Vaika.* The vanity of these felines!" He twirled the ends of his moustaches.

"Are you still in the Navy? I mean, are you on leave?"

"No, Mister Sexton"—so he did hear my name after all—"I left the service at the quietus of hostilities." He drank again.

"You fought in the war?"

"I did, sir. Or didn't. We patrolled and escorted here in the Caribbean. We did not find any Germans."

"I imagine the thought of having to fight in one of those things must be ... unsettling, though."

"Unsettling? Not much shoots back at a submarine, so perhaps you could say no, not like the fools on the ground, charging up some hill with nothing between them and the bullets but the buttons on their shirts." He gestured towards the painting that hung over the bar. "But then again the wrong thing happens in a sub and the sides punch through and you're sunk like a stone, and say your prayers loud because by God you'll be saying them through water. Do you know what water pressure is at all, Mister Sexton?"

I told him that I did not.

"Gravity pulls down on the water, squeezes it tight. Air and water don't lie on the earth, they hug it. That's science. So we push our bubble down into the water, and the water pushes back. The deeper you go, the stronger the push. Down a couple hundred feet, it pushes quite hard. Go down too deep, and...." He snapped his fingers.

"What?"

"You get crushed." He leaned forward. "You die."

"Oh. I see."

"And then of course there's the ... moral question." He made a wry sort of grimace.

"The moral question?"

"I suppose sugar men don't have to face too many moral questions. Soldiers and sailors do, though. Now, those men, up on the hill, they knew they were in a battle, they knew what they faced, and they accepted that. That's called being a soldier. Us, though, I mean to say the submariner, we see a little German boat bobbing along, not paying attention, well, we fire, and here are all those sailors not knowing they're even in a fight. Maybe they're playing *schapfkopf*. Maybe they're reading letters from their little fraus and kinder. And do you know how fast a torpedoed boat can sink? I wonder if you know that."

"I do not know that."

"Well, I should not like to be the one to tell you. All I will say is that if you're on a warship and want to have a nap, I suggest you take it in the lifeboat. Drink your rum, sir, for I can't pour you a second while the first still lies in the glass."

I was very much disinclined to have more of the rum but I complied with his wishes nonetheless. This time I could not help coughing out some of the volatile fumes. Vionaika clicked her tongue but Captain Adamski did not comment.

"Well," I said, "I believe that all men must face moral questions, but I take your point. I think, though, that Christ understands that a man must sometimes fight."

"Not fight," said Adamski, "kill. Does Christ understand that a man must sometimes kill? There's a difference, you see."

"Well, I believe ... I mean to say it is my belief...." The rum was already going to my head, and I struggled for the words, but then they rushed out on their own. "You see the picture of Justice, the woman holding the scales and the sword, and she has a kerchief or scarf tied over her eyes, because Justice is blind, a rule in a law book is blind, it doesn't care about circumstances or what's in your heart. But is Christ blind? He is right here! He sits right next to us! What doesn't he see? What doesn't he understand? But," I said to Vionaika, "that also means that he cannot be fooled. You cannot fool Christ."

"*Está hablando de Cristo*," said the other woman, pursing her lips and looking upward in a face of sour sacrosanctity.

"*¡Que mala suerte!*" sighed Vionaika, brushing dust off my sleeve.

"Don't you think that's a bit blasphemous?" asked Adamski.

"Why? What do you mean?"

"Are you trying to tell me that Christ spends his time in saloons?" His laugh rocked the air like a gunshot.

As if on cue, Vionaika suddenly spoke to me in English. "Do you like girls, meester?"

"Why," said Adamski, "do you know any?"

"*¿Qué?*"

Adamski growled into his glass. "I mean to say I only see a couple of old hags." He took another sip and bit a new lime. "Anyway," he said petulantly, "the Germans did it first."

"*¿Qué? ¿Qué?*"

"I'm sorry, I didn't mean to make you speak about matters of such, er, gravity. I just find the topic of submarines very interesting."

"Quite natural," said Adamski. "I do as well."

"For instance, I understand from the newspaper that you just recently captained a scientific expedition."

There was a pause while the captain studied the near-empty bottle of rum. In time he said, simply, "yes, that's true."

"Who supplied the ship? Is it yours?"

Adamski laughed. "Me? Rich enough to own my own submarine? Ha! The underwater pay is not as good as all that. And what would I do with it even if I could buy one? I'd be better off playing with a bucket in the bathtub. No, she's a Navy ship. Decommissioned. C-7."

"Sea seven? You mean … the seventh sea?"

"The letter C and the numeral 7." He drew this with his finger in invisible ink on the table. "That's her name. Formerly U.S.S. Coelecanth. I was her captain then. Used for training out of Coco Solo now, but the Navy leased it to the folks from Argoyle University."

"For the expedition."

"For the expedition. Excuse me for one moment please."

While Captain Adamski was gone I signaled to the bartender and pointed to the empty bottle. Emboldened by the sight of my money, the older woman shouted that we also wanted a plate of crabs. "*¡Cangrejo! ¡Queremos cangrejo!*" For some reason The bar erupted into laughter, and there was some rather rough talk between the painted woman and the rest of the patrons until Captain Adamski returned. I poured him another drink. "So Argoyle University hired you as captain."

"Aye, and together we were able to scrape together a skeleton crew of ex-submariners, or something that passed for that. So, they had their submarine." He silently raised his glass to his former employers.

I leaned across the table. "Captain Adamski," I whispered, "what were you looking for?"

A shadow passed across his face, and suddenly he seemed not himself; the brass and confidence were drained away, and he looked at me with a strange high nervousness, as though flinching away from something. "How should I know?" he finally replied. "I only steer the ship." His glass hung in the air halfway between mouth and table; he seemed unable to move at all.

"Okay, but … let me put it a different way: *what did you find?*"

He sat there still, pinned, almost I would say helpless. "You want to know what we found?"

The words jumped out of my mouth. "Damn it, I do."

He rubbed his face with a thick hand, sank back in his chair, and then told me his story.

Out beyond the peninsula, halfway to the Caymans, there is a peculiar reef, discovered only recently by the U.S. National Oceanic and Atmospheric Administration Commissioned Corps—how's that for a jawbreaker?—in the course of their mappings of our Caribbean here. At that time the seamen on board happened to notice some strange what you call fauna in the vicinity, I mean to say fish and sea animals and what have you. Strange fish, large, primitive-looking, like armor-plated, and not too observant of the boat above, despite having more eyes than is customary for fish, three, sometimes five. Also when they haul up the sea anchor they find a severed arm caught wrapped around it, like an octopus's, though from the size it would have been a big one, bigger than most. This much I heard from the university people, who had caught wind of it somehow and so of course felt that it would reflect well on them as a hall of science and bring them some little measure of fame if they could capture and name a whole barrel of new species all in one go. So, they outfit their entire biology department with all manner of fancy diving equipment and down the fellers go.

Now what do they find? Well, the fishes of course, and some crabs like no one has ever seen, as wide as a railroad tie and striped like tigers. Unfortunately the fish turned out to be a bit too slippery for the eggheads, rather a bit more sly than expected, and there was more of a chance of the crabs catching *them* than the other way around. They had to satisfy themselves with coral and anemones, which were also strange and unheard-of, aggressive little barnacles with razor legs that could leave scoring on steel, or so they said.

But they found more than that. From the surface, the reef is just a shallow patch, not even a danger to ships except in bad weather, but seen from below of course it's a mountain, a peak heaving up from the edge of a great undersea cliff. On the south side it drops down and away to, well, who knows? The abyss as they call it. The bottom of the world. So one of the divers swims over to that side, chasing one of those three-eyed fish I suppose, and, shining his light into the depths, what do you think he sees halfway down the mountainside? He sees a great yawning cave, but not just a cave, no. On either side of the opening, like gateposts, are these two pillars. Obelisks. Cleanly polyhedral, symmetrical, geometrical. What I mean to say is man-made, or else made by a very smart lobster with a plumb line and a chisel. What did it all mean? The ruins of some ancient city, sunken beneath the sea by an earthquake or what have you? The only problem was that the obelisks were too deep for the divers, being one-fifty or two hundred feet below the surface. But not too deep for a submarine.

So, one year later the university people outfitted C-7 with underwater lights and cameras, ones mounted on the outside that could be triggered by a portable radio wave transmitter from within the ship; we were to try to take photographs of the two obelisks and to see what else of interest might be there at the edge of the cave. Down we went, my crew plus Riesling, the engineer from the university who was to snap the photos, and Straworthy, the head of the bunch; the other two cooled their heels up top on the tender that towed us. We made our way using the echolocation device as best we could. There's no windows to look out from in a submarine, you understand! Nobody goes down in a submarine to enjoy the view, you're steering with your brain and your gut, not your eyes. We made it down there, though, almost two hundred feet down, and it was a pretty piece of navigation if I must say so myself. We had ourselves lined up with *something* according to the man at the Fessenden machine—the echolocation device, you understand—so we make any God's number of passes past the place and Riesling snaps a bunch of photos and back up we go. On the surface he dismantles the boxes mounted on the bow and goes off to play in the little darkroom he had set up down in the hold of the tender. We all wait in the galley, playing at cards and listening to the science men talk, and finally at suppertime he comes back out ready to bust his rivets, starts handing out copies of photos to anyone who'll look at them. Sure enough, his jury-rig worked like a charm, and on the few pictures that he happened to snap off at the right moment you could see these pillars plain as day, or at least parts of them. Everything about them had the look of having been hand-carved; they had flat faces and corners, and upon them were carvings like hieroglyphics or hydrogriffins or however it is that you call them. They were not quite letters and not quite pictures, but strange arrangements of wriggling shapes and circles, but somehow meaningful, like you could almost figure out what they meant to say if you stared at them long enough.

There was one other photo he had brought out which at first we ignored but, at his insistence, gradually captured our interest until it eclipsed that of the others; it was taken during what must have been a very close pass (in fact you could say that we had very nearly killed ourselves and not even realized it), and what we were looking at was a photograph taken directly into the mouth of the cavern. What surprised us initially was the roominess of the space, for the cavity did not become smaller as it deepened but, after a short, tunnel-like passage, it apparently broadened and increased in size. There seemed to be a large empty space there just inside the giant reef, the cave walls strangely smooth and regular, and then just at the farthest edge we thought we could make out *a second pair of obelisks*. Then Riesling pointed out something that had particularly piqued his interest: the picture gave a reasonably good view of the top of the cave, and in the open space the end of the tunnel, just at the last reaches of our light, the rocky roof widened and then unaccountably it disappeared and was replaced by a flat, reflective surface, as if it were the skin of a giant bubble. An air pocket!

It didn't take long before one of our university friends wondered aloud about the possibility of steering the submarine into the cave and surfacing—so to speak—at the far end, where the signposts led. Well! I was quick to inform him that this was a rather drawn-out and complicated method of committing suicide, and that surely we could all simply tie rocks around our necks and jump overboard and thus avoid the loss of the submarine and all the other expensive equipment. Seagrave—for I think it was he who had suggested the idea—backed down immediately, saying that of course I knew best and that the safety of the crew was paramount and all of that sort of thing, but the idea had been planted, planted in soil which had already been tilled and made ready by those damnable photos of the carved monuments come from who knows where. I could see the boys in the crew mulling it over, thinking how the adventure might just be possible with a little luck, and truth be told I was thinking the same. Off in corners I could hear them talking of discovering Atlantis—in tones of jest, but at the same time trying on the words for size, practicing, curious to see how they rang in the open air.

The next morning I could see that every man on board had chewed the notion over all night in his bunk and that it was only a matter of time before someone broached the subject. Perhaps a better man would have bellowed at them all, swatted their heads and instructed them to go to hell on their own, for I would not lead them ... but I did not. Looking back on it now, I can see that there was something in me too, some reckless mood that wanted this madness, this all-or-nothing turn of the wheel. For where was I headed, now that I had left the Navy? I'd spent the war patrolling the home front, I was no hero. I was lucky to have even had this job, not to put too fine a point on it, and I chafed at the thought of living out my days tootling along in some miserable steamer, some backwater tug, serving every man but myself. So, when Straworthy asked if it would be possible to risk entry into the tunnel, I said that it would be.

By nine o'clock we had reassembled in the sub, this time with all four university men as passengers, Straworthy, Riesling, Seagrave and Chaplin. We were able to scrape together a fair sort of expeditionary outfit, including lanterns, compasses, a camera, an inflatable rubber raft and even a breathing apparatus should the air in the pocket be unwholesome. The scholars all sat in a huddle up by the torpedo tubes, hugging knees to chests, and we worked as best we could around them. It was no small thing we were about; may I remind you again that there is no window in a submarine, these being at cross-purposes to the necessity of keeping the ocean on the outside. We had only the Fessenden oscillator to guide us, and once we approached the place where we thought our cave lay, any freak current could have pushed us up against the rocks and compromised the ship. Regardless, we moved down the side of the mountain, and then suddenly our man at the headphones says he found an empty space where there once was a solid wall, and we hoped and prayed we had found our cave and not merely some other depression, for otherwise we would be moving directly at the side of a mountain.

We moved forward, as slow as possible, sailors and passengers alike on tenterhooks, expecting at each moment for the walls to stave in and water to come gushing in upon them; I imagine that every man aboard was fighting off a panic, a voice in their head screaming at them to turn back, to give up this mad idea. I stood close by the men at the controls to watch for any sign that they might flinch and throw the boat in reverse. They in turn watched the man listening to the oscillator, whose primary function I think was to alert us should we be about to die. He did not do so however; instead he told us that we were closed in on the sides and clear straight ahead, and so we went forward. Then there was a frightful shout; an obstacle dead ahead. We reversed the engines and the ship slowed to a stop. We had Riesling shine the radio-controlled lights now, and I manned the periscope; slowly we rose, and I watched for any sign of a rocky ceiling coming down to crush us, but there was only emptiness and water. Then we breached a flat, shimmering plane, and I realized that we had done it: the submarine had surfaced—inside a mountain two hundred feet below sea level!

We yet had a terrible risk to take in merely opening the hatch, however, since we had no idea as to whether the air in that pocket was breathable or poisonous; if anything, chances favored the latter, since if the reef had been formed from a volcano, then the trapped gases were likely to have come from deep within the earth and be laced with all manner of vapors and acids. One of the more reckless members of our crew volunteered to open a ventilator and take a sniff. He did so, with the rest of the crew and myself secretly holding our breaths. He reported that the air was stale and had an odor, but it did not burn his nostrils or cause any lightness of head. As a final precaution we struck a match and drew it close to the pipe, since we would have to use lanterns to see in the darkness, and so needed to know if there were any combustible gases without, but the flame only flickered as usual and then guttered out.

Two of my men went topside with a lantern to drop anchor, and I followed soon after, with Straworthy and Seagrave behind me. I had worried earlier that the periscope and conning tower would be pinned against the rocky roof of our cavern, but to my surprise there was only darkness above us; in fact, there seemed to be nothing but darkness—darkness and silence. There was not even the familiar lap lap lap of water against our hull, for the surface was as smooth as glass, and I tell you now that it was as if we had traveled back to chapter one of the Holy Bible, except instead of the spirit of God hovering over the waters, the formless and emptiness, the darkness over the deep, it was our little submarine. Ha! I say it in jest but He knows himself that it is the truth.

We stood there looking about, not knowing precisely what to do, almost afraid to speak, and then, as my eyes became accustomed to the dark, I saw something out there, just at the very edge of the light. I walked out to the farthest tip of the bow, lantern in hand, and turned my face to the unknown, and finally I could see them, those damned things, those pylons, again, upon a faint shining shoreline, with their fairy script carved upon them. It took my breath clean away, I tell you, whether from triumph or awe I cannot say, but my companions soon crowded around and saw the same things too, so they were no mirage. Straworthy began calling for his rubber dinghy and I knew that we were going ashore.

Fifteen minutes later I was paddling in the dark with the four professors and seaman Kine, paddling towards the ghostly monuments floating and bobbing in the darkness before us like a will-o'-the-wisp, if you know what that is. The echoes of our oars passed back and forth over our heads, bounding away and then coming back at odd intervals to frighten us. At one moment we even halted to make sure that there was not indeed two boats, ours and some phantom in pursuit, but there was only ourselves and the submarine and the gate in the darkness.

Finally we struck land, and it made us shudder to do so, for only now did we understand the size of the things that had led us here; they towered over us like two great trees, their tops lost in the dark; I could fit my entire hand into one of the carvings near the base, and I had to stretch myself to the last unfurling of my person just to reach it. My two arms outstretched could only just encompass one side, and the edges and faces were not chipped and marked with pocks like ruins but still had a smoothness to them. No wonder, said Riesling, for what was there to erode it? Not wind nor rain could harm it here. And I tell you I would have no more tried to make a dent in the things than I would kick a sleeping tiger, so there they sat. For a while the university gentleman made sketches of the hydrogriffins and I sat on the ground and watched them, until we heard a yelp from Kine, who had been poking about the surrounding area. What he showed us was that the ground was uneven and rocky where it rose up to the left and right of the gates towards the darkness, but there was a long, wide ribbon of flatness extending from between the pylons and out away from the shore—in other words, a thing that had every appearance of a road, heading off into the darkness.

By this time our scientific friends were on the verge of giddiness, prattling away at each other in their own kind of talk, and before I had a moment to think they had announced their intention of following that road wherever it led, provided it was not over a precipice. I proposed that Kine and I should make camp between the obelisks and await their return, as I did not like the idea of all six of us marching into the darkness and leaving the men on the sub to wonder and worry at themselves. We checked our watches and they agreed that they would return after two hours to report their progress, and then a second expedition would be discussed if we felt it was warranted. After a round of handshakes, Kine and I watched the four depart; there was a slow rise beyond the monuments, but then the ground dipped and wound down into what looked like some kind of valley. There at the top of the ridge there were no obstructions to block the light from their lantern, and so Kine and I watched every step while the men became smaller and smaller, until they were no more than flickering moths before a candle spark. Then Kine and I both gasped together, for the dim distant light now shone upon what looked like a collection of smooth walls and cornered angles. Dwellings?

The Satanic Bridegroom

Then the lantern disappeared behind a shadow and was gone.

Kine and I waited, but there was no more sound or light from the valley. Instead we investigated the immediate surroundings, but found only rocks and empty space, so in time we walked back down to the water and simply sat on the ground and waited. I hallooed back to the ship the best I could, trying to tell them the situation on the shore. I heard a halloo back, but whether they heard all that I had said I was not sure, for the crossfire of echo and counter-echo confused all speech at that distance, though in truth they were really not so very far away. When this was done with, the silence soon became oppressive, and we found ourselves clearing our throats or scuffing our feet just to chase it away. Every once in a long while we would hear what sounded like a far-off sound from the valley, but as soon as it came it was gone. What amazed us both was that through all this we had seen barely any hint of a ceiling; down by the bay (or so I was calling it in my mind by then) I had thought I had seen a far-off shimmering reflection of the light on the water, but here on the shore there was nothing, like a starless sky. I took a walk off to the right and could just see in the lantern glow the side wall rising out of the water, but the rocks simply rose up into darkness, only curving slowly overhead. Repeatedly we went back up to the top of the hill to see if there was any sign of life in the valley beyond, but there was nothing. It was like the cave had swallowed them up.

In time I sent Kine back to the sub in the raft to inform them that it would be some hours' wait and not to worry themselves on our accounts. I gave him instructions to come directly back, and he said that he would, but even so those long minutes of solitude on the banks of that midnight world began to work against my nerves. I fancied that I heard things, muffled bumpings that were at once close by and miles off, but I couldn't be certain they were anything more than my own heart beating in my ears. I paced back and forth like a rat in a cage until finally I saw the little raft detach once again from the sub and make its way back in my direction. I could only stand on the edge of the shore and stare at its coming, so desperate was I for company in that lonely place. I watched and watched. Then, strange to say, as I faced that little boat on its way, I became terrified at the thought of turning back around to look behind me, for it had been so long since I had glanced that way that I began to imagine that surely *something* must be waiting there now, some fiend of the depths that had already torn to pieces the other four and which now crept up to take me as well, silently stretching itself to its full height, waiting for my terror to reach its uttermost peak before it fell upon me and pulled me apart by the limbs. Oh God! It was horrible!

But finally the boat reached the shore, and I was surprised to find that it was not Kine but Lionel Jackson who had returned, my previous companion having decided that his presence was necessary back on the ship. Young Jackson was eager to see the great stone things, and he inspected every surface with many comments and speculations as to their origin. I was only happy to have another soul beside me, and the more talkative the better.

And yet time ground on, like a millstone, crushing the minutes one by one. Two hours had long ago passed and presumably the university men were returning, so we stood at the top of the ridgeline and looked down, but still there was nothing. After a time we became jumpy and unsettled up there on the edge of the darkness, and so retreated back down to the shore where we could at least see the lanterns on our sub.

Finally a full four hours had passed, but still we were alone. Now, it did not surprise me that the explorers would have stretched their curfew, being eager, no doubt, to coo and jaw over every new vista before returning, but in the intervening time I found myself making imagined appeals to the absent men to return to the sub and quit the place for good. Fortunately Jackson had had the happy idea of bringing victuals with him, and so the two of us sat down to eat our salted pork and soda bread. The food lifted my spirits, until I considered that our missing companions had nothing in the way of provisions with them, and that surely they must be getting hungry themselves. Their canteens of water, too, would not last forever.

Some time after that it seems that I fell asleep, despite my intention to stay alert in that strange place. I remember terrible dreams, dreams like I had never had before. I was lost, far from men and their history; somewhere their trials and fighting continued on, but not here; it was as though I had returned to some antediluvian time when mankind's actions went unrecorded, except to say that they were mad and brutish and scorned by God, and indeed I did feel that remote from our world. As I cowered there in that lost place, ferns and vines reeling out of holes like fire hoses, colossal armored insects perched shining and terrible on high rock pinnacles, I felt monstrous presences about me, enormous but invisible. The presences were the true horror of the dream, for I knew that they could see me, could see *through* me—could, if they wished, tear apart not just my body but my very soul, stretching my consciousness on a

55

rack until it snapped and broke into pieces. And I knew I disgusted them, like a bug, like a mouse trapped on a cellar floor, but I was beneath their notice … for the moment. Desperate to hide, I pushed myself into the empty recess of a rotten hollow stump, only too late realizing that it was no stump but the remains of some other animal destroyed by the presence, some ancient bearlike creature reduced to bones and leather. Still I cowered in the rotting cavity where its entrails had once been, its bare ribs the bars of a cage, its head suspended over mine, the mouth torn open in a final shrieking scream....

The scream was my own when Jackson shook me awake, and it took some time before I realized that I was now back in my own senses and not still in the nightmare. It was hours later, nearly eight since the departure of the university men, and Jackson had heard something moving in the dark.

We took a moment to collect ourselves, and then together we walked up over the rise, the lantern held out before us like a bow light. Shadows bounced across the rocky terrain as I strained my ears for any sound, barely daring to breathe. Sweat covered me like ghosts' tickling fingers, and I felt like I was walking to my own execution, except that somehow I was advancing towards it of my own free will. The frontier of the light's edge moved forward, and each second we expected it to reveal something monstrous, but there was nothing, only tumbled stones and silence. Then we heard it: a shuffle or a pant, just a little ways off to the right. We swung the lamp, and off on a rise, on a little hillock, we saw a great crumbled stone block, and, lying in a heap at the base of it, was Mordecai Seagrave.

The Satanic Bridegroom

We ran to the man, calling his name, but he did not rise or turn his face. He seemed instead to be in some vacant state of mind, terrified, or out of his wits; he did not show any sign of recognizing us, or even speak at all, but simply looked at the empty space before his nose and panted raggedly, blinking somehow hurriedly, as if he were afraid to shut his eyes for even a moment. He had some small object clutched in his hands, but his pack and equipment were missing; how he had made it back this far in the darkness was a mystery. We tried to talk to the man, to bring him to his senses, but our words had no more effect on him than a gust of wind; repeatedly we asked about the others, shaking his shoulders, shouting, but it was of no use. He was like a man destroyed.

We shone our light in every direction to look for sign of Straworthy, Riesling or Chaplin, venturing away from the giant stone as far as we dared, but the landscape was dead and empty, and there was no sound save for Seagrave's strange breathing. Oddly, despite our worry, neither of us had dared to shout; unspoken between us was some acknowledgment of fear, and the possibility that there was something out there in the dark besides the men. Finally, though, I caught Jackson's eyes and read my own thoughts in them: it was the final step we had to take, because once taken, we could then return to the submarine and leave the damned place where we had found it. We steeled ourselves, and then I took a deep breath and shouted. "Straworthy!" The word shot around us like a flock of bats, echoing and amplified by every angle; it disappeared and then returned again, weirdly altered, so that I was not sure that the voice was still my own. It tacked and wheeled about the vastness of the chamber, and before it had died Jackson had one of

Seagrave's arms and I had the other and we were running over the hill. We threw him in the bottom of the boat like a sack of flour and our paddles struck the water, I on one side, Jackson on the other, the lamp blown out and only the silhouette-on-gold of the submarine to see by. Never in my days as a midshipman with the threat of a beating hanging over my head did I ever work like I had that day! We near leaped out of dinghy the moment our deck was in reach, all but kicking it away.

"Shan't we stow it?" asked seaman Lamb, who was idling on deck.

"Leave it to the devil, you fool, we're getting out!"

The crew was stunned, near exploding with questions on what had happened—all except Kine, of course, whose surprise appeared to be of a somewhat milder degree—but I waved them off and began bellowing orders. "Weigh anchor! Turn her about! Lamb, to the fore with the lantern, and hold tight! Put those filthy pylons behind us and then we dive!"

It was no easy task, for while the bay was large it was still yet small for a submarine, but by alternating between forward and reverse we were able to turn the sub about face without incident. Happy I was to give the order to dive, and all but forgot about the danger of the tunnel, but instead urged my men on to make our exit. When it finally seemed that we were well and truly out in the open sea I felt as though I had returned from the land of the dead, and I wanted to kiss my shipmates and dance. The only thing that stopped my celebration was young Seagrave, who, when we began the process of resurfacing, unexpectedly let out a choked kind of shriek. By God, the crew jumped then! We stared at him in wonder, but he was silent after, staring off into nothing, as if listening to some far-off voice; then spasms rocked him, a look of fear, and he clutched his head with his hands and buried his face in the corner, his legs kicking. Something rattled on the deck and at my feet I saw the object that Seagrave had been clutching in his hands all that time; it was some kind of relic, some little carved thing, and I stuffed it in my pocket and went to help tend to the man. Seaman Henry tried to get him to take some whiskey (and be sure that I wondered how he had smuggled that aboard, let me mention in passing), but I think he sooner would have swallowed a baseball, with a bite of the mitt for good measure. I should like to say that it was us who eventually calmed him, but truth be told I think it happened of its own accord; in time he unclamped his ears and his yelling was replaced by the same frightened stare, twitching, flinching—listening, it seemed, listening to the churn of the engine or something beyond.

Now, here on dry land, you might judge us cowards, or even murderers, having left the other three behind, and you can be sure the same thought ate away at me as we reached the tender and birthed ourselves out from the sub and the sea. Were they still alive, and only lost or sleeping or down in some ruin where they couldn't hear our shouts, then we had condemned them to die of thirst or starvation, trapped in the darkness—forever! It stabs at me, day after day! Not for one moment have I forgotten those men! All the rum in the world will never drown that out! But then … then I remember what it was like to be down there … buried … stranded on that shore, stranded at the gates to the abyss, the obelisks. I remember Seagrave gone out of his wits, I remember the look in Kine's eyes when we returned, a look that told me that if I wanted him to go back I would have to tie him up and carry him screaming. I remember the dreams, and … I can't say how, and I can't say why, but by God, I knew those men were dead.

It was late when the captain had finished his story. Vionaika had settled her head on my shoulder, eyes drooping, her arm curled through mine; the other leaned against Adamski, quietly smoking a cigarette, playing with a lock of her hair. Between us all lay a plate of broken crab shells, gray and translucent. The rum bottle had weathered many forays but now it was at its last gasp. The captain was tipsy, looking unsteady in his chair, but there was a fire in his eyes, a tenseness to his face, and he looked at me as though I were the one who was supposed to provide an answer to *him*, as though he were looking to me to judge what had happened and what he had done. What *had* he done? Was any of this even true? I suppose his crew would corroborate some or all of it, unless … certainly there remained the possibility that Adamski was a murderer, and that his crew were lying on his behalf. Or.…

"Did it ever occur to you that Seagrave may have gone mad and murdered the other three? Or perhaps he was always mad? Really we … that is to say you … know very little about the man, no?"

"Aye, that it did," said the Captain. "Though I must say that he struck me as an ordinary enough fellow when I first met him. Young, enthusiastic, thoughtful … a pretty fiancée, too, I later found out. Girls like that don't marry madmen, that much is for sure. I was introduced to her in fact, gave her the object that her young man had carried out of that place."

"What was the object?"

The Satanic Bridegroom

"Just a piece of carved stone, but not carved fancy like a statue; it was just a circle, or rather what you call a cylinder, like a stubby, fat, gun barrel, one end all curved and smooth and the other topped with a flat ring coming out of it sidewise."

He was describing the object I saw in Miss Pulver's hands two days ago. "Like a pendant?"

"A what? Ah, you mean like what a woman might put on a necklace to wear upon her bosom." He winked and then nudged his drinking companion, who had drowsed off and now woke up with a start. "Yes, very much like that, though perhaps a little heavy for that purpose. It was very plain, however, not worth much, I'd say." He stared past me for a short while and then spoke again. "Did he go mad? To be sure he did. Did he kill his companions? That I cannot say. Certainly it would be the easy explanation. Or perhaps he broke away from them, ran into the dark, and by some crazy happenstance he found his way back and they did not? Perhaps they stumbled into a pit in search of him? Yes, these things are all possible, but...."

I waited, but the Captain did not continue. He was staring off beyond me, or perhaps I should say through me, his face transfixed, as though he were listening to some distant voice. "But?"

His eyes did not move, but in time he spoke again. "The dreams ... that place ... at times I think it touched me too. I felt it. I *feel* it. Sometimes I think I hear things ... not loud ... I can't make them out. But they're speaking to me. Me! I'm out of there, it should be better, but at times I think it's only getting worse. No ... no more under the sea!" The captain suddenly became more animated, grabbing the sleeve of my jacket and holding it tight. "No more under the sea! I'm finished with that! Land! Dry land!"

One of the other drinkers spoke softly in Spanish: *he's getting bad again.* The barman's voice rang out like a warning shot. "*Señor.*"

Captain Adamski looked up, then let go of my sleeve and collected himself. He stood and grabbed the bottle off the table, drained its contents, and then swept up the older woman by the arm. She patted her clothes to make sure all was in order. The captain was glaring at me. "Who are you?" he asked with a snarl, eyeing at me like a tiger. I opened my mouth to speak. A coin rang on the table.

"Go to Hell," he said, and they were gone.

I offered Vionaika a ride back to town, and she accepted. We strolled outside together like an old married couple, arm in arm; I do not know why. I should have stood apart, spoken to her about the moral dangers of her trade, but truth be told I liked the warmth and the softness, I liked how neatly she fit into the crook of my arm, and in it there was some grain of shared kindness that fit in somehow with Christ's teachings. After all, did He not treat Mary Magdalene with the regard of an apostle? But of course I am not Christ ... perhaps it is even sacrilege to compare myself to Him. I do not know.

Captain Adamski was nowhere to be seen when we exited El Club Huracán, but I was pleased to see that my driver was still there. Unfortunately it appeared that he had been passing the time by drinking, and all on credit in anticipation of his fare—the man was stinko, not to put too fine a point on it. He instructed me to pay his money to a third party standing hard by, and then he collapsed in the rear of the cab. I drove, Vaika drowsing on my shoulder, and though it was now past dusk and the road awash with darkness the horse knew which way to go. My mind was churning with thoughts of the captain and Seagrave and that cursed reef under the sea, of mystery and excitement and three men lost, but at the same time my heart felt easy and free. The air was cooling and a breeze blew across my skin, carrying with it quiet sounds of nighttime. The silhouette of the land was still beautiful, curved in nature's way, suggestive of frontiers of discovery and idyllic groves, heights from which to look down and lowlands to call home. My cares seemed far away, and once again I allowed myself to indulge in the fantasy of the aimless traveler wandering through some paradise, unmapped and unstained. Eventually the woman departed at a group of wooden shacks on the outskirts of town, where a waiting boy of twelve or thirteen stared at me with frank hatred. She did not look back, and I went on alone.

Saturday, March 13

An unsettling day.

I lingered long upon my couch this morning, having stayed up late to write down my experiences of the previous day, until finally Ayana knocked and entered with a tray of coffee and buttered rolls. I welcomed the simplicity of the meal, as my stomach was still unsettled from the rum. I had not heard the usual calisthenic thumpings from upstairs, and I asked the maid if our housemates were absent or ill; she let me know that they were to spend the morning sightseeing in the city before visiting the young man in the hospital in the afternoon.

I had no engagements scheduled for the morning, and so I decided that I might do some roaming as well; perhaps I would by chance encounter the two ladies and strike up a conversation. I would only have to be careful to not too quickly reveal how much I already knew about Miss Pulver's affairs, lest she find that off-putting, and understandably so.

I did however discover in an alley shop of religious paraphernalia a small but remarkable painting of Saint Raphael the Archangel, patron saint of healing. The picture depicted a tall beatific being with long drooping wings; its hands were outstretched and were casting some sort of fanged, hairy beast into a jagged hole in the desert floor. The two creatures were of titanic size in relation to the bug-like humans who prostrated themselves before the scene or fled in terror. The shop owner, a tiny, almost dwarflike man, saw me handling the icon and told me that the painting had powerful healing properties; it had hung in the bedroom of an old woman who had been crippled by a winter breeze, and in time she was able to rise from her sickbed and return to work. It had also been instrumental in returning many choleric infants to health, and those that did expire while under its influence passed uncommonly peaceably. As the price was not so very much for such a powerful relic, I decided to purchase it; I thought that I could bring it to the hospital and hang it in the room of young Mr. Seagrave that very morning. Miss Pulver would be sure to see it, and it might serve as a conversational starting point at some later time. And of course if the proprietor were to be believed, it might well heal the young man entirely; at the very least it would surely do him no extra harm.

It took me a fair span of time to find the hospital again, as it seemed not to be in precisely the place that I remembered it, but, once inside, the same female functionary I had seen two days prior recognized me and gave me permission to proceed by way of a curt smile and a jerk of her head. I made my way through the maze of wards until finally I found room 619; the door was slightly ajar, so I pushed it open and entered.

To my surprise, Mordecai Seagrave was out of bed. He sat on a chair facing the window and was looking out over the streets and buildings that rolled down to the bay, and then the hills beyond. His posture was lax, his face turned away; as before, he looked like a doll that had been unceremoniously dumped by a child and lay where it had fallen. This time, however, I could sense something different about him, some silent alertness.

"Mr. Seagrave?"

There was no answer. I took a step into the room, but my foot hit something which clattered across the floor, banged against the iron bedpost and caromed off into the corner. The man did not flinch or turn his head, but sat as silent as a statue.

I walked over and picked up the object that I had accidentally kicked; to my surprise it was a light, inexpensive crucifix. I remembered now that these hung over all the beds in the hospital, and this one must have fallen to the floor. I cleaned the scuff marks off the statuette with my handkerchief the best I could. When I looked up, I jumped; though he had not moved his head, Seagrave's eyes had swiveled around and now regarded me.

"Mr. Seagrave," I said, "can you hear me?"

"Yes." The word was flat and hoarse, breathed out quickly and then silenced.

"Do you know where you are?"

"Yes."

"You were on a submarine, under the ocean … do you remember?" It was a too-frank question, perhaps, but my curiosity had gotten the better of me.

His eyes moved slowly back to the window, and then they returned to me, but he said nothing.

"Was there an underwater cavern? Did you find something there?"

He continued looking at me for some time, then glanced down at my hands and spoke. "Do you worship that God?"

I was taken aback by the question and the flat, detached way in which it was asked. "Yes. Yes I do." I walked over to the wall and returned the cross to its nail. "Do you not?"

Seagrave looked out the window. "I could tell that you worshiped it." There was a pause. "It seems a poor choice."

This surprised me. I could not see his face, and so did not quite know how to take the remark. I returned to his side, though I was careful to keep myself out of arm's reach. "I don't understand. There is only one God."

There was another long pause, and then he spoke again. "He is a quiet god. Quieter than a mouse. It seems we have not heard from Him in quite some time." The voice was neither contentious or mocking, but only flat, somber and distant.

It occurred to me that the young man must have been terribly shaken by his ordeal, his mind perhaps in a precarious state, and so I tried to adopt a positive and reassuring tone. "I believe you are mistaken. He is all-powerful. He created us all. Even if he is silent, he is everywhere." I smiled in what I hoped was a sympathetic way.

Seagrave's face remained as inscrutable as a basilisk's, and he looked at me with eyes like wells. Out the window, beneath him, the city whirred and ticked, turning slowly around the sleeping bay, but here in the room there was a hollow strangeness, like a haunting. I wanted to feel compassion for the young man, but I instead felt dread. His arms and legs still hung limply, one foot cocked on its side, one hand turned upward in his lap, and his back slouched against the chair, and yet his breathing was slow and deliberate, like a jaguar in the bush. His face did not turn away.

I remembered then the heaviness under my arm: the painting I had bought on his behalf. Now I felt awkward about it, but it seemed too ridiculous not to give it to him after having come for only that purpose. "I brought you this...." I held it out to him.

Finally, some flicker of emotion crossed the young man's face: his brow furrowed as he looked at it, his eyes roving everywhere quickly, taking in every corner. Attention changed to perplexity, and then, abruptly, fear. "What is this thing?" he asked hotly, hoarsely, his eyes wide. An arm came up as if to ward off a blow. His stare was locked onto the beast that was dropping into the blackness. "Get that away! Get it away!" With a sweep of his arm he knocked the painting out of my hands and onto the floor. He was tense in his chair now, breathing hard, staring off blindly into space. He seemed to be gripped by terror, and his hand clasped at his throat as though he feared it being cut. I was alarmed, truly, and was about to rush out of the room to call for a doctor, but already the attack seemed to be subsiding; gradually his muscles relaxed, his respiration slowed, and he settled back into his seat. His face became flooded with a torpor even deeper than what I had seen before; his half-closed eyes stared into nothing and his lips parted. Once again he was like a cataleptic, like a marionette with the strings cut.

"Mr. Seagrave?"

His eyes blinked excruciatingly slowly. Close. Open. I was shaken. I picked the picture up off the floor and left.

When I returned to the boarding house later that evening I heard an animated discussion taking place in the parlor, and so I investigated. Doña Calvo y López was holding court, and arranged on the sofas and chairs around her were Miss Pulver, Miss Karas and a fair young gentleman I had never seen before.

"Ah, Mister Sexton"—pronounced *says-ton,* as usual—"I am very pleased to see you. You have met Miss Pulver and Miss Karas I believe. This is another countryman of yours, an acquaintance of Miss Pulver's, ah, *cómo se dice?* Betrothed?"

The acquaintance stood up briskly. He was tall with sandy hair and a broad, handsome face. He wore a white linen suit which I judged to be of recent purchase, and in his hand he held a soft sailor's cap. "Percival Lamb." He shook my hand with excessive vigor. My arm rattled painfully in its socket.

"Why Mister Sayston," said Miss Pulver, looking at me catwise, "I didn't realize you were an American. You were terribly quiet during our dinner together." She was wearing a gray skirt and a pearl-colored silk blouse with oversized buttoned cuffs. Her teacup upraised, I could just glimpse the skin of her arm within, glowing softly. Her face appeared even more pretty than I had remembered, now that it was turned towards me. I could tell with a glance that Lamb had also noticed the young woman's charms. His eyes were as wide as saucers, and his hands clenched his cap nervously, crushing it all out of shape.

"Sexton," I corrected with a smile and polite bow to our host, "I do apologize for my silence yesterday. As I recall, you and your traveling companion were having a *tête-à-tête* and I didn't want to intrude. On top of that my mother would have been quite indignant if word had ever gotten back to Baltimore that I had been talking with my mouth full."

"So you preferred to remain quiet and eavesdrop," jabbed Miss Karas. "What is that you have under your arm?"

I showed them the painting of Saint Raphael Archangel. "I was in a shop and it caught my eye. Also, I was told that it may have certain magical properties." I chuckled and shrugged.

70

The Satanic Bridegroom

"Mister Says-ton, I am disappointed in you," said the Doña tartly. "These shopkeepers will tell you anything to sell you their garbage. This picture is in bad taste, I think. I hope you are not planning to hang that in your room." She waggled a finger at me.

"The painter had a vivid imagination, I must say," said Miss Karas.

"I am afraid to say that that picture is rather a bit grisly, Mister Sexton," confirmed Miss Pulver. "What is it that the angel is doing?"

"I believe it is casting the demon Azazel into a pit."

"Ay, Mister Says-ton! No talk of demons, please! Not in my house! Ayana!" She ordered the sleepy-looking maid to take the painting away and fetch another teacup.

"Ah, well, I don't want to intrude...."

"Nonsense, sir, sit with your countrymen, I insist it, we are having an interesting time and you should join us."

I sat across from the two young women, with our hostess on my left and Mr. Lamb by the doorway on my right. "What brings you to Cuba, Mister Sexton?" asked Miss Pulver.

"I'm an agent for an association of sugar importers."

"I told you he was sweet," winked the hostess at Miss Karas, who scowled.

"That sounds very interesting."

"Quite. And ... you ladies? What is it that brings you to the beautiful island of Cuba?"

"We are here visiting a friend that is ill," said Miss Karas.

I am not a person who can easily countenance the idea of lying, but at that moment I found it necessary to dissemble somewhat. "I know of one American in the hospital here

71

in Santiago, a young academic named Seagrave who was taken ill during some sort of underwater expedition that was reported in the newspapers."

Miss Pulver blanched. "Yes, that is my fiancé," she said.

"Ah, I am terribly sorry to hear that. Some sort of shock to the system, I suppose?"

"Just so."

Our hostess interjected. "I am having a mass said for the *novio* at La Iglesia de la Cruz Sagrada tomorrow, Mister Says-ton. I hope you will attend." She swiveled to Miss Pulver. "Tell me, Miss Pulver, were there long romancings between you and Mister Seagrave? How did you meet your heart? I am interested in these stories of love." The Doña fancied herself to be fluent in English, and specified as much when advertising her boarding house, but the actual results of her attempts were varied. "I hope you do not mind this women's talk, Mister Lamb," she added.

Miss Pulver sighed. "We have all known each other since we were children. Well, of course Irene and I knew each other, we are cousins, second cousins."

"We share a pair of great-grandparents," elaborated Miss Karas.

"Our families live not so terribly far away from each other, in Connecticut, which is up in the northeast part of America. Mordecai and Irene are from the same town, and when I would visit her we all played together in the woods and fields. He was such a beautiful little boy, and so sweet. He had a little museum in his room of arrowheads and birds' nests and snails' shells, he was so proud of them. He would only show them to me, no one else. Then his mother would set out a picnic dinner and we would all eat together and play games, and it was terrible fun, do you remember, Irene? Everyone was so much simpler and kinder in those days. If you had said that in ten years everyone in the world would be lying in trenches and killing each other no one would have believed you, and now of course his elder brother Jeremy is dead, killed in France, and back then he was still climbing trees and dropping acorns on us."

"I disliked that," said Irene.

"Irene wanted to climb that tree herself! Of course we girls weren't allowed. I suppose you could climb a tree now if you wanted, you minx."

"I might just do that. And if there are any acorns, I assure you, I shall save the largest for you."

"Then I shall carry an umbrella. Mordecai never climbed trees, of course, he was always so thoughtful and quiet. He would sit reading at the windowsill all day if we'd let him." She looked up off to the corner of the ceiling and a smile played along her mouth. "I was taller than he then, but not now of course, he's just the right height, I think. As children I would insist that we were to be married, and of course none of us knew what that meant, and he took it all gravely and seriously and sometimes we would quarrel about it and other times not at all."

Doña Calvo y López chuckled. "I was the same way! Ah, if only we knew."

"When we were older we were the best of friends. Some people thought that odd, but why? Can't a man and a woman be friends in the same way as two men or two women? We would talk for hours, play cards, go on outings. Then we were separated … he went to the university, I to a girls' college. The Christmas before last he gave me a pair of pearl earrings and asked me to marry him. He was so serious, but so handsome … and I thought, who better to marry than your best friend? Don't you think so?"

The older woman looked at the mantel, to the portrait of the late Don Calvo y López, a stout man with Brilliantined hair and teeth like a graveyard after an earthquake. She smiled serenely. "We were locked inside as girls, we did not know the young men. It was a dangerous time, not like now. I was told who I was to marry, that was the way." She lifted her eyebrows and shrugged. "I had seen more beautiful men, but he was from a good family. His mother was French, but that is not so very bad, and his father's father was from Catalan, like mine. I hated him sometimes, so stubborn! *Asno!* I would yell at him, and I would kick his shoes that he would leave all over my house. Ay, that made him angry, but I was angry too! But he was a good man, and a good father to the children, and I loved him very much." She reached out and put her hand on Miss Pulver's, squeezing. "I do not know if it will be easy for you because he is your friend, but if you love him, then marry him."

"Thank you," said Miss Pulver. "Was that your husband's name, Asno?"

Had the old woman enough blood left in her I believe she would have blushed. "Ah, no, my dear, it means, ah, you know, the animal, what do you call it?" she looked at me.

"Donkey," I said.

"Oh dear," said Miss Pulver.

"*Olvídeselo, señorita.*" She patted her hands and sat back. "Now mister sailor Lamb, tell us, how many girl-friends do you have in the ports? No lying, please, this is a Christian house. And if you've forgotten their names we shall toss you in the street, because that is not a romantic way to be."

Mister Lamb was in the so-called hot seat and he looked it. "I don't wish to disappoint you all, but I'm afraid I don't have even one girlfriend. I suppose I've been at sea too long to have made many friends."

"Shall we say that the sea is your mistress?" asked Miss Karas. "I believe that is customary in these situations."

"Ah, Mister Lamb, that is no good. You do not want to be an old unmarried bachelor like Mister Says-ton. No one to take care of you, to make you feel happy when you come home from your voyage." She gave me a mischievous look, and then glanced at Miss Karas, who glared at her tea.

I thought it might be expedient to change the subject. "You say you are an acquaintance of Mister Seagrave's, Mister Lamb?"

"I was just telling the ladies that I was on that same submarine expedition," said the young man.

"You? Great God!" This outburst escaped me quite by accident. And then I suddenly recalled that the Captain had mentioned a seaman Lamb in his story.

"Yes, it's true. I saw Mr. Seagrave brought in, saw his state of mind when we transported him back to the surface," said Lamb.

"I heard a rumor, a rumor of an undersea cave, and an air pocket therein. Is that really true?"

Mr. Lamb took a deep breath. "It is true, sir."

"Fantastic! And ... no one knows what happened to the other three men?"

Mr. Lamb shook his head. "The four of them left in a dinghy along with the captain and another member of our crew—the rest of us stayed behind. After some hours our shipmate returned, telling us that the four university men had gone off down a … well, a road, or so he said. Another one of our mates went back to keep company with the captain. Four hours later only three men returned, and the captain told us to get underway. Full speed ahead."

"Fantastic," I said again.

Miss Karas was watching the young man closely through narrowed eyes. "And what of this captain and the other crew member, the second one. Do you know them well?"

"I do, perhaps better than most," said Lamb, straightening himself in his chair. "I sailed with them both, here in the Caribbean, in that very submarine, in fact. Jackson and I both left the Navy after the war, after our tour of duty, as did Captain Adamski."

"Well, do you think either of them capable of—and I'm sorry to ask this—murder? For money? Or in a moment of drunkenness, from spirits or from some kind of, I don't know, toxic volcanic gas?"

Mr. Lamb looked somewhat offended, but his answer was measured and polite. "I would say that they are both good men. In fact I looked on the captain as a … as a kind of second father, I guess you might say. He looked after me, encouraged me, kept me out of harm's way. You say that perhaps they killed them for money, but if there was anything of value taken from that cave, it must have been something exceedingly small, for I did not see it brought onto the vessel, and the captain did not seem inclined to ever return to that place. Beyond that, I know that the captain would have wanted the expedition to be a success, for certainly his name would have been made as well as those of the university men. That could be more valuable than any one diamond or nugget of gold. If you suggest rather that the men ran amok from drunkenness, well ... Captain Adamski is no teetotaler, but he did not tolerate any alcohol on board his vessel when we were in the Navy; certainly I didn't see any drinking that day, and both men were stone cold sober when they returned, of that I am certain." He rubbed his chin for a moment. "Toxic gases, however ... I must confess that that is a possibility that had occurred to me as well. Initially I wouldn't have thought so, because I myself stayed up on the deck for many hours out in that air and felt quite all right, and at first nothing seemed wrong with any of our crew who had accompanied them. However, Captain Adamski has begun to act ... strangely."

A chill crossed over my skin as I remembered the captain's behavior the day before, after he had told his tale. *He's getting bad again*, they had said. "Strangely how?" I asked.

The young man sat forward in his chair and began talking in a hushed voice, as though there were others who might overhear. "I don't know quite how to describe it. I visit him at the tavern where he now spends all his time, and mostly he is himself, though somewhat more touchy now, perhaps. He seems to be afraid of something, however, or it's as if there is some idea that is haunting him, some thought that he can't send away and which horrifies him. Sometimes he becomes erratic, one moment talking of fleeing Cuba, the next swearing that he'll *never* leave. Sometimes when I see him, he embraces me as though I were his brother, as though he were a drowning man and I the lifeline, nearly breaking into tears, but then ... the other times, the bad times, he looks at me as though he had never seen me before, shrinking away from me as if I were a ghost. When I press him as to what the trouble is, if he is feeling unwell in his body, or if there is some circumstance that is pressing on him, a debt or an enemy or some such thing, he becomes fearful and waves the question off. At the worst moments he flinches away from phantoms, something unseen, something that he is hearing or thinking."

"And you believe that there could be some connection with Mr. Seagrave's ailment?" I asked. "You think perhaps something in the air poisoned them both?"

"I don't know ... I'm only trying to understand it all myself."

"There could be any number of reasons why your captain is experiencing emotional distress," opined Miss Karas. "Too much time spent in submarines? The horrors of war? Perhaps some feeling of, I don't know, guilt?"

"Ah, but I tell you there was nothing wrong with the man before that expedition. I admired him! He was a good man! What would he have to be guilty about?"

"That is my question, sir. For example...."

I interrupted Miss Karas before she said anything to further agitate the young man. "Excuse me, but did he say whether anything had happened to him while he was on that shore? Something that had frightened him, or...?"

Lamb considered the question. "At first he was quite talkative about what he had experienced," he said, and then he told us a concise version of what the captain had related to me last night—of the road between the monuments, the four men walking down it, the lantern light disappearing, never to be seen again. "Returning to Cuba he told us much about the great stone pillars, and the dark, and the quiet. Later, in the tavern, he told me about the fear that he had felt, though he knew not the cause. Now he says nothing."

The Satanic Bridegroom

Mr. Lamb stared at his hands for a moment, then spoke again. "Until last night ... and what he said and how he was then frightened me. I saw him very late, at the cantina; he was sitting in the dark, with his back to the corner; his shirt was unbuttoned, and his cuffs looked muddy. He recognized me, let me sit down with him, but when I tried to talk to him he would not answer, and only glanced around as if I were not there at all. Suddenly he began speaking of the university men, and asking me what they had found, as if I would have known. He was extremely distressed about this point, and then ... he made a cry and clamped his hands over his ears. The other people at the cantina started to become alarmed. He grabbed my hand and stared into my eyes; he asked me to save him, as if he were in peril. He held me so tight he hurt me." Mister Lamb held out his hand and showed us lacerations on the ball of this thumb, perhaps from fingernails. "Then, suddenly, he just stood up. His face was blank, now completely calm, but as if distant. He started walking away, then stopped. He looked down at me, and drew a pistol out of his jacket pocket. The women began screaming, the men were yelling ... but he simply stood there, looking at me, holding it in the air, as if considering some question. Then he put it back in his pocket and walked out. The barman held me back, insisting that I should pay the captain's tab. When I finally broke free and ran outside Adamski had disappeared."

"*Dios mío!*" said our landlady.

"I have not seen him since," said Lamb. "I had the hotel open his room this morning, afraid that he may have done some harm to himself in the night, but he was not there. His belongings are all in place, but as of a few hours ago he had still not returned."

Miss Karas wore a look of deep dubiousness, but Miss Pulver's face showed honest concern. "How terrible, Mister Lamb. I do hope he's all right. Is there anything that we can do?"

Lamb blushed slightly. "I don't think so, Miss Pulver. However, as I said, it had occurred to me that perhaps the captain and your friend Mister Seagrave are suffering from the same ailment somehow, and so I wanted to ask if you had learned anything from the doctors regarding your friend's condition. That was actually the reason for my call here today … I hope I haven't upset you and Miss Karas in coming here. Certainly I'm concerned for Mr. Seagrave as well, and … and … well, if there is anything I can do to help, then, by gosh, I would surely do it."

He and Miss Pulver sat for one moment staring into the other's eyes, each with their own separate look of hope and concern. It was Miss Karas who broke the silence. "I'm not upset in the slightest," she said lightly, examining the back of her glove. Then she regarded Lamb from scalp to shoes and back again with two speedy flicks of her dark eyes. If she approved or disapproved of the young man, her face did not show it.

Miss Pulver sighed and smiled. "Thank you, mister Lamb, it means a lot to me to have your friendship in this matter, and certainly I hope that we can help each other. You'll be happy to know that Mr. Seagrave is doing better today. When we went to call he was out of bed, and he even spoke a little, though …"—she paused a moment, groping for words—"… he seems still not quite himself yet. Not very … talkative." She gave another faint smile.

"Did he speak at all of the expedition?" asked Mister Lamb.

"I'm afraid he did not, though I would have sworn that there was a moment of recognition when I asked him about it. However, he simply didn't answer. He just ... retreated, into a shell, like a, what do you call them?"

"A mollusk?" offered Lamb.

"A what?" asked Miss Pulver. "I was going to say a tortoise. Do you mean like a clam?"

"How very charming," offered Miss Karas. "Clams are always inside their shells, though, no? Perhaps he merely meant a limpet."

Mister Lamb shifted in his seat and stammered. "Ah, well there are all different types of mollusk, of course, some of which are very interesting creatures, really." I had to chuckle to myself, for I think the lad hardly knew what he was saying in his nervousness, and yet he prattled on. "Why, there is a thing called a nautilus which has a shell that is quite beautiful, like a multicolored spiral with tiger stripes. Quite good swimmers too, or so I hear. If you break the shell open, the inside is a maze of little rooms, each smaller than the other, curving away into infinity."

"I can understand how you would feel a connection to those creatures, Mr. Lamb," I put in. "Mr. Verne named his fictional submarine after them, no?"

"He did indeed!" He seemed about to say more on the subject and then stopped and thought for a bit. "Strange creatures, though. I saw a dead one preserved in a jar once. Its face is all little wriggly tentacles, like a cuttlefish, but many more than eight. Even fifty, perhaps. I found myself wondering if it knew each one, in the way we can move every finger one by one, if it had a name for them all, or if they all moved together with a thought, like when you pick something up without thinking." He looked at his fingers

81

and waggled them. "Strange eyes. Just a hole, really. Must seem rather monstrous to whatever makes up its diet, I'll say!"

Miss Pulver listened politely, brows raised and eyelids blinking expressively, in that way that women do when a man has been talking too long about hunting or automobiles. A mischievous smile twitched one corner of her lips. "Well, I am relieved to hear that you found my dear friend Mister Seagrave not at all like a clam and only like a monster cuttlefish. Thank you for setting my mind at ease on that point."

Percival Lamb looked as though he had been shot through the heart with some large-caliber bullet, or perhaps a cannonball. I tried to hold back my laughter, but the young women burst into merriment and I tumbled along with it. Thankfully, Mr. Lamb laughed as well, blushing and looking sheepish. I decided that he was a good sort after all, and quite likable.

"I'm only joking, Mister Lamb, please forgive me. You seem to be quite the naturalist."

"I've never called myself such, but I do find the natural world fascinating. Don't you, Mr. Sexton?"

"I do indeed," I said. "Speaking of which, let me ask you something: you say that you went topside when the submarine surfaced in the cave. As a naturalist, what were your impressions of the place?"

He seemed to consider the question seriously, and then he spoke. "It's interesting that you put the question in precisely that way, sir, because truth to tell there was something *unnatural* about the place; what I mean to say is that it was all too accommodating. I don't know what else you've read about our adventures, but perhaps you know that there were markers, you might say guideposts, outside the cave, and then again at the far end, and then a third pair up on what you might call the shore, within the air pocket. These were man-made, that much was clear even from the distance I was at, and of a very large size, so some certain amount of coördination and engineering must have been involved. The cave itself had a rough surface, but if one took a broad view of it, it was actually quite regular, with no obstructions. Once inside, you could have hardly asked for a better harbor. To be sure, it was a bit tight for a boat as long and difficult to maneuver as ours, but we had no serious trouble. On top of that, the captain and two of my mates agree that there was a road there on the shore. So, in short, there was nothing natural about the place at all; perhaps once upon a time it was some kind of habitation or meeting place. Perhaps in aeons past it was at sea level, and then a cataclysm sunk it, or else it was drowned in the biblical deluge."

"Why, Submariner Lamb," said Miss Pulver, "I believe you have some hint of the poet about you. You have inspired me to compose a verse. *Attention, s'il vous plaît.*" She closed her eyes, thought for a moment, and then declaimed:

> In aeons past
> The sea did rise
> It drowned their cave
> And claimed their lives.

Submariner Lamb was tapping a finger on his lips. "Yes, very nice! Here's another:"

Their hallowed ground
Submerged it waits
For us to pass
Its stony gates.

"Edgar Allan Poe would be jealous," I said, "but tell me, gentle bards, who is 'they'?"

"Ah," said Lamb. "That is a good question."

Helen sighed. "I think that's what Mordecai wanted to find out."

"Don't worry, Miss Pulver," I said. "He may tell us yet."

Miss Karas sniffed dubiously. "I wonder if he knew us at all. Mordecai looked at me like he had never seen me before."

"Irene!" Miss Pulver suddenly exploded from cheerfulness into anger, her face as red as a washed beet, her lips compressed together in a fierce line. She glared at her friend through a wave of stiff blonde hair, her little hands two balls in her lap. Mr. Lamb was visibly alarmed and our hostess was looking back and forth between us all with goggle eyes. For myself, I'm ashamed to say, I could only think: *by God, she's even more pretty when she's angry*. Ha! Damn my foolishness. But to be sure she was.

For once the stoic Miss Karas looked flustered. She spoke quickly and quietly. "I'm sorry, Helen. I'm very sorry. I shouldn't have said that. I only meant...."

To our surprise, Helen Pulver slapped her. Her engagement ring flashed in the lamplight.

Irene Karas sat for a moment in shock, a hand poised beneath reddening cheek. Then she stood up. "You needn't have done that, Helen," she said in a trembling voice, then walked stiffly out of the room and stomped up the stairs.

Miss Pulver buried her face in her hands and a moment later was sobbing. The three of us reflexively rose from our seats, but Ayana appeared from nowhere, put her arm around the girl, and started saying reassuring nonsense in Spanish. Doña Calvo y López spoke to me in Spanish as well, sotto voce: *these girls are very high-strung, no?* Then she prattled a bit about young people and their strange manners.

"Well, now I really have made a mess of things," the young man said to me forlornly.

"Not your fault, Mister Lamb, I'm sure," I said. "Miss Pulver, it sometimes takes time for the mind to recover from a shock or a traumatic event. If your fiancé is in a ... well, confused state, it may be only temporary. It may well be that it is partly due to the fact that he is in a foreign place. Perhaps if he returns home to familiar friends and surroundings, then his personality will be restored to him."

Miss Pulver was wiping her eyes and cheeks with a handkerchief and taking long, slow breaths to relieve the hitching in her breast. Black mascara had been rubbed onto her eyelids like kohl, giving her face a mysterious look. "Please forgive me. Of course you're right, Mister Sexton, and to be sure I am very much looking forward to bringing him back to the States—as soon as his health allows, of course. I was very much reassured seeing him today, though, as Irene suggested, he seems still to be rather distant."

The young woman appeared to have calmed down, and there was a pause in the conversation. Something was nagging at my mind, however, so I put a question to

Submariner Lamb. "I wonder, sir, did you have any other impressions about the underwater cavern?"

"I'm not sure what you mean."

"I'm not sure what I mean myself. I suppose what I'm asking is, did it seem in any way, I don't know, dreadful or unsettling?"

The young man thought. "It was very quiet, and to be sure that was unsettling, as you say. I would not even say that it was like a tomb, for even within a tomb there can be tokens of remembrance, and in any case a tomb is still something familiar and human. No ... it was like...." His eyes drifted away for a moment, and then returned. "It was like being on some other world, some world not our own ... stranded, with nothing familiar and no way home. Or perhaps like a land of ghosts. Or perhaps it was like being dead, with the curtain rung down between us and everything that we love; I can tell you that I almost cried when I saw the sun again. There was indeed something terrible about that ... emptiness."

"What of your fellow crew? Did they feel the same way?"

"No one spoke of it, but I would bet all the money I have that they felt the same to a man. In fact, once the novelty of the situation had run its course, most of the men stayed inside the submarine, and preferred to pace around that enclosed space rather than stand on deck in the dark."

"How about the fellows who went on shore with the Captain?"

"There was not much time to speak to Jackson when they returned, beyond to find out how he and the Captain had discovered Seagrave, and we did not have any opportunity to talk once we quit the sub. Kine was also tight-lipped; he did not speak of anything odd or unusual … except.…"

"Except what?" asked Miss Pulver.

"Except that when he returned in the dinghy he announced that he would not go back, and he had a look in his eyes that said that if any of us were to insist otherwise, there would be trouble."

"Do you think that the strangeness of the situation might have affected their minds, Mister Sexton? That perhaps something like isolation or claustrophobia drove them mad, and that is why the other three men disappeared?"

Indeed the thought had crossed my mind. "It's hard to say, Miss Pulver, but at the very least it seems to be a possibility. I hear that isolation can have strange effects on the mind. I have also heard of cases in which people who survived the ordeal of accidental burial were driven mad with fear."

"Mister Says-ton! Please!" protested our host.

"Ah yes," said Submariner Lamb. "Mister Edgar Allan Poe wrote a very interesting story on the subject. Have you read it? No? Ah, but you must. And then of course there is his 'Fall of the House of Usher,' and those, heh heh, 'low and indefinite sounds.'" He shivered gleefully, like a boy in a spook-house.

"You seem to be quite the expert on strange literature, Submariner Lamb," said Miss Pulver.

"Pardon? Oh, no, not at all, not at all. Though," he leaned over to me and said, in a half whisper, "I have just read a very interesting novel by a certain Arthur Machen entitled *The Terror*.…"

Doña Calvo y López shrieked and covered her face with her hands. "Ay, Mister Lamb! No more terrors and gravings, if you please! Did we not have enough horror in the newspapers during the war? All those strong young men exploded into pieces! Ah, if you like terror, you should have grown up with me, here in Cuba! Always there was fighting! We saw many men and women buried, and none of them, I think, by accident. But I can see nothing changes." She turned to Miss Pulver. "These men, they are impossible to live with. Will you help me throw them out? If we do it together, I think we can put them in the street, just let us do it one at a time, I am an old woman." Miss Pulver, for her part, was shaking with laughter, and Lamb and I did our best to keep straight faces and feign contrition.

"I can see that I am becoming a bad influence on this company," said Submariner Lamb, and he stood up from his seat. "I do hope, however, that you'll let me call again, so that I might inquire as to the health of your friend, Miss Pulver."

"But of course, Mister Lamb." Miss Pulver stood and shook his hand seriously, and then brushed away a lock of blonde hair that had fallen across a cheek.

"I suppose I should retire as well," I said. "*Buenas noches*, Doña Calvo y López. I am very happy to have better made your acquaintance, Miss Pulver, and if there is anything at all I can do for you, please be sure to ask. It would be no trouble at all, I assure you." She bade me a good night, ringing out the simple phrase of politeness with her own charm, that mixture of sweetness and sadness that I was coming to know and like so very much. Ah, if only...!

One last encounter before bed, of course; I could see two white shoes on the stairs beneath the landing above mine, and looking up I saw a glum Miss Karas sitting, arms crossed on knees, cheek on her wrist.

"Hello, Miss Karas. I'm so sorry you had a quarrel with your friend."

"Give it no thought, Mister Sexton, we often quarrel. It's nothing, I assure you. Perhaps I deserved it."

"Ah, well, I don't...."

"No, perhaps I did. My frankness gets me in trouble sometimes, but I am a person who likes to tell the truth. I cannot help it, it wants to come out, even when it would be better to be silent and let people believe what they will. Do you understand, Mister Sexton?"

"I think I do."

"I'm not a mean person, and I care for Helen very much. But sometimes I feel compelled to say the way things are."

"I understand."

She reached out and touched my shoulder, leaning down towards me now. Her face was quite near mine, and I could feel her breath on my ear. "And this is the truth, now: something is wrong with Mordecai. I'm telling you there is something wrong."

I could feel my face blushing, partly because the odd young woman was so close to me, her blouse open at the breast, her skin moving with her heartbeat, but also because I knew she was right but could not say it.

"I think...." Her eyes moved across some invisible plane, looking inside herself. "I think I am afraid."

I squeezed her hand. "Thank you for telling the truth. You could be right ... let's be careful. Let us all be careful."

She nodded and returned to her vigil on the stairs. I entered my room, struck a match to light the lamp, and immediately had to stifle a scream. Ayana had left the painting on a chair facing the door; the beast was leering at me from out of the hole. I took it down and turned it to the wall. Pfft! Stupid girl!

Sunday, March 14

It is now late in the night, halfway to morning, but I will try to put down all that happened this day, as difficult as that may be. Sleep is lost anyway, for I fear what dreams would come.

To begin, I tried in vain to attend the mass dedicated to praying for the recuperation of Mister Seagrave, but I must have misheard the name and address of the church that our landlady specified, since there was only a tobacconist's at that location and no one had heard of La Iglesia de la Cruz Sagrada. Some passersby suggested possibilities, but my searching and inquiries all came to naught. Late, lost, and worn out from walking, I finally took my chances on a small stone church in a side street where I could hear the services just beginning; it was humble to look upon, but it had an air of dignity and welcome that yet gave me hope. At any rate, I had to attend mass somewhere, and while one has the luxury of being sectarian in one's own familiar territory, I believe that when traveling any Christian house of God is serviceable; even if points of liturgy differ, surely the intention is the same.

I sat in the rear, in the furthermost pew, and looked over the congregation of mantillas and bowed, oiled heads. There was a mixture of whites and negroes attending the mass, the two races even sharing pews with one another. In fact, a black man sat across the center aisle from me, well-dressed in a white linen suit and high collar that made his skin look even darker in the gloom, a hue indescribable, like obsidian. He noticed me looking at him, so I bowed. He gave a short, dignified bow in return, like a host at a dinner party, and resumed his devotions.

Joe Gola

The celebrant was a small, serious priest who I judged to be of partial Indian blood, though it was difficult to say in the dim candlelight. The narrow stained-glass windows like arrow-slits were in the shade of the buildings situated cheek-by-jowl on either side of the church, and so there was a close, cave-like atmosphere within the space. The darkness was intensified by the somber paintings of the Passion of Christ that hung on the walls, all apparently created by the same hand. These shared an unusual technique or quality by which the Savior always seemed to be at a certain remove, the cross terribly high, his face indistinct. He was subtly outsized, like a destroyed explorer in a land of pygmies, and beneath the crucifixion the people were as a swarm, followers weeping, rabbis arguing, soldiers gambling for his clothes. The eye was drawn down to the churn of this horde while the pale pinned figure hovered in the air, all but blended in with the steam-like clouds to become a feature of the sky.

There were peculiar aspects to the mass as well; the psalms and ceremonies were unfamiliar to me, and there seemed to be no missals anywhere. Perhaps the congregation was illiterate? I followed along the best I could, and of course the Gospel does not change so very much from church to church, or so I thought; I was surprised to hear a passage being read that I did not recognize, a cryptic episode from the life of Christ involving a visit to a tomb in a place called Danaea; at the conclusion, this reading was attributed to something called the "Gospel of Simon." Meanwhile, I had noticed a heavy, blood-colored curtain at the rear of the altar; throughout the service I had assumed it to be ornamental or something to a utilitarian alcove, but at the end of the mass this was drawn back with ceremony while the congregation knelt and hid their faces. Behind it was a woman.

At first, I mistook this apparition for an idol; she sat still as a statue on a gilded chair, and she was clad in golden robes that were covered in shining medallions, polished to brilliance. Her face was painted like a mask, the eyes exaggerated, the mouth defined with a draughtsman's line, but subtly it moved and I saw it was alive—a living Virgin! The woman was still and silent as the congregation prayed before her—even the priest bowed and kneeling now—but then there was a quiet sobbing; an older woman in black stepped forward, her face buried in her hands. She voiced a lament that I could not hear and moved towards the blazing figure; when she reached the edge of the carpeted altar she clumsily tripped and landed face-down. Alarmed, I rose to help her, but then realized that none of the people in the church had moved, or even flinched, least of all the figure in gold. The woman picked herself up and continued upon her knees to the feet of the Virgin, and now the stifled sobs turned into a piercing wail of sorrow. She lay her head on the lap, one arm thrown across, the other gripping the knee, and I could see tears running down her face. Fast, hot words came from her mouth, but I could not hear what they were, and all the while she sobbed on, drenching the woman in the golden dress in sorrow.

From the corner of my eye I saw a glint of white, and I turned to see the negro watching me. His eyes fixed mine and he shook his head solemnly, and then he bowed in reverence with the rest. I was not supposed to be watching. Blushing, I bowed my head too.

* * *

When I returned to the house there was a great busyness taking place; I could hear Doña Calvo y López giving orders to someone in the kitchen, and out in the dining room Ayana was in her cleaning-day clothes and was polishing silver at a furious speed. When I asked her what was the occasion she told me that the doctors were releasing Mordecai Seagrave from the hospital and that Miss Pulver would be bringing him to Sunday dinner. In his honor we were to have a ham, and there would be a bottle of port as well. I told her to expect my attendance, after which I ascended the stairs to my room.

Strange occurrences and customs had so become a part of my daily routine in recent days that I was only mildly surprised when I heard a great thumping noise at the landing and spied a pair of white rubber-soled sneakers running in short steps on the stairs over my head. I leaned across the banister to investigate and was treated to the sight of Miss Karas in short pants and a grey cotton undershirt bouncing up and down on the stairhead above. She faced away from me, climbing forwards and then descending backwards, and as she bobbed up and down I could see her pistoning a medicine ball to and from her chest. Her coarse black hair bounced around unfettered, and there was a great huffing and puffing as though a locomotive were passing by.

I stood staring in amazement, partially because I was struck by the strength and agility of the girl, and partially, I must confess, because her movements were mesmerizing; her calves and triceps were like smooth elastic, and her backside bounced like a pair of bagged geese on a buckboard.

"Good afternoon, Mister Sexton." I blinked and realized that the young woman had ceased hurtling herself about and was now looking at me over her shoulder.

"Ah, Miss Karas. I had heard a rumpus, that is to say a noise, and I was, ah, investigating the, well ... what I mean to say is ... am I to understand that this is your exercise regimen?"

"Quite so. Catch!"

I was not aware that medicine balls were quite so heavy, and I suddenly found myself on the floor. When the pinpricks of light had swirled out of my vision I found Miss Karas standing over me with her hand outstretched.

"Mister Sexton, I'm surprised at you. I would call that very poor coördination indeed." She helped me to a standing position but did not let go of my hand. "Squeeze please." I did as instructed, and with her other hand she palpated the muscles of my arm, then released me. "Satisfactory," she pronounced, "but with room for improvement, I should think."

"I apologize for staring, I was just curious about your exercises."

"Quite natural," she said, still puffing somewhat from the exertion. Her face was wet with perspiration, tendrils of hair sticking to her cheeks and neck; that aspect was unattractive, but at the same time the flush on her skin gave her somewhat horsey features an alluring vitality. "People think of health as merely the absence of sickness, but in our modern world with its convenience and conveyance and communication by wire our bodies are rapidly slipping into atrophy. In one hundred years the human race will all be a pile of damp rags. I tell you now, Mister Sexton, and I will prove it later, that strength training and stamina exercises

95

will eradicate all these diseases that we coddle like pet lambs. Feel that," she said, pointing to her stomach.

I carefully touched the material of the cotton shirt. "Yes, light and breathable. Proper exercise equipment is very important, I'm sure."

"No, sir, the muscle." She grabbed my hand and briefly pressed it to her belly. "What do you feel? Not much slack, I dare say. Abdominal strength is generally overlooked in fitness regimens, but in my opinion … oh dear, Mister Sexton, are you quite all right? You face has gone all red. I am sorry I threw that ball at you. That was unfair of me. You weren't prepared."

"No, Miss Karas, I'm all right, I merely bumped my head against the wainscoting."

"Poor circulation, more like. Would you like me to leave the ball with you? I can easily do without it, and I'm inclined to think that you could benefit from it. You're never too old, you know! I wanted to pack my dumbbells as well but Helen thought it impractical."

"Miss Karas, I am touched by your concern, but I would sooner remove my head and dribble it about the staircase like a basketball than deprive you of your exercise machinery for even a moment."

"Mister Sexton, I rather doubt your head would bounce very high, if at all."

"Speaking of heads, I hear that Seagrave is to be released?"

The girl froze. "Yes. We'll all be going home soon," she said stiffly.

"And is it really true that he's coming to dine with us tonight? Miss Pulver will be bringing him here?"

The Satanic Bridegroom

The athletic force that I had seen on display a moment ago abruptly vanished; the girl seemed oddly small of a moment. "Yes. In fact I must get myself ready."

"Do you think she can bring him here by herself? Might she need any help?"

Miss Karas picked up the medicine ball, tucked it under her arm, and started to return up the stairs. "You'll have to ask her yourself, Mister Sexton," she said with her back turned. "Except I expect that when we next see her she will have already either succeeded or failed, so I suppose the point is moot. Let us hope for the best. Good afternoon."

I fell asleep that afternoon and dreamed of strange things. I saw the wayward Israelites in the desert and their golden calf, all framed in a red sky with craggy mountains and campfires like blood. Then within the dream I woke to a room high above a stone city held in the jaws of a jungle valley. Towering over the ramparts on a great pedestal was a terrible creature the size of a mountain, a calf reclining, but with a horrifying, awful head, its eyes sweeping in different angles, the mouth open to a red maw. Its fur writhed like a flood of snakes, stretched as it was over unfleshed, shard-like bones, the ribs great looming claws. Beneath the thing, insect-like people carried offerings, moving forward in a terrified wave, and everywhere there was fire. I awoke for real, then, woke to a terrible wind blowing from the east, roaring over the mountain, and through the window dark purple clouds boiled overhead like ink. The shutters of Santiago trembled in fear of a storm to come, and below on the street I could see the city men holding their hats and peering up in wonder. I felt shaken and confused, a disloca-tion worsened when I discovered that my father's pocket

watch had stopped; near trembling, I put on a clean shirt and
went downstairs to find out the time.

It was dark in the parlor; no lamps had been lit, and the
stormlight entered the room eerie and perpendicular. Ayana
stood by the window, watching the trees struggle in the
wind. Beside her the clock on the mantel said twenty-three
minutes after five; I did not have much time before dinner.
Then, calamity: I had set my watch and had just begun to
wind it when suddenly there was an odd twanging noise, the
back popped open like a jack-in-the-box, and a shower of
tiny brass gears erupted and flew away in forty different
directions. In the sudden instant I froze as I tracked the
golden comets, but as each spark flew farther from its
source and was swallowed up by the darkness I felt within
me a terrible sinking. The watch had belonged to my father,
now deceased. How could this have happened?

I howled and dropped to the rug, seeking and feeling.
One tiny wheel I found, thin as paper, and I had to tease it
up out of the nap where it was held down like a fly in a web.
Ayana rushed to my aid, and I told her what had happened.
She knelt on the floor beside me and searched, but it was of
no use. I stared at the dead clock. My poor father ... he was
a good man ... a better man than I could perhaps ever be.
When I was a boy he held it to my ear and I heard the
ticking ... his lap was broad then, or so it seemed, his
waistcoat with its pockets and loops like a secretary with its
cubbyholes; here there was tobacco, there a scrap of
scripture, and then receipts, snapshots, lozenges, an agate,
his pennies. And here was I, thirty years old, far from home,
no wife, no sweetheart, no son of my own, not even a
pocket watch to mark the time. I felt indescribably sad.

The Satanic Bridegroom

It was just then that there was a great crash from the hallway and a burst of light and wind shot through the house, leaves and pinprick dust crashing upon us like a breaker on the shore. We leapt to our feet and rushed to the hall.

Miss Pulver had arrived. She had her back to the door and was trying to push it closed against the wind; the embroidered hem of her dress blew up and whipped at her knees, bluebird stockings on show. Her feathered hat had tipped forward over her face in a comic fashion, but with a terrific shove of her shoulders and backside the door slammed closed.

"Golly!" she said.

Next to her was a long, dark shadow standing motionless like a great stretched spider. Then Ayana struck a match and lit a lamp, and the shadow became Mordecai Seagrave. He wore a somber brown suit, his face now shaved, his hair combed but uncut. He seemed not to know where he was, or rather not to care; despite the fact that we stood before him, he stared off dully, as though any one corner was as good as another. Gone was the vacant, hollow stare of the first day I saw him, and yet still I sensed an unsettling remove; I could not quite describe it to myself, but it was as if he were sleepwalking through some dream of famine and blood and we were only the shades of strangers within.

"Come, Mordecai, come," said Miss Pulver brightly, taking her fiancé by the wrist and leading him towards the parlor. "Hello, Ayana, hello Mister Sexton, isn't it marvelous? Mordecai is here with us now. Just this way, dear." We followed her to the parlor, where she steered Seagrave into an armchair. She took out her hatpins and started rearranging her hair, which had been teased out of its usual tight formation and had been blown to all the compass points. "Mordecai, this is Mister Sexton, a new friend of ours, a fellow American. I think you will like him very much."

Seagrave's head did not move, but his eyes swiveled over and upwards to me. There was no look of recognition, but flatly he said, "I have seen this man before." His voice seemed to come from a very great distance, like a bell rung in a basement.

Miss Pulver seemed briefly perplexed, but then continued on as before. "Oh, I think you may be mistaken, Mordecai, but of course anything is possible, Mister Sexton has been here in Cuba for some time, I understand, and people cross paths every day." Mister Seagrave made no further comment, and Miss Pulver asked Ayana to let Doña Calvo y López and Miss Karas know that her friend had arrived. No sooner had she said this when our landlady appeared and began making a terrific fuss over the young man, who at first recoiled at the commotion but then settled back into the same eerie stillness. She asked a hundred questions regarding his health and spirits, all of which were answered by Miss Pulver. The subject of the expedition was mentioned only glancingly, and the disappearance of his three colleagues not at all. Seagrave only looked about the room with sullen indifference. A crack of thunder then rolled through the house and the door banged again to admit my neighbor, Don Peppo; he raised his hat to the company and in Spanish was informed by the hostess of the importance of the occasion. With his usual conviviality the widower pumped Seagrave's hand, and the victim of this bonhomie betrayed a look of startled confusion, as if the new acquaintance had instead taken hold of his nose and waggled it back and forth. I excused myself and ascended to my room to ready myself for dinner.

When I returned downstairs I learned that the ham would be delayed, but that the residents of the house were nevertheless assembled in the dining room to make ready for the event. Port wine had been decanted for the men and sherry for the ladies, and instead of lamps our hostess had produced two silver candlesticks to add intimacy to the gathering. The Doña sat at one end of the table, her back to the tall garden window, with Don Peppo, the eldest male, facing her at the opposite end. At the hostess's left, at the far wall, was Mordecai Seagrave, and next to him was his fiancé, Miss Pulver. Miss Karas sat on Don Peppo's left, and a place was reserved for me at her left elbow. As I entered I could tell that the conversation was centered on the upcoming nuptials between the two young people.

"June is nice, of course," said Doña Calvo y López, "but perhaps a bit rainy. April is best, I think. I'm sure that Don Peppo will agree with me." In Spanish she asked the gentleman what month he and his late wife were married, and he confessed that he did not recall, the event having taken place some time ago. She shot him a dark look and continued on as before. "He agrees, April is the best."

"Ah, but Connecticut is very pretty in June. So many flowers, and butterflies. The carriages to the church will pass by a meadow which is a sea of daffodils, a sea of them! Do you remember that meadow, Mordecai, just by the old stile?"

Mordecai Seagrave was staring off into the corner, but he turned and gave the woman a glance with a slow blink of his eyes. "No." He sat with his hands in his lap, the glass of reddish gold before him untouched.

"Really, Mordecai, the one next to the Sanford farm-house," interjected Miss Karas peevishly. "What's the matter with you?" I risked a look over at the girl; she was staring at Seagrave and trembling slightly, whether from annoyance or fear I could not tell. Seagrave turned to her and stared back, a hint of tension in his jaw now.

The Doña seemed to be about to speak but she was cut off by Miss Pulver. "Don't be cruel, Irene, he's had a shock, he's doing the best he can. He needn't remember every little field and pasture." The words came fast and hot, but her tone was almost a pleading one. She curled her arm through Mordecai's and tried to slip her hand in his where it limply lay. "You'll have plenty of time to rest when we return home, dear, and in our old familiar surroundings things will come back to you. We can forget about this whole terrible trouble, we don't ever have to speak of it again. Don't strain yourself now, things will be better, I know they will."

The pathetic, hopeful look in her eyes touched my heart, but to my surprise I thought I saw Seagrave recoil when she mentioned a return home. Then the stony look returned to his face and he shrugged her hand away. "Oh, what are you talking about, woman?"

Miss Karas gasped, and the landlady began to glance about nervously, no doubt out of her depth. For a moment Miss Pulver looked stung, but then composure returned to her face. "But you do remember that we are to be married, you and I? You do remember that, Mordecai, don't you?" Warily she touched his shoulder, her eyes searching him. "You asked me, and I said yes."

Mordecai Seagrave's face was twitching now with ill-concealed vexation. All signs of his former torpor seemed to have disappeared, and yet still he was distant, like a man who was being importuned by someone else's children, or worse, by some kind of speaking barnyard animal. He finally did collect himself, however, and answered. "Yes … I do remember that."

There was a pause, then, and my curiosity got the better of me. "I heard you undertook a rather unusual expedition under the water, Mr. Seagrave, do you recall that as well?" I could not help myself.

There seemed to be a flash of something like fear or panic on the young man's visage, but he brought himself under control quickly and his face changed to a mask of dark intensity. "I know this one," he said, pointing to me. "The Christian." It was such an odd utterance that no one seemed to know how to respond at first. Only Don Peppo, who was entirely oblivious to what was being discussed, retained any kind of self-possession. He smiled and lifted his glass of port in salute to our hostess, but no one followed his lead.

"Well, we're all Christian, aren't we?" asked Miss Karas.

Again the finger pointed at me. "No, this one is different." He looked away, off towards the door, as though expecting someone. Then he continued in a low, trance-like voice. "That is an old god. A god of the desert. In the jungle, in the black valley, they worshiped another. They knew much; they knew of the lands underground, and of the stars. Do you understand? *Their* god spoke. Not silent. It *spoke*. It had a face! A face … in the valley … I have seen it.…" Seagrave drifted away for a moment, and I glanced around me to see masks of confusion and dismay staring back at him. Miss Pulver opened her mouth to say something but he hurried on, speaking, it seemed, directly to me. "The world

103

we come from is from the valley too, from Ur, boiling out, and before that from the god-kingdoms of the Sahara … but here in the West, there was a mirror-kingdom with its mirror-god. You cannot have the light without the dark, do you understand? They say the dark is but the absence of light, but that is a lie, the greatest lie, the greatest conspiracy ever dreamed! And their world was no less than ours. They built cities, temples, grandeur—but only the most unholy knew that the true center was the black valley, hidden away … silent … until … and then … and then.…" His eyes stared off to some unknown horizon, bulging like boiled eggs, the candles reflecting red in the whites with a single pinprick of fire in the black. His mouth was stretched in a grimace, the teeth sharp and white.

The table sat in silence. At the ends the two Cubans were baffled and embarrassed, whereas the young women looked stricken and aghast. The terrible truth had finally made itself known, an ugly, terrifying flower blooming in a cowering garden: the young man, their friend and loved one, seemed to have gone completely mad.

Slowly, carefully, Helen Pulver reached out and put her hand on his sleeve. At the moment of contact he flinched. "Everything is going to be all right," she said. "We're going to go home. We're going to go home and everything will be better. You'll see."

"Home…?" asked Seagrave, again staring at her as if he had never seen her before.

"To America."

His eyes narrowed and his voice emerged in a growl, like a beast from its hole: "you understand nothing."

It was at that moment that Ayana suddenly appeared in the room carrying the ham. She placed it triumphantly before our landlady and directly in the path of Mordecai Seagrave's gaze. He stared at the piece of meat for a moment, mesmerized, and then we heard his stomach growl. I almost wanted to laugh, and I thought I saw a silly, approving grin drawing itself on Don Peppo's face, but to our surprise the young man suddenly stood up, grabbed his fork, and stabbed the haunch with it. He picked up his table knife in his other hand and began to awkwardly saw at the meat. The company was stunned.

"Oh, really, Mordecai, let's, let's...." Miss Pulver reached out feebly for the tableware, but he showed no sign of relinquishing them, and so she was pinned there with her hands outstretched.

Coolly, genteelly, but not unkindly, Doña Calvo y López stood up at her place and smiled at him as at a child. "Ah, Mister Seagrave, please remember we must first say grace before we serve the food."

He stopped and stared at her. "What?" he snapped. Again, the tone of menace had returned.

She fluttered her eyelashes, made a show of composing herself, and spoke again. "We must thank God for this food that he has given us."

"Fool!" On his lips was a sneer. "Thanking God for your slaughtered pig! Ha! For all He cares! Your bloody meat! You may as well thank the Devil!" He stabbed the table knife deeper into the ham.

The Doña stood there as if struck by lightning. "What did he say? ¿Qué dijo él? ¿El Diablo? ¿El Diablo?" She looked to each of us, her head twitching back and forth. As the color drained from her face, slowly outrage flooded in. "No, sir! No! Not in my house! Blasfemia! That is blasphemy!"

105

"Go to Hell!" snarled Mordecai Seagrave. The women gasped.

Doña Calvo y López stared at him in open-mouthed disbelief, and then she exploded. "Blasphemy!" Her voice hit the ceiling as though she were calling down the lightning itself. "Blasphemy!"

"*I said go to Hell!*" With a sudden sweep of his arm he grabbed up the heavy candlestick and smashed it down onto her forehead. Ayana screamed as though she had been ripped through with a knife. The old woman dropped like a stone. I swear by God she was dead before she hit the floor.

Those of us who were sitting shot from our chairs, and those of us who were standing reeled backwards as if struck. Seagrave slung the candlestick in the corner, picked up his chair, and flung it at the window beyond. Glass shattered, and the chair was trapped in the mullions; the killer leapt at it like a battering ram and with a great tearing crash the window exploded outwards, and he and the chair with it. Meanwhile the fallen candle had landed on the table and ignited the tablecloth; Miss Karas slapped at the flames with a napkin. Ayana was already at the side of her fallen mistress, shrieking. Helen Pulver stood at the wall with her fist in her open mouth, eyes wide and staring at what lay beneath her.

Don Peppo suddenly appeared at my side, staring into my face and clutching my arm. "*Asesinato! Murder!*" He pulled me and we ran into the kitchen and then out the rear door into the garden. The pouring rain was deafening, but we could just hear footsteps hammering through the alley and into the street. We followed, the puddles exploding beneath our feet, and then we broke out into the open, where I saw something that halted me. Someone had stopped Seagrave beneath a lamppost, holding his elbow and looking down into his face. Seagrave returned the gaze, his brow furrowed with confusion. It was none other than Captain Adamski. The pair stood like that for a moment more, and then they began to run away, together, side by side. Undaunted, Don Peppo charged after them, his belly bouncing like a piston, and I ran after Don Peppo.

For a stretch of time there was only the sound of rain and running and the heavy breaths of Don Peppo as he barreled downhill towards the two fleeing silhouettes in the dark. The empty streets flashed past, one beyond another. Shadows and reflections multiplied the two forms ahead, creating angular fragments of movement that twitched across the glistening surfaces of the canyon-like streets, while overhead all was of a lowering darkness. Then with a final gasp Don Peppo collapsed panting onto a lamppost; he urged me onwards with a wave and cried weakly into the night: "*Asesino!*"

I called after the two men as I ran—"Seagrave! Adamski! Stop!"—but they only charged forward, onwards to the bay. My lungs burned, and the rain flowed down my eyes, my nostrils, my mouth; I felt close to drowning in it. I was hatless, and my crown and shoulders were as if struck by bullets, the drops pelting me mercilessly. As we crossed a great plaza I began to slow, no more able to take the pace, but at the same time I saw the two fugitives slowing too; though Seagrave was young and wiry and the captain large and athletic, the former had spent a week as an invalid and the latter as a drunkard. Their movement gradually became less fluid and more stiff, liquid speed replaced with a pained, bouncing gait. When the streets once again swallowed them up they had made their way to a mercantile area; just as I entered the lane I thought I saw two figures at the far end dodge into an alleyway.

I slid to a stop before the long, narrow tunnel of darkness. At the far end I could see rain streaking through the golden glow of lamplight, and silhouetted before it were rubbish tins, crates, and other objects—but no men. I doubted that the pair would have been able to make it to the far end of the alley and run out before I had reached the entrance, judging on how labored their flight had become, but there was only the sound of rain. Or was there something else?

I took a step into the dark, but there was a terrible tension growing within me. It was as though there were some electricity in the air, for despite the patter of rain and the gushing of drainpipes I sensed a chilling stillness about the place. It was as when I was a boy walking in the woods and suddenly came upon some unsettling quiet, something eerie and unnatural that stemmed from no visible cause, until my advance rousted some great bird of prey from its perch in the limbs above, wings battering the air as it passed like a specter through the trees and my heart leapt into my throat.

Suddenly a figure disengaged itself from the shadows. It was tense and predatory, moving sideways like a wolf. Long hair hung down in wet, ropy strands, giving the silhouette a horrible, animal look. It stopped just at the edge of the light, and I could see then that it was Seagrave. Held over his head in his right hand was something heavy—a brick. He took a step towards me.

A new jolt of energy shot panic to my arms and legs, and I glanced about me for something with which to defend myself. Before I even knew what I was doing, I had reached for a long metal slat that lay discarded in a barrel; it was thick and angled along its length, giving it weight and rigidity. I yanked it free and swung it out before me like a sword, its length giving me the advantage. Seagrave took a step back but then stood still.

"Christian," he said in a mocking voice. "Say goodbye to this world. Another god comes to take the place of yours."

"Call him what you will, there is only one God," I replied.

"No! There is another." In the dimness of the light I could suddenly see two bright rows of teeth smiling. "It sleeps, now, but the thrashing of mankind has stirred it. When it awakens, it will hunt down your Lord and tear it to pieces like a lion. *Then* we shall know war!" His voice dropped low like a purr. *"Then shall we see blood."*

I had the urge, then, to strike him down, to lunge out and crush his skull. He was a murderer, and insane. How many more might he kill in his frenzy?

And yet, it was this same thought that gave me pause. The man was sick. The Doña was gone, and nothing could bring her back, but could he not be saved? A blow from me might well kill him, and was it my place to hold his life in the balance? No—that is God's prerogative. We are but men, and our only charge is compassion.

These thoughts were but a flash in my mind, sparking one from the other in two halves of a second's tick, but from it I gained resolve. I saw that I only needed to defend myself and hold the man here until the help arrived. The rest would be up to God.

I was wrong, however; the rest was up to Seagrave. He recklessly lunged towards me, diving under my panicked, reflexive swing, and knocked me flat to the ground with

Joe Gola

him on top of me. My head hit the cobbles painfully, and the ground beneath me swayed as sunbursts blinded my eyes. Then Seagrave grabbed my neck with one hand while heaving the brick high in the other.

I forced words through my lips. "You don't have to do this," I gasped. "Run, Mordecai. I won't chase any more."

The young man paused, and for the second time I saw the crooked, horrifying flash of a smile. "I'm not going to kill you because I *have* to. I'm going to kill you because I *want* to."

I cannot describe how my blood went cold in that moment; something pierced my soul like a dagger, and I realized that the end of my life was suddenly at hand. There is nothing that prepares a man for the sight of that doorway, and, once seen, it can never be closed again all the way. I did not die, however; suddenly there was a burst of footfalls and whistles from the street beyond, and Seagrave leapt to his feet, the brick dropping heavily just an inch from my head. A second figure, Adamski, bolted from the shadows in the opposite direction, and Seagrave followed, two hunted dogs running for their lives. A moment later men had surrounded me and rough hands pulled me to my feet.

And suddenly now I am tired. The pen feels heavy in my hand, the very shirt on my back seems to weigh me down. I can only say that I returned to chaos and grief; I spoke not to my housemates, but only to the police. The younger officers winked and slapped my shoulders for my brave attempt to apprehend the murderer, and the older ones scowled and shook their heads to express their sorrow that there was no cure for a fool, but each response stirred within me equal disgust and unease. The moment I was free I stole

110

away to my room, looking neither to the right nor the left, but even so I saw a thin, still object carried out on a pallet, something small and ruined hidden beneath a white sheet stained with blood.

Monday, March 15

The sky is clear now. There is no hint of apology from the clouds for the fuss of the night before. They ease white and puffy across the north as if to say "who, me?" Sorry, dear fellow, can't hear you, too much air between. To the starboard gulls wheel, or else pace upon some long, low, scruffy island, witless, unaware. One finds a crab, tries to escape unnoticed with the silly, spidery thing dangling helpless beneath. The other birds see, and follow, and a fracas ensues. Everyone eats.

I left Santiago; I had done what I could, and further labor was unlikely to produce any result. It was unsatisfactory, but there was little use in throwing good hours after bad. I am returning to Havana now, and we shall see what we shall see.

It was a stark morning in the house of Calvo y López. A son of the late landlady had been contacted, and he was returning from the north; I left a note instructing him how to contact me for the remainder of what I owed.

I had stayed long in bed, getting up closer to noon than sunrise; downstairs I found not only Miss Pulver and Miss Karas, but also Submariner Lamb. The police had informed Miss Pulver early that a skiff had been reported stolen during the night and that two white men fitting the description of Mordecai Seagrave and Captain Adamski were spotted leaving the mouth of the harbor at daybreak. Perhaps they were heading for Port-au-Prince, from there to make their way up through the Bahamas to Florida. Captain Adamski was also being sought by the authorities in connection with a fire that had destroyed El Club Huracán yesterday afternoon just before the storm.

Joe Gola

I found it difficult to look Miss Pulver in the eyes this morning; she sat quietly in an armchair with a handkerchief clutched on her lap, while Miss Karas kept by her side and did her best to not look lost. However, I could well imagine the thoughts that would have been struggling their way into the light of their minds. Who could they talk to? Where should they go? Should they remain in Cuba and hope to hear word, or should they return to the States? More importantly, at the moment Miss Pulver was engaged to a murderer. What would happen if he fled to the U.S. and Cuba asked for his return to stand trial? I do not know. Did she still love him? I did not know. Surely theirs is no whirlwind romance that would dissolve into air the moment the storm of infatuation blows itself out, but....

As I stood before her, struggling to find words to say, I saw that she was playing with the odd little totem that Seagrave had brought back with him from under the sea, that thick, black, glasslike cylinder that I had seen on the first day I met her. Someone had supplied her with a thong to thread through the loop to make a necklace. She stared at it, seemingly unaware of anything else, and then as I watched she slipped the leather lanyard over her head and let the thing fall to her breast; it lay quietly upon the silk like some sleeping bottle imp curled upon her bosom. It gave her a wild and foreign look, a traveler of the stars. Finally she looked up at me with eyes the color of the Caribbean sea and breakers of tears ready to spill down her cheeks. Her beauty now was so close, I ached to put my hand on her cheek for just that moment, but it was as if a great chasm had been torn between her and the ordinary world, and that now she was drifting away to some dark and strange place where I could not follow.

The Satanic Bridegroom

"May God be with you," I said. Then I left.

The gulls glide with us now; by some trick of the wind they hover impossibly, like stones in the air, just out of reach. I do not know what to think of this land of pirates and Indians and conquistadors and forts and guns and rum and swine and the great pincushion palm trees prickling the hills. The men who I represent need only the sugar, not the rest; these impurities must be sloughed away. Remove a cube of Cuba, wash it, boil it, burn it with acid until all that remains is glittering crystal.

A porpoise breaches. And what of the Fisher of Men? Are we brought to Him as we are, with our familiar impurities, or only some refined essence? Or are we to refine ourselves, stripping away all that makes us our own self until there is only left a clear hard melting sweetness? Or does He love as we love, coming to cherish the colors and sounds and breathing, awkward and unlovely as they may be?

Now to the east I see that mainland, the rolling hills a sleeping maiden, head resting on one plump outstretched arm, the other cradling a full bosom. Delicate ridges of rockhair course down to the ripples of the sea, a smooth haunch poised against the sky in that slow soft curve that only nature can make. Behind me the great gulf of the sea roars, a churning emptiness where sailors are lost for years, dead from thirst, boats smashed, nothing between them and the abyss but a bark of wood and everywhere there is salt and drowning. Over my head still hangs the single white bird.

God forgive me for when I have been less than I should be. Save us all from danger. Please someday bring me home, for I have so very much left to do.

The Satanic Bridegroom

I

By the great glowing bollocks of Jove, there was nothing to do, I swear it, and so I was resolved to go forth and make mischief upon the world and myself in my own familiar way. There was a tavern I knew, down by water, smelling of pine tar and pukings, and yet for all that it was an agreeable place to splay one's frame and drink rum until the blood swims in the eyeballs. The sailors all come in with their tall tales of voyage and death and the all-night girls, brown and white and yellow like canaries, sweet ports for every battered ship—ah, how I love those yarns!—and of course the old familiar lies that really honestly happened to them and not the other fellow, The Piper in the Straw, The Girl Who Cried Hold, The Bare Ass at Daybreak, The Dairy Lass and the Manxman, and that old foolish favorite, The Gay Sailor and the Virgin Chocolatier. The barkeep there was a friend of mine, a grim fellow who had lost his nose in México, and for a silver dollar he would lift the dented tin hood that covered his face like a raven's beak and reveal to the spectator a living skull that would frighten the shit out of a stone statue in daylight. O! Now that was a laugh for you.

I told my valet Squatley to run to the office to tell my secretary to tell my brother that I would be as indisposed in the afternoon as I had been in the morning (having been too asleep to welcome the arrival of midday) and to continue to run affairs without me as he had been doing since the death of our father four years ago. This arrangement suited us both, for though he looks on me with dim disapproving, I believe that this is his preferred state of mind anyway, as it affords him a certain pleased self-regard that might be

119

absent otherwise. I filled my pockets with my little jade box and what cash monies lay closest to hand and sallied forth into the grisly light of day.

I elected to walk rather than ride to the south shore, the way being downhill and myself still sober, but I soon regretted the decision, as here in Belize City one's path is always obstructed with horses, beggars, pedlars, perambulators, water carts, great steaming heaps of dung and casual acquaintances; I believe I was accosted by no fewer than four business associates, three after-dinner companions, two protégés and one maiden aunt, the last inviting me for dinner, which I politely declined, having already made plans to be drunk and unruly at that time. It is disheartening that in a city of this size a person will eventually come to know a full ninety per cent. of the population, seventy-five per cent. of whom were born tiresome and a full eighty-eight per cent. of whom are unsuitable for appeals for sexual intercourse due to blood relation, age, aesthetic flaws (height, girth, broken teeth, palsy, inconsistency of skin tone, et cetera), lack of imagination, excesses of religious fixation, or catastrophic inappropriateness of gender.

After a seemingly endless trudge, during which I calculated that I inhaled sufficient fresh air for the rest of the day and the night following, I arrived at the familiar grey, paint-peeled corner pressed hard between the shipwright's office and the farrier. The door opens on naught but a stairway leading downwards, through which the aspiring drunkard must descend to a stone basement lit only by cracked pissedupon windows at scalp-height. Hard upon the left is the long mahogany bar, shaped from a tree which may well have been purchased from my family's firm back in my father's day; bitter tears he'd have shed had he known the fate of such a fine specimen, for it has been the buttress for any God's amount of malfeasance and criminality. Behind this Jericho stood my noseless friend Sniffy, as he was called, though not to his face, such as it was. The plate over his nasal vacuum was buffed to a high polish, and at my appearance he produced a special bottle of rum in which certain local weeds had been steeped along with a green tumbler; I thanked him and crossed to my favorite table, the one beneath the vivid oil painting of a matador murdering a bull. The subject of the canvas is slender and smoothfaced; local tradition tells that the model was the infamous Clara María Suárez, professionally known as "Aboranto", a mysterious lady bullfighter from the previous century who disguised her sex with men's clothing both in the arena and without. The legend held that she ultimately eloped with the daughter of a nobleman, but after a stormy and confusing wedding night the bride returned home in tears and complained to her father about the deception. The nobleman's retinue pursued Aboranto with the intention of capture and trial, but the young woman threw herself from the face of a cliff and was destroyed upon the rocks below. In any case, it was in this corner that it was my habit to sit and watch the souls of the underworld come and go, the unsteady travelers from the land above who, oppressed by the weight of the sun, had stolen away to quaff a dram of nighttime. For some these odd fugitive moments would lengthen into great lesions across the skin of time until the daylight world became an enemy state, hostile territory to be passed through on the way from one darkness to the next. Within this domain there existed a great confraternity of conspirators against the light, a second shadow world of shared jokes and alternate economies, all human standards adjusted for depth and lack of radiance.

On this day one individual attracted my attention in particular, a beefy man with a drooping moustache like a drowned cat and short no-color hair that may have once been blonde. His clothing I estimated to be of fair quality and recent cut but badly abused, and his face and forehead were ruddy and scarred by the sun. He had that arrogant yet childlike self-assurance common to Americans, like a little boy in short pants who struts into a neighbor's garden party with his popgun and lolly. An adventurer down from some mountain, or in from the sea, I imagined, and as I watched him I could see him watching me, and so it was that we were watching each other. Finally he tipped an imaginary cap and I raised a real glass, and he took that as a sign of invitation, lumbering his way across the room with many side-glances. In the meantime I gave a quick nod to Sniffy, who showed that he understood my communication by demonstrating that a demonic Bowie knife was ready beneath the bar should there be any misbehavior from this particular specimen of humanity.

"Good health to you sir," I said, pouring him a drink from my bottle as he sat down before me.

"Ah, you speak English. Thank God for that!" came the deep reply. He drained his glass, and I watched as his face convulsed while he expelled some malignant spirit from his lungs. "Jaypers, what's in that stuff?"

"Nothing that would kill a sinner," I said, pouring him another. "By the sound of your vowels I would guess you to be an American. Have you been long in our dreary little city, Sir?"

The Satanic Bridegroom

"I would ask you to disregard my vowels, sir, but no, I have only but arrived in this place."

"I see," I said, watching him closely. His eyes were like two rats wading in brine. "A cosy place, this, no? Convenient to both the waterfront and the brothels. When the air is still you can smell them both."

My new friend looked about as if he had not properly observed his surroundings until that moment. "Good enough," he said at last, then continued on in quieter tones. "In point of fact, I do not expect to be in the city long. I will be making my way into the interior very shortly." He touched his nose.

A long pause and a knowing look suggested that he thought I knew what he was signifying, but this was far from the case. "I wouldn't presume to ask what business you might be about, but if you are searching for gold or silver, I'm afraid you may be disappointed. The rivers here in British Honduras are...."

"Not from any river," he interrupted.

"I don't understand. Are you planning a career in banditry? Certainly the desolation of the jungle will keep you safe from capture by the authorities, but perforce you will also have fewer victims to rob. I can assure you, if the natives had anything worth stealing besides their trees, King George and the British Honduras Company would already be stealing it."

"Gold, but not from any river," repeated the man. "I am talking about the treasures of a lost age. Have you heard of the Maya?"

I informed him that I had in fact heard of this ancient people, as their exploits had achieved no small measure of renown in these parts.

"I have knowledge of a temple, a temple at a sacred place to the Northwest called Aoxoa, hidden and undiscovered deep in the jungle. The treasures found within are beyond the imagination."

"I see. Where did you acquire this knowledge, if you'll forgive me for asking?"

I expected my interlocutor to be coy with his answer, despite the fact that his information very likely came from the same traveling salesman who had sold Jack the magic beans, but his reaction was odder than even what I was expecting. His face twitched strangely, as if an imp were plucking at his brain matter like a Spanish guitar; finally he winced at some fearful thought and then simply blurted "no matter."

"I was only curious because it seems to me that it would be odd that a person would pass this information on to you rather than take advantage of it himself—men being the mercenary animals that they are, present company excluded, of course."

He looked back at me emptily for some time, and then finally said "no living person."

"Say no more, my friend, I understand completely. Here you are, or should I say there you were, an adventurer in our pretty blue basin, casting about to see what you could lay your hand to. You strike up an acquaintance—much as we have done here—with some peculiar stranger, a fellow fortune-hunter, and perhaps with him you embark on some fascinating enterprise. But disaster strikes! Your friend is laid low—malaria, snakebite, a machete in the back—ah, the poor devil. With his last breath he beckons you closer, presses something into your fist—a treasure map drawn by Cortez himself, precious information tortured out of the brown devils, but information which the conquistador was unable to act upon because of pressing business elsewhere. And so down the centuries it passed from hand to hand, no one suspecting the incredible meaning of this tattered parchment, until, by the grace of Mammon, it fell into your waiting arms."

"Something very like that," said the American, "in fact you have just about hit upon it exactly."

"And now you are venturing off into the jungle to rob some ancient Mayan cathedral. An excellent undertaking! I wish you good luck."

"All I need is a backer, sir."

"Aha!"

"A person to defray some of the expenses of the expedition; naturally that person would receive a share of the profits, which are all but assured."

"But of course!"

"Perhaps *you* would be interested in such a business enterprise?" He leaned forward, his fish eyes wide and vibrating.

"I'm afraid I would be unable to participate in such a venture, as my capital is needed elsewhere." I stood to leave.

"Ah, ah, ah, if I could just have a chance to explain a bit further, I'm sure I could convince you, sir. You see...."

He made to stand up as well but I stayed him with a hand on his shoulder. "Each of us has his own treasure to pursue, my friend. In fact I must seek mine even now. This very night I hope to see something golden and precious beyond measure—perhaps a trifle to others, but to me, all. I venture on alone, as every man must do in the final end. Eris be with you. I bid you a safe journey."

Joe Gola

As I walked away I could sense at my back a seething agitation, some animal emotion that threatened to tear the surface, but already I was ascending the stairs and breaking through the doors into the horrible, horrible daylight.

I did indeed have serious enterprises before me: that evening found me in the Grand Holzusz Theatre assaying a traveling company's performance of *Don Giovanni* and clandestinely munching on a certain infamous jungle fungus named "The Door of Patmos." The theater, which was supposedly built on the site of an ancient cursed ball court, was decorated with a bastardization of Mayan temple artwork, the proscenium arch a riot of plaster whorls and faces, the audience dwarfed by giant glaring warriors painted upon the walls in profile, the fresco overhead an exploding sun with concentric rings of multicolor angles and diamonds. My coign of vantage was the family box seat, which was styled to resemble a bulbous stone carving of Kinich Ahau, myself in the great grinning maw like a wobbly tooth.

I had been present for the previous night's performance and those of the week before as well. The music itself was a desperate sawing and warbling, notes flying in every direction to collide with each other in remote unlovely alcoves … voices cracked, strings broke with a cacophonic twang, the man in charge less a conductor and more a truant officer. It mattered little to me; I was there to see, not to hear. It was an actress, of course: the Elvira. She was like a light shining upon the stage—young, terribly young—as shy as a fawn to be out in the open before so many eyes, her voice filling a room of empty ears, but perhaps also thrilled with the realization that the curve of her bosom peeping over satin could stop the men's breath in their throats, that they might gaze in wonder at her, each pair of eyes reflecting the milk-and-honey curls that tumbled down and touched her cheek. Ah, that hair! How it squeezed softly between chin and bare shoulder when she turned her head away, how it coiled about her throat like the tail of a playful cat when she raised her face in defiance! And her hips! And her arms, the flesh so plump and smooth! Once a night she passed one of these perfect arms across her face in a moment of sorrow, bare inches away from her lips, and the thought of that tender friction drove me mad; I would picture it in the night, in those spaces of wakefulness, and then other meetings of her flesh, thighs rubbing together as she sat, or reclined....

I had contacted her, of course, sent her bouquets and sweets, silk gloves, perfume, eau de toilette, sent her passionate letters praising her beauty and skill. Finally I gained ingress, as they say; I had bribed the stage manager and revealed myself in her dressing room after her performance, showering her with gifts, explaining that I was her secretive admirer. I could see that she was frightened, trembling like a calf, but then also pleased with my appearance, I think; she was not being importuned by some terrible functionary—warty, bloated and wheezing, coal dye staining his hairline and trickling down his nape—but a gentleman with a fine coat and some recent memory of vigor and spring. I could see too that the little present of money I had sent the night before had softened her somewhat as well. On my part I felt one string of my heart sour and snap when I noticed, for the first time, a certain dullness in her eyes, as though I had opened some pricy and mysterious leatherbound tome only to discover it to be a dictionary, but at the same instant her physical grace and the smell of her skin shook me like a rat in a dog's jaws. Briefly I considered forcing myself upon her there and then and afterwards paying whatever amount would assuage her chagrin, but then there was a flash of inspiration, and in a passionate rush I instead proposed a novel bargain to the girl. At first she was shocked, of course, and briefly I feared that she might faint away entirely, but after explanations, entreaties, declarations of amour and an upwards revision of the price offered she hesitantly and embarrassedly agreed; for tonight's performance, she would appear on stage secretly and completely unencumbered by underclothing of any sort.

Now, in the theater, I watched my Elvira run in terror across the stage from Don Giovanni's approaching fate, my imagination running riot, and I nearly collapsed upon my chair thinking of her pale pink thighs swishing in that dark perfumed place under her costume. The ecstasy was brief, however, for that dreadful knocking rang out, the same knocking of last night and the week before, and now my heart began to crash about in my chest and I felt my palms wet with perspiration. It was the statue of the commendatore, and he would not be denied! *Quand don Juan descendit vers l'onde souterraine....* Before, the costume had seemed paltry and ridiculous to my eyes, but tonight—no doubt due to the purple and gold mushroom I had consumed earlier—the grey figure seemed to grow and vibrate, the bass voice booming out from the yawning mouth of the stage like the crack of doom. He locked his hands about Don Giovanni, stone fingers closing in upon throat, and now the fabric of what I saw suddenly rippled like cloth, and then torn along the seam came a great blazing hole. Fire licked upwards to the rafters, and with a bone-crunching grip of iron the great statue, now alive, dragged the mortal down through the floor. For a moment I thought I could see from my perch above the churning, boiling lake of fire skittering black imps dancing with knives, the howling flayed skin of faces still living screaming soundlessly as they stretched across leagues, naked humans beaten with chains, chips of flesh and blood singing through the air, and last a horrible mad devil exulting over all. Then down Don Giovanni went, straight down to Hell.

Panting, I fled the vision and leapt through the red velvet door behind, down into the gullet of Kinich Ahau. I had to put the hallucination out of my mind and race now, race down to her dressing room, to get there before the curtain fell. I could not give her time to deceive me, for I needed to see the proof of our pact while she was fresh from the stage. I burst into the empty chamber just at the breaking of far-off applause, my chest heaving from the flight. The approbation of the crowd surged and waned, and I faced the door and waited.

Some silent minutes nocked past then, but finally with a click the door opened and she entered. Her face and neck were white with paint, sharp angles for eyebrows and a red bauble of lips, but the wave of blonde hair was a beauty inexpressible, a cascade of light, each ringlet a sleeping dove to be caressed and fondled. For one moment she looked surprised, but this passed, and, eyes down, she silently closed the door behind her and slid the lock. She passed to the far corner with short, stiff strides and stood by her table with her face turned away, to the left, quiet, passive.

"Show me," I commanded.

She glanced at me without moving, and I saw in her eyes the flash of a spark of pride. Her chin tilted upwards with a rebellious coquettishness then, but just as abruptly she was gone, her mind retreated to some other place. My Elvira lifted her skirts.

What I saw was a knife in my heart. I had been expecting a pretty little haystack: a blooming of furze, a trim tow-colored thatch of down to match her golden locks. What faced me now from the quiddity of her nudity was an unruly thicket of darkest brown. Deceived! I almost groaned from sorrow.

And yet, it did have its charms, that little softness, that and her haughty silly face turned away in profile just so.

Later I sat on the floor at her feet, one arm curled around her thigh, my cheek resting against the cool skin of her backside, her skirts on my head, she facing the opposite way, her elbows upon the desk, reading a gazette and eating chocolates. I felt a sadness within me, a melancholy restlessness drowned beneath fatigue. What a waste! Why had I come here in such a heat? I no longer remembered. Her allure was like tissue paper, ripped in two just from handling, and now I saw her for what she was: an actress, no more fascinating than a gazette—a picture reflective of the moment, designed to catch the eye, but once caught ephemeral and of no substance. She had nothing more to say than I, and now everything was spent. The room was dirty, the plaster stained, and beyond all it spoke of deadly dullness. She would leave, another would take her place, and then leave, and then another, and so on. I pictured an endless ratcheting of dropping money, dropping clothing, painting and wiping, a monotony only broken by the dullness of defended virtue in a stagebound sawdust world where no one cared, of interest only as an oddity.

I cared even less for myself, my sick stomach, my headaches and pains. Did I even deserve the animal warmth of this skin pressed against my cheek? I rose to my feet and left the girl with what little surprise and mystery that I could muster, one last rush of blood: I pinched her bottom. She yelped and threw a box of powder at me. Ghostly and alone, I left.

That night the wind raged upon the town like a hurricane, a great booming animal winding through the streets and bashing at the stanchions. In my dreams I cowered in fear from a padding catamount, a nightcolored beast who pursued me through a great mansion; I would run into a room and find a corner in which to hide only to hear the beast coming on once again, invisible and relentless. Panicked, I ran through one doorway and the next, winding myself ever deeper into the maze, but always the hunter was just behind. In the end I made my way to a lonely storeroom piled high with rubbish and draped with cobwebs. There was only one exit, and I barricaded it with urns and tables, but then behind me there was breathing, and without looking I knew that it was *there with me*. I tried to bolt, but my legs would not move, and finally it jumped....

I awoke in the dark, disoriented and afraid. I could feel the familiar surroundings about me, angles of darkness sketching out the confines of my chamber, but something of the dream remained, clinging to me like smoke on clothing. Was there yet a panther pursuing me, was some mortal disaster about to drop from above? Then with a fright, I realized it: I could still hear the breathing. I was not alone.

There was a flash of lightning just then, followed by darkness and thunder, but etched in eyesight upon the black I saw a frozen image of two men advancing, hollow-eyed and desperate. One I recognized immediately: it was the adventurer from the bar, his burned face as red as fire in the ghostly light. Slightly behind and off to the right was the other, smaller, thinner, and with longer hair. His face was obscured in shadow, but in his hand I saw a glint of metal.

Despite the fact that I was so recently dreaming—perhaps *because* I had been dreaming, and so anything seemed possible—I neither quailed nor fled but instead leapt forward towards the danger and lunged for my bedside table. The drawer contained a pistol, a Webley-Fosbery, and in an instant I had it. For a horrible, fear-clenched moment I could not tell which end was which, and I fumbled in panic, but then the grip slipped into my hand and my finger found the trigger. I frenziedly cocked the machine and fired. The roar was incredible, and in the flash of light I caught another glimpse of the two men, now closer, flanking me like wolves, their eyes deadly and wide. I found myself dropped to a crouch with my arms flung before me, ready for the attack, but no assault came; there was only the ringing echo of the blast, followed by running footsteps that receded through the house and into silence.

The alarm caused by the report is imaginable; shouting arose from every quarter, and in moments the butler Albion was leading a phalanx of servants charging though the house in their nightshirts. Lamps were lit and the doors thrown open. I explained what had taken place, and Squatley ran to the police station to fetch whatever officers might yet be sober and alive at that late hour. Later it was discovered that a hole had been bored through the wall of the bedchamber, and then also through the opposite wall of the adjoining hallway; after much searching it was found that the bullet had finally come to rest in the forehead of a large stuffed Jesus Christ lizard that was poised upon a pedestal in the upstairs library. However, apart from a jimmied window, the disappearance of some small silver *objets d'art*, and muddy footprints, no sign of the intruders remained.

II

When I finally made a tentative expedition from the bed the following day, I was informed by the valet that my brother had come to inquire about my health but had left after hearing that I was still asleep. In time other relations and business associates also sent cards and messages expressing relief that no harm had come to me, though none ventured to appear at my doorstep in person, perhaps having correctly guessed that I had somehow brought the fracas upon myself through recklessness or the keeping of disreputable company.

As for myself, I lay upon the sofa in my study, the gun in my hand, hour upon hour, periodically taking aim at the portraits of my forebears. There was a blankness inside of me, something cold and the color of newspaper, but there were also prowling things strange and unsettled. The image of the two men advancing upon me was never far from my mind; every step of their progress I could see fitting into some larger unseen web of cause and effect—every motion predestined by economics and criminal psychology—and yet I could not shake the dread sensation of having been stained by some kind of madness, having been marked by some supernatural hunter who curled among the rafters like a shade and only waited for nightfall to regain form and return. I aimed my pistol at the two heads in the lightning flash, my gun now the thunder, and in my mind's eye they exploded with a glittering coxcomb of blood and gore, their frames thrown splayed in ecstasy from the violent copulation with death. Or: coolly, in the daylight, firing shots in quick succession, like pipping buttons off a priest's cassock, knee, stomach, heart. Bang bang bang! But the second intruder, the faceless one, now fires; I hear the bullet scream past my ear like a train. I dodge to the ground, roll, return fire! It hits him in the shoulder, spinning him, dropping him, his pistol flung to the corner. I brush off my knees, advance. I stand over him, looking down. His face is hidden by long hair, but one eye glares at me through the oily strands that heave with his quick, animal breath. I point the gun at his face. In the audience the women's eyes are shining, their lips parted.

And then my mind betrays me! This specter's hand clutches my leg, his teeth bear down! I scream, I fall, the gun won't fire, he is on top of me!

I very nearly fired the real gun off into the ceiling, carried away by the daydream, but a quiet knock at the door interrupted me; it was Squatley, bringing the news that there were two visitors who wished to speak to me about last night's encounter—two young women, in fact. Quickly I returned the firearm to its drawer and put on my jacket. Dusk was settling, and so I lit the lamps. My skin tingled strangely.

Squatley ushered in two young girls, one fair and one dark, each only of about twenty years of age. The blonde stepped forward, smiling, her hand outstretched. Great blue eyes simmered beneath a matching cloche hat, her cheeks pink and round, her lips as if carved in marble, but sensual and alive, as some creature whose only purpose on this earth was to be kissed once and then die. Her dress was a simple travel costume of a sky-blue jacket and skirt with a blouse the color of honey, and beneath its contours I sensed as she walked the outline of her hips and thighs. My mind sparkled like fireworks at the touch of her hand and visions assailed me: the queen of a harem, recumbent in silks, playing between her lips the tip of a nozzle, its black hose coiling across satin cushions and the bared buttocks of courtesans to a green bubbling hookah. The hand was soft and alive, like a bird.

The lips moved. "Helen Pulver."

The other was a fair piece of horse meat, though not quite as winsome as her companion; upon coarse black hair was perched a geometric sartorial nightmare, a squat purple cylinder with a brim as flat as a saw blade, all topped by an explosion of ivy. Her teeth seemed slightly too large for her face, and it was all she could do to keep them penned in between her lips and prevent them from escaping into the room like a chain gang of albino cretins. She was less pleasingly curved than her friend, though there seemed to be an animal vitality to her, and I had a brief fantasy of inviting her to a mud hole and staging an impromptu bare-chested wrestling match, or else yoking her to a plow and watching her haunches work as she tilled some little garden in the rear of the estate. Would she take the bit? Not likely. A lash might have to be employed. I squeezed her hand, and she told me that her name was Irene Karas.

Tea and coffee were served, and I invited the women to sit down. "How very delightful to have visitors! And a pair of new faces at that! Our city is not very large, and I am entirely starved for lack of novel company. I am going to guess from your accents that you are citizens of our vast neighbor to the north. How many states is it that are united now?"

"You are correct, sir, and I believe the count is now at forty-eight," said the brunette.

"Bravo! A great and progressive country, or so I am told, though I think I would find its attitudes towards spirits not quite to my taste. In our corner of the world an outlaw-ing of rum would be tantamount to revolution, you see."

This remark brought Miss Karas's chin very high indeed, and I had a clear view into her two nasal cavities. "We are hoping to begin a new age, sir, one of healthy bodies and healthy minds."

"Spirits unhealthy? Can it really be so? I don't believe it! They are relaxing to the brain and a boost to the constitu-tion. In fact, I have it on good authority that moderate use can strengthen the pancreatic thalamus and drain unhelpful humors from the renal arterial organ."

I had baffled the brunette into an open-mouthed silence but bubbles of laughter escaped the blonde. "Please forgive me, sir, but I suspect that you invented some new anatomy just now."

"I can't imagine what you mean. All the best people have pancreatic thalamuses (which is to say thalamatti), and with a little exploration we might find yours as well. But perhaps it is only the quality of your local product that is unhealthy. Would you like to try a little of our own Belize City rum? I think you will find it quite delightful. Entirely beneficial to the mental state, I might venture to say."

"Thank you, but no."

"Ah, well. At the very least let me pour you each a cup of coffee, which I think you may find preferable to the ditchwater that I hear is served in the progressive and healthy in mind and body united forty-eight states of temperance. I must play the ambassador, you see, for it is not often that I am visited by foreign ladies from distant enlightened lands. In fact I must confess that I am veritably tingling with curiosity as to why among all the men on

The Satanic Bridegroom

Earth I should be quite so lucky as to receive a call from two such charming young Americans."

Helen Pulver relocated a lock of blonde hair which had fallen over her right eye and composed herself into a businesslike attitude. "We have come to see you today because I have read in the newspaper that your home was forcibly entered last night and that you were menaced by two men."

"Precisely that!" I cried. "It was quite horrible and a terrible shock to my system. I regret to say that at least one of these burglars was a fellow countryman of yours, in fact. And now I suppose the American government has sent you here to me to offer a formal apology. Well, I can assure you that I am quite all right, Ambassador Pulver, and if you would be so kind as to convey to Mr. Wilson that such a gesture was entirely unnecessary, quite unnecessary, though sincerely appreciated...."

"Mister Stirgil, please believe me when I say that I appreciate your sense of humor and the brave face with which you have confronted the situation," interrupted Miss Pulver, "but the reason I have come here is one that causes me a certain amount of anxiety, and I only wish that I could explain everything to you quickly so that certain worries and concerns could be put aside."

"But of course! Please forgive me. You have my undivided attention."

"Would you be able to describe the men who attacked you?"

"Yes and no: one of them quite well, the other not as much. I had met one of them in a social establishment earlier that day, you see; he was a bulky fellow of average height, broad-chested, fair hair turning to grey, the hair itself cropped short, and a round face with long grey moustaches that drooped down over the corners of his mouth like the notorious Fu Manchu. His cheeks and forehead, I noticed, had been quite badly burned by the sun, and I suspect that he may have recently arrived in town via sea. The other man I only saw by a single lightning flash; he was much thinner, shorter, and younger, I think, and he had long hair, like a romantic poet. I could not see his face at all."

The young women shared a tense glance with each other.

"Are you ... acquainted with these men?" I asked.

Miss Helen Pulver straightened her back and fidgeted with a pair of gloves. "I believe one of them may be my fiancé, Mister Stirgil. He has suffered a terrible mental shock, and we believe that he may not be entirely, ah, that is to say, that he may not be fully *aware*, of, of...."

"No need to elaborate, I understand, of course," I interposed. "And the other man is your fiancé?" I asked the Karas woman.

Had I sneaked up behind her and surreptitiously poured a bucket of eels into the seat of her underpants, I could have hardly evoked a more violent reaction from the girl. "Good Lord, no! I hardly know the man!"

"He is a former captain in the U.S. Navy," said Miss Pulver, "Captain Adamski, and it is possible that he has suffered from the same mental shock as my fiancé. You see, fourteen days ago we were all in Santiago de Cuba; they stole a small boat, and we believe that they may have sailed here together to Belize City."

"Aha." I busied myself for a moment with the coffee service in order to hide whatever look of incredulity might be crossing my face. "Well, I think we can resolve your mystery right here and now, Miss Pulver. You suspect that your two men, alone, sailed all the way from Cuba to British Honduras in a small boat. Forgive me for saying so, but I find this somewhat doubtful. Do you understand how overwhelmingly unlikely that is?"

"After we learned that they had departed from Santiago, we contacted authorities throughout the Caribbean and offered a reward for any sighting. Four days later we received word by wireless that two similar men in a similar boat were seen in George Town, and supplies were stolen and a man injured. Their last bearing was said to be west by southwest; we chartered our own boat and followed. Four days after embarking we encountered a mail steamer halfway between the Caymans and Belize City, and their captain claimed to have seen a small craft with two men traveling in that same direction. These men did not respond when hailed, despite the fact that they were far from any shore. So, where else could they have been headed? Even if their intended destination were further up the coast, surely they would stop here in Belize City for supplies. Meanwhile, we were told that during all that time there was clear weather and a steady wind from the east."

"But don't you see, my very trusting friend, that you have been cheated? It pains me greatly to say it, but I must inform you that there are some governments here in our beloved Caribbean that are not fully and completely worthy of trust. It's no great mystery: you offered money, and someone in George Town thought they may as well claim it before some other liar took the opportunity. Meanwhile, the two men seen by the mail boat could have been any two fishermen who had lost their way."

"And yet your description of your attacker fits Captain Adamski to a T," interjected Miss Karas.

"Be that as it may, the Caribbean is a very large place, it is entirely possible that there are two Americans within it who fit the same description."

"But you said yourself that he was terribly sunburned," she persisted. "Just like a man who had spent ten or twelve days at sea."

"Sunburned, yes, as any fair man might be in these latitudes," I said. "You two yourselves look to have acquired a shade of color on your journey, if you'll allow me to say. Luckily yours suit you more than his did he."

The brunette Karas threw up her hands. "Well, it seems that you're determined to gainsay every argument we offer."

"Please don't imagine that I have any desire to vex you. I only wish for you not to suffer from over-exaggerated hopes," I pleaded. "I only want to impress upon you the incredible unlikelihood of what you're saying. Why would your two men even come to British Honduras at all? If they had simply wanted to leave Cuba, surely they could have more easily traveled to Port-au-Prince, or even Jamaica. If their intention was to return to the United States, they would have sailed round the coast to Havana and then on to Florida. Why on Earth would they come here? Given the danger and risk of such a journey for two men in a small craft, it seems a very strange choice. Perhaps you will say that the shared shock that you have alluded to has clouded their reason, but from my experience with the world I will tell you that it is a rare thing when two people who have been unbalanced by some insult to the mind's function will act so closely in concert; in sanity we are all dreary and predictable, trudging side by side, but when we stray from the path of reason, we tend to strike off alone into our own private madnesses."

Regrettably, I had gone too far in trying to explain this high-flown idea, and in so doing had forgotten my audience. Miss Pulver was now trembling slightly; her eyes were shining, and with a little snap! she suddenly pulled a button off of one of her gloves. "Mordecai is not mad, Mister Stirgil. He is not. He is only … confused."

"Of course, please forgive me, I was merely speaking in theory, that is to say theoretically, I mean to say that I was only theoretically speaking. Of course; why, more likely your friend is merely under the influence of this sea captain. Yes, it may well be that this Adamski is some kind of Svengali and he has bamboozled an otherwise exemplary young man into some desperate scheme." I was not entirely sure what I was blathering at this point, so anxious was I to keep the pretty young woman happy.

"Thank you for understanding," she said, simply. I noticed, however, that behind her Miss Karas was rolling her eyes incredulously.

"Of course. However, we are still left with the question, 'what scheme?' If your two men and my two men are one and the same, then there would have to be some purpose for their risking their lives to make such a journey."

Miss Pulver shook her head sadly. "I don't know. I simply can't imagine. Perhaps México is their destination and they only stopped here for further provisions … but I suppose that leaves us with the mystery of why they should want to go to México, and we are no better off than we were before."

Miss Karas was leaning her elbow on the arm of the chair, her chin in her hand, seemingly lost in thought, but then she spoke. "You say you met the heavy-set man earlier that day. Did you speak to him? How did he act?"

I rubbed my nose and thought. "I took him for a confidence trickster, to be honest, and not a particularly gifted one. He told me he knew of an undiscovered Mayan temple, deep in the jungle and filled with riches, and that he only needed financial backing to mount an expedition. Now, how it is that some American who had likely just fallen out of a boat would know the location of an undiscovered Mayan temple he did not specify, or rather it would be more accurate to say that I did not give him an opportunity to invent a story. So, in short, he wanted to extract money from my person, and I imagine that after receiving a polite denial there in the tavern he and his accomplice decided that it would be more expedient to take it by force."

The two women appeared to be at a loss to reconcile this information with what they already knew. "An odd lie for a man to tell," said Karas.

"Mayan temple indeed," I snorted. "And yet...." Some stray thought was anxious to make itself known, but I could not quite lay my hand to it.

"Something gives you pause," said the young woman.

"Yes, just so. But what is it? Something the man said, something that made me curious ... well yes, of course, now I remember: Aoxoa."

The women stared at me in mute puzzlement.

I continued. "When he told me about his temple, he mentioned Aoxoa, to the northwest, and in fact that is a real place. Moreover, it is a place which not even a born-and-bred citizen of our city would necessarily know of, as it is somewhat remote and unremarkable; I am only aware of the name because of my family's logging operations in the hinterland. And to be sure, there are many ancient temples located in the jungles of our little peninsula, and it would not surprise me one jot to learn that not all of them had been catalogued by White Man."

"I find it difficult to believe that Captain Adamski is any kind of authority on ancient temples," retorted the Karas girl. "In fact I would posit that his areas of expertise are limited to the piloting of boats and the ingestion of rum."

Suddenly Helen Pulver's features became alive with excitement. "Not Captain Adamski, Irene, Mordecai!" She was very nearly bouncing on her seat, which was a rather attractive spectacle from my point of view. "Mister Stirgil—my fiancé, Mordecai Seagrave, is a student of archaeology, which is the study of ancient civilizations from the remnants they leave behind. He *is* an authority on ancient temples! Well, not ancient temples per se—and I don't recall him ever mentioning your country or the Mayans—but even so, it all makes sense now."

"Except why would Mordecai suddenly take it into his head to go on an archaeological expedition?" asked Miss Karas. "Especially now, after...." She did not finish her thought, but instead pursed her lips, and Miss Pulver too clamped her mouth shut tight. There was some detail they were choosing not to tell me. No matter; I too was withholding a piece of information for their sakes, which was that their young man, if it was indeed he, had come into my bedroom armed. Perhaps it all amounted to the same thing: their friend and lover, Mordecai Seagrave, whatever he had been in the past, was now very possibly a dangerous man.

III

Before the women left I inquired as to which hotel they were occupying, in case any new information came to light that might be helpful, but upon hearing their reply I sent Albion to transfer them to a cleaner and more reasonably priced one. They had no definite ideas on how to proceed from their current point; certainly they would keep in contact with the police, but there remained the possibility that the young man would be compelled to spend time in a jail cell. Were they at home in the United States, they might enlist the services of a detective agency to try to find the errant fiancé, but there was no one in Belize City who conducted business in that capacity. For myself, I sent for Beppo, one of our foremen, to come serve as bodyguard for the night; it was said that Beppo had once punched a man with such force that the victim thereafter whistled like an oncoming train whenever he breathed through his nose, and such a talent seemed useful for my purposes. When he arrived I instructed him to capture without harm the younger of the two intruders, should they return, and that he could do what he liked with the elder. Beppo installed himself in a chair in the corner of the main hall and waited, a hulking silent shadow in the gloom. I, of course, kept the pistol.

I passed an uneasy night of visions and waking dreams, though, strange to say, the pictures in my mind were not of panther-like prowlers but instead the face and body of young Helen Pulver. Innocent enough they began: I re-envisioned her countenance from this angle and that, just as she had been on that day; I tried to reconstruct the precise curve of her mouth, each curl of hair, her little movements,

147

how she looked when she smiled. An hour or more I spent in this manner, until the inside of my skull began to ache. Her body I then explored speculatively, as best as I could from the vague hints and outlines suggested by her clothing. I was determined to be realistic, adding little marks and blemishes, unlovely attitudes as she moved this way and that, but it was of no use: she had been of an admirable plumpness, a creature who had hit that apex of womanhood with overpowering force, poised at the peak, her skinny knobkneed girlishness behind her and boxy matronhood unseen before. She was a spectacular flower in full bloom. I envisioned her lying before me, nude in the grass, unfolded, lids swooning, tips of fingers brushing her lips, passive, unafraid, waiting, dreaming. I crept to her, hung my face between her breasts, not touching but for the silver-invisible hairs, inhaled her scent. Every inch was perfect! She rolled onto her belly, her cheek on crossed arms, smiling through her hair, feet and toes in the air, brushing lightly the rushes, a glorious round backside bare to the sun. Ah, but for one bite! One slap! And then....

> *J'eusse aimé voir son corps fleurir avec son âme*
> *Et grandir librement dans ses terribles jeux;*
> *Deviner si son cœur couve une sombre flamme*
> *Aux humides brouillards qui nagent dans ses yeux*

For hours I lay enraptured thus, a delightful game, and every so often I chuckled at myself, ready at any moment to cast the dream aside for some other, but as night wore on to dawn I found my head swimming, and the vision began to take on a strange, unhealthy kind of urgency. It was clutching at me, pulling at my stomach and heart and loins; in time I felt genuinely unwell. When I finally quit the bed and ventured downstairs I could not even bring myself to upbraid Beppo for being asleep in the hall (and not merely asleep but actually face-down on a rug and snoring, the curve of his great flabby back like a sugarloaf mountain rising from the sea). I decided that I would throw myself into my daily routine to shake off the sickly feeling that had gripped me, until I recalled that I had no daily routine, and that I did as I pleased every day of my life.

Though it was only just past sunrise, I finally hit upon the odd, paradoxical idea of visiting the hotel to cure my obsession; it struck me that I would only need to see the girl's real face, the unimagined one, and I would be cured of the sickly-sweet visions; the frank reality would clear the fantasy from my eyes and set me back aright, as a drink of clear, cold water refreshes after a night of too-sweet wine. At first I thought to awaken the men to prepare the carriage, but this seemed like an impossible, tiresome delay, and so I instead decided to walk. I broached the outside world, and the servants and workmen of the morning must have been rather puzzled to see me sally forth at that hour instead of returning. One familiar fatherly shopkeeper went so far as to inform me that I was heading in the wrong direction. Perhaps they imagined that I had invented some new advanced variety of vice, one so outrageous that it only begins deep in the night so as to intermingle perversely with the ordinary existence of the day.

After a long hour of walking (I had underestimated the distance) I reached the hotel pop-eyed and out of breath only to learn that the two girls had already left on an outing. Ah, Helen, how could you? At this hour? To where? I rushed precipitously into the street in hopes of catching them somewhere nearby, but there was nothing. The shops and cafés were empty of Americans, the plazas were deserted, and even the dull doorway idlers who see every coach and pigeon had no memory of a beautiful blonde with a body like Venus and her tall toothy friend. Wheezing and defeated, I made my way home.

Beppo's position on the floor had changed from prone to supine, but otherwise during the intervening hours he had remained as insensate as when I had first left him, his rhythmic snore vibrating the wood paneling and causing the chandeliers to tinkle. On the peak of his stomach lay an envelope addressed to me, delivered by the Belize City S.T.C. Messenger Service, and in it was a short note from the missing females informing me that they had had an early morning conference at the police station and had gleaned new information which, as a courtesy, they would to impart to me later in the day, were I to be at home.

Without delay I whipped the household into a maelstrom of activity. Curtains and rugs were removed from their places and beaten out of doors. Flowers and biscuits were sent for. Hasty repairs were attempted upon a bust of Gérard de Nerval, which had had a crystal decanter broken over the bridge of its nose the January before last.

It was a quarter after one and I had only just begun to sulk when the women were announced. Rushing into the hall, I nearly collided with Miss Pulver, who wore a shining white blouse with white scarf and tweed skirt. In tow was Miss Karas, her wiry black hair blown into a Valkyrie's halo by the wind. My new friend pumped my hand up and down with a hearty handshake. "I'm so glad we found you in, Mister Stirgil, so very glad!"

The Satanic Bridegroom

My head felt oddly disconnected from my shoulders. "I'm very, very pleased to see you both as well. Why don't you come into the sitting room and have some coffee with me?"

"Surely, but we can't stay long, because we have rather a lot to prepare for."

I ushered them to a settee just as Albion wheeled in the trolley with the urn and cakes. "Prepare? I take it there's been a development in your situation, then?"

"There's to be an expedition," blurted Miss Karas proudly.

"Wait a minute, wait a minute, we must tell everything in the proper order, Irene."

"An expedition? To where?"

Karas leaned forward, beaming. "The jungle!"

"Ah, just look at her," marveled Miss Pulver. "Like a little girl on Christmas day!"

I could not quite comprehend what was going on. "The jungle? What jungle? This jungle? *Our* jungle? But, whatever for?"

"To follow my fiancé, Mister Stirgil," said Miss Pulver. She closed her eyes and took a deep breath, then regarded me again with a new firmness. "We were informed this morning that food, tools and a pair of mules were stolen from a small plantation on the outskirts of the city, and subsequently two white men were seen traveling upon a similar pair of beasts on the Northern Highway; one of the men was described as being young and thin, with long hair; the other was older with long grey moustaches. Both men were said to be badly sunburned."

"Fantastic! Why would they possibly want to do that? There's not much of interest up that way … Boom, Bakers

… Orange Walk, eventually … surely they don't intend to cut across the peninsula on muleback?"

"Aoxoa!" said Miss Karas. "What else could it be?"

I could only repeat my previous response: "fantastic."

"As far-fetched as the scheme might seem to us, regardless, it appears that that is their destination," said Miss Pulver, "or at the very least they are headed to that area for *some* purpose. In any event, I just wanted to inform you of what we have learned so as to put your mind at ease that there will be no further break-ins, and also to let you know that we will be hiring some guides and leaving Belize City as soon as possible."

"The police have set out on horseback to try to recover the missing mules," interposed Miss Karas, "but due to the many hours' head start, and the fact that the plantation-owner in question seems to be a *persona non grata* with the local government, it seems likely that they will pursue the matter only as far as is reasonably convenient for them."

"I don't wish to speak badly of your government here, Mister Stirgil, but it appears to be true," said Miss Pulver. "In fact, we overheard that the deputy or whatever you call him stopped for a second breakfast before riding out in pursuit."

"They said that he ate an entire chicken."

"With potatoes."

"Well," I said, "perhaps he was anticipating a long journey without rest or material comfort."

"They said that he got a shoeshine and bought a newspaper."

"Ah," I said. "Well, I will admit, that does seem a rather excessive exhibition of sangfroid for the leader of a posse."

"Exactly our thoughts," said Miss Karas.

The Satanic Bridegroom

"And so...." The beautiful Miss Pulver was now standing and gently placing a half-empty coffee cup in my hand. "We must bid you good-bye. We have rather a lot to get in order before we depart, and I'm sure you can understand how anxious we are to get underway. However, we are very grateful for your help and your friendship, and we will be sure to send word to you when we return."

"If you promise not to have Mordecai arrested," added Miss Karas, who was now also standing.

"Yes, that would be awkward for us," said Miss Pulver.

For a moment I could only sit and stare at the pair of them, from one to the other—my mouth open, I dare say—and a saucer and cup in each hand. "My dear ladies, you are talking about some rather rough country."

Valkyrie Karas with her tornado of black hair looked down her nose and shrugged one shoulder. "What of it?"

"We shall hire horses," explained Miss Pulver. "We are both experienced riders."

"And if their trail leads off into the jungle...? There is no proper road to Aoxoa, you know."

"Then we walk," said Karas.

I nearly dropped the china on the floor. "What, through the jungle?"

"Through the jungle."

I tried to feign some show of composure. "My dear girls, I'm not certain what the jungles of America are like—I imagine they're equipped with soda fountains and crossing guards and public telephone booths—but here in the British Honduras they are perhaps rather more jungle-ish than you are used to."

"Jungle-ish?" said Miss Karas. "What on earth are you talking about?" She threw up her hands. "As far as I know there is only one kind of jungle. Anyway, what of it?"

"Well, it's no place for two young women," I blurted out.

Miss Karas looked at me coldly. "This is 1920, Mister Stirgil, and we are a new kind of woman."

I looked her up and down, but she appeared to be the same kind of woman I was already acquainted with. "I'm afraid I don't understand."

"We have at long last reached the era of the physical, Mister Stirgil. Natural science. Biology. The mind and body working as one. Helen and I follow a strict, scientifically designed physical fitness program. Of course, some of us follow it more strictly than others...." She prodded her companion's belly with her finger.

Helen flushed and snapped back in a shrill schoolgirl voice. "Leave that alone! It's not polite to poke people, you know!"

"We believe in personal betterment through physical training and exertion, Mister Stirgil," continued the girl. "It seems to have been some kind of mark of social standing for the women of your nineteenth century to live lives of enforced idleness, like hothouse flowers that are afraid of sunlight and a stiff breeze. Like helpless calves waiting to become veal. What did they get for it? Chronic dyspepsia. Muscular atrophy. In short, they were a bunch of flabby-asses. We are not that kind of woman. In fact, I dare say I exert myself physically more than some of you men do."

"Well, that may well be, but I've been in the jungle whereas you have not, and what I'm telling you is that it's not comfortable. It's hot and wet. There are biting insects.

There are snakes. There are vicious catamounts that are liable to pounce upon you and eat your livers if you're not careful."

"Catawhats?"

"I mean to say jaguars and pumas and ocelots, those fellows. Or you could trip over a mountain cow or some kind of lizard. You could get washed down a river. You could become entangled in vines or step on a venomous toad. God only knows what the natives will think of you."

Miss Pulver crossed her arms over her breast. "It might interest you to know that I reached the thirteenth rank in the Girl Scouts of the Golden Dawn, and Irene is an active Rover Scout. We are both in the mountaineering club of Childbras College, and even if the mountains of Connecticut are not very tall, we did in fact climb them. I can read a compass and I can build my own fire. I have fired a point-twenty-two caliber rifle at any God's number of tin cans and will fire one at a leaping ocelot if absolutely necessary."

"I once killed a stag with a bow and arrow and made a little jacket out of the hide," interjected Miss Karas.

Miss Pulver started. "Good Lord, Irene, did you really do that?"

"Yes I did, Helen. And I made you a pair of gloves, remember? For your birthday?"

"Well, that *is* distressing. I rather liked those gloves, but now that I know that you hunted and killed the animal personally, it takes some of the joy out of wearing them."

"I can't see how that could possibly make a difference, Helen."

My temples were beginning to ache and I felt a pressing need to have the two young women stop talking at that point. More importantly, some dark idea had now taken hold of me; the sticky-sweet vision of Helen Pulver that had clouded my consciousness the night before had returned like an ague, but I now saw a new scene: us, lost among the great fan-like ferns and low palms, the birds and animals pressing close around us, odors and heat, and then a pouring torrent of rain, soaking us to our skins. I grab her shoulders. She strikes out and gasps. The sound is lost in the deluge. I pull her to me and…. Finally I could take it no more and threw up my hand, erasing the phantom scene before my eyes and silencing the two chattering girls before me.

"Are you really determined to do this thing? To chase two desperadoes into the wilderness?" I asked Pulver.

The young woman tensed her mouth and put her hands on her hips; clearly, her will had been challenged. "Yes, I am," she said gravely. "Mordecai and I have known each other practically since I was in swaddling cloth, and at long last we are engaged to be married. I do not take these things lightly, Mister Stirgil, and I will not take others' word for what I can and cannot do. I am going to save Mordecai from this man and this madness if I have to bind him hand and foot and drag him bodily out of the jungle to do it."

"Very well," I said. "That being the case, then, I will insist that you allow me to be your guide to Aoxoa. As I have said, my family has had logging operations very near there, and while others may claim to know the way, I can give you assurance that I do. I have access to all the materials and personnel that would be necessary for such an expedition, and I can have us on our way at daybreak tomorrow. You seem to be young women of very great willfulness, and I commend you for that. I recognize this because, despite appearances, I am a man of some willfulness as well. So: permit my request; allow me to accompany you, and together we will bring our separate energies to bear on the problem, and so shall the deed be accomplished."

The two women glanced at each other uncertainly. Finally, Miss Karas reached out with her hand and took Miss Pulver's. Helen Pulver looked back to me, and humbly nodded.

"Thank you."

At dusk I was alone in the garden. Word had been sent to my brother that I would be borrowing men and horses. Albion was in town, buying provisions. A bottle of port was close to hand, and one of rum. The stuffed lizard was lashed to a gate, a weird serpentine silhouette in the gloom. I fired a shot, and a puff of sawdust winked up off its shoulder. Then it became a black puma, leaping upon its helpless naked prey. Rapid fire, one shot after another, the recoil cocking the gun for the next hammer strike. Closer and closer to the heart: the machine was ready, and my aim was true. By morning, I would be ready as well.

IV

The valley of Aoxoa lies some thirty miles Northwest of Belize City, and perhaps ten or twelve miles due west of the Northern Highway. I knew this because my family's timber operations lay to the south, and in the course of exploring the surrounding area with my father and brother we had once found our way to the edge of that remote spot. I remembered that it had elicited a fair amount of discussion and storytelling among our Mayan guides, and yet, for all of that, we were pointedly steered around it. The little men seemed disinclined to even say the name of the valley too often, perhaps because when pronounced correctly it sounded like a painful hacking cough, as though one had swallowed a handful of twigs and then afterwards thought better of it. The place itself made some impression on me as well, though what the meaning of that impression was I am not certain. Cartographically speaking it was not much as valleys go, as there were no inclines of any particular steepness, and yet when one looked upon it there was indeed a distinct feeling of *down there*-ness. The trees seemed to lean inwards upon it, like the teeth of a lamprey, which made the place darker than it should have been, and there was a certain quiet upon it as well, as of a cellar, or a graveyard. My brother paid it no mind and continued forward, always with an eye to what lay before him. My father stopped for a moment and assayed the trees, frowning, a quizzical distaste in his eyes.

I remember then at that moment I suddenly and somehow forgot where we were and what we were doing; I cannot quite explain what happened, I only knew that I was standing in the world's thickest forest with my ancestor, the backs of our guides moving away. I remember that I grabbed the tweed sleeve of his jacket then, and that he started and pulled himself free.

"Walk on your own two feet," he growled in his typical manner.

"Which way?" I asked, for I did not know.

He started again at this strange question, and then a moment of rare perplexity seemed to cross his face. His beard and hair bristled as he looked about himself in every direction, his pipe hand suddenly dropped to his side, the ashes flickering down into the brush. He saw the Mayans through the trees. "Those men, the brown ones, I think they can show us...." He could not get the words out, but he took a cautious step in their direction. He grabbed hold of my elbow and took another step, and then another, each more sure than the one before, and then in a moment we were over the rise and gone from Aoxoa. Then he let go of my arm and it was as if nothing had happened.

Adamski and Seagrave had had a full day's head start on us, but they were riding mules and we had horses. I planned for the women to ride in my carriage while I rode my much-neglected filly, Peaches. Accompanying us would be the doughty Beppo and two other men from the mill, these three to function as muscle or pack-bearers as required. Possibly we would overtake the two fugitives on the road, but we had to be ready to brave the forest if the need arose. We had rope, rifles, matches, maps, food, and water; meanwhile, Albion was able to extricate and fumigate the old bell tents and tarpaulins that had survived from a more adventurous time. I felt strangely energized by the prospects of the excursion, even to the point of mania, and seeing each detail to its home intensified the sensation. For the first

The Satanic Bridegroom

time in years I was eager to see the sun climb over the ocean, and even the sickly aftereffects of my drinking the evening prior seemed insignificant in the fearsome blazing light that shone inside me.

Naturally the face and form of Helen Pulver were close to mind throughout that morning, and as the time for our departure approached I stood at the portico waiting for the carriage to return with my two charges. I tried to imagine what sort of traveling costume they might be wearing; no doubt the pair would be more suitably dressed for a jass-party or a shopping campaign than a march through the woods, and I was tickled by the idea of watching two suncolored frocks become increasingly torn and soiled as the girls picked their way through the trees. I could picture pinwheeling crinoline tumbles into creeks and naughty monkeys pulling at gauzy bows; bedraggled, the two lasses would finally appear before me in hangdog tatters, and I would chuckle and lend them some clean linen shirts to wear, after which they would scamper across the forest like a pair of barelegged nymphs. Ah, the fun we could have! It was only the shoes that worried me, for women are notoriously impractical in that regard.

When the carriage finally did return, however, my initial supposition was that my conveyance had been commandeered by French legionnaires, for I was hailed by two grinning individuals wearing slouch hats, jodhpurs and puttees; it was only after a great deal of squinting and confusion that I realized that the soft-faced expeditionary youths were in fact my adopted charges, Miss Pulver and Miss Karas. There was a third passenger as well, a towheaded young man who it turned out was an acquaintance of the women from the island of Cuba and who had in good-

Samaritan fashion pledged to accompany them and aid them in their mission. I felt a dark stirring within me on meeting the boy, as I had not planned on having an outsider attending or defending the two girls. Regardless, I welcomed him with what warmth I could muster and offered him a horse of his own, which he declined, explaining that he was more accustomed to the piloting of boats than beasts. His name was Percival Lamb.

One final discussion and rearrangement of supplies took place and then the seven of us embarked on our journey. We rode out in train, with Peaches and I in the lead and Beppo just behind, followed by young Lamb and the millworker Arthur on the box of the carriage and the two young ladies in their jodhpurs within, and finally Oliver bringing up the rear on an old grey pack horse laden down with bags. Or was it Oliver on the box and Arthur behind? It was impossible to say. The two creoles were notorious pranksters and were known to suddenly exchange hats and coats and take each other's places. They could impersonate policemen and messengers and clergy, and at one time they even shared a false moustache which they would pass back and forth with the light-fingered skill of the prestidigitator. The foolishness had been allowed to continue because, truth to tell, nobody much cared which of the two they had on their hands, since as far as skill and ambition went the fellows were as identical as two peas in a pod, and so it hardly mattered if it were Arthur that sharpened the blades and Oliver that swept the yard or vice versa. The moustache, however, was ultimately confiscated by management and sealed in a jar. One had to draw the line somewhere.

We rode out of the city, then, out upon the Northern Highway. Our goal for the day was the camp that my father had constructed as a way station for those work crews traveling to and from the interior who could not be accommodated by boat. It was set in a clearing in the trees a quarter mile down an overgrown trail off the highway, and it consisted only of two padlocked bunkhouses, a circle of stones for a fire, a water pump, and a privy. The windowless wood buildings were rough and unpainted, warped and drafty, but sturdy and safe, and not without a certain rustic charm. They were rarely used for legitimate purposes now, of course; for the most part they only housed whichever of my own private social gatherings were too erotically progressive to be held within city limits, the smaller foremen's quarters for intimate occasions and the barrack for rowdy group excursions. My mind's eye was yet narcotized by the tableaux it had recorded there in that place, breathing sculptures of infinite beauty and sexual dramas of undefinable moment.

Beppo rode alongside me on a sturdy-looking roan that was accustomed to dragging sledges and so could handle the man's corpulence. His face was as impassive as that of a Buddha, the image only dispelled when he would dredge up a snotrag from his rear pocket to produce a fusillade of honks and nasal explosions. I had explained to him in vague terms the purpose of our mission—that we were in search of an impressionable young man who was under the influence of a seagoing anarchist—and that his role would consist primarily of ensuring that the captain did not cause us any inconvenience or harm. For this reason he carried an old, notched rifle slung on his back, though judging by certain silences and rollings of eyes he seemed convinced that it was all a fiction that I had invented so as to add a dramatic plot line for whatever tomfoolery would take place in the confines of the camp.

In time the town houses gave way to farriers and saloons, and the two bouncing ladies in their safari garb drew open-mouth stares at every doorway, and in some cases hasty signs of the cross. Just as we were reaching the outskirts proper we happened to encounter Warwicker, a social acquaintance of mine whose bearing and fine features were offset somewhat by his insistence in wearing cuts of clothing that had gone out of fashion the century prior. Today he had on a cerulean pork pie hat with matching tailcoat and a collar that nearly folded his earlobes.

"By the great glowing backside of Juno, is that Stirgil, out here, in the daylight?"

"Your eyes do not deceive."

"I almost didn't recognize your face with the sun on it like that. Be careful, man, you're likely to become disorientated. In point of fact you're headed directly out of town. Do you realize that? You should watch out, you might fall into a boggy hole."

"I am entirely aware of the direction in which I am pointed, and 'in point of fact' I am leading an expedition into the interior."

He threw a glance behind us as he trotted to keep up. "Is that so? And who are these two vestals you have in tow? Is it a picnic? I do so love a good picnic. Say, is this your horse? Why haven't I seen her before? Why not let me buy her from you? I could use a horse like this." Here he ducked down to take a look at the hooves even as they walked along. "I say, this girl is limping, you should let me take her off your hands."

The Satanic Bridegroom

"First of all, this horse has never limped a day in her life, you outrageous cheat. Secondly, these are two young American ladies of my acquaintance, and you will kindly not interfere with them. Lastly and foremostly, I must inform you that we are headed into the wilderness on a dangerous life-threatening mission and for that reason I am fully armed against roadmen and swindlers such as yourself. However, upon my return I am prepared to meet you on the ground of your choosing for a duel with whiskey glasses at twenty paces."

This response left Warwicker momentarily speechless and agape, and as I watched an iridescent beetle took the opportunity to fly directly into his mouth and down his throat. He convulsed into red-faced fits of coughing as our party marched past, and the last I heard of him was a croaking "Three cheers for President Taft!" in the wake of the carriage. The two ladies looked at each other in bewilderment, and then Miss Karas stood up in the seat to make a correction, but a bounce very nearly sent her out of the conveyance. If she had not been able to hang onto the side and scramble back in like a monkey she would have become intimately acquainted with a rain barrel, a sight which would have afforded me no small amount of pleasure.

The journey began something like a sightseeing tour as the road wound out past the mangroves, and the young people pointed and chattered each time the prospect cleared to show us the sea down beneath. The blue of the water was like a slap to the gaze, deep like the ether between the planets, deep like tourmaline. Once a long knifelike fish leapt from the spray and flashed in the sun before dropping down beneath the waves again. Arthur and Oscar told them pirate stories of the Caribbean, adding colorful details of macaws and gold and pretty brown slaves. Torture and sackings there were, men and women hiding in the hills, cities put to the torch, and always the same yarn of the captain smitten by the wife of a wealthy landowner, courting her with silks and jewels even as he held her captive, until finally he could stay himself no longer and took what he wanted by force. Even Beppo was inspired to contribute, though I may have been the only one close enough to hear: "the tourniquet of eyes ... they lashed a leather strip around the head, the villains, and twisted it tighter and tighter until the eyeballs burst. People nothing but screaming meat. Evil."

The road followed the river away from the sea then, and the mangroves gave way to forest and farms. Still the young women looked all about, eager to know everything about the birds and trees, and Lamb and the creoles did their best to fill in what details they knew and invented the rest. In time this talk ceased as well, and there was quiet on the road except for the hooves and the wheels. At noon we found ourselves standing about the well of a good-natured veteran of the Mesopotamian campaign and his gravid wife, the former admiring our horses and the latter marveling at the Americans' *jungle couture*. The blood in my head was beating hot and loud by this point; there had been too much drinking these past days, too much of everything except peace and quiet. I also suspected Peaches of having tried to sabotage me by bouncing me on her back like a pea in a pan, and more than once I had caught her purposely steering me towards a low-hanging branch as though she were going to deal with me like a nettlesome itch. I had long noticed that the horse was a proud thing with an inflated sense of self-worth, and riding her could occasionally be a demoralizing experience.

Miss Pulver had removed her hat and was using it to fan her flushed cheeks, her hair, now loosening from its rigid architecture of rococo waves, fluttering like golden feathers. It turned out that we had the very same subject in mind.

"Mister Stirgil, I admire your horse very much."

"Why thank you. I agree, she is a fine thing, to be sure, though she perhaps suffers from a touch of hauteur that is not very attractive in animals."

"Oh, I don't know," she said, looking out to the road where Oliver and Arthur were holding the mounts. "I like a filly with spirit."

"That is your famous American character, I should think," I replied, not entirely sure what I was talking about. "Do you ride?"

Miss Pulver reseated her hat, put her hands on her hips, and gave me a beaming, satisfied look. "I do, Mister Stirgil."

"Helen is excellent with animals," interjected Miss Karas, who was consulting a compass. "She had every stray dog lying at her feet." She threw a glance at Mr. Lamb, who was squinting up at the sun for some reason.

"Well, would you like to take the rein for a while, Miss Pulver?"

"Oh, I don't want to take your mount away from you, Mister Stirgil, I wouldn't dream of that," said her voice, though her face was saying something rather the opposite. She looked over at the horse once again and clapped her hands together with glee.

"Miss Pulver, I insist. In fact I demand it. I have long thought that women as a class have been insufficiently exposed to the equine arts, and it would encourage my heart to see you as an exception. Even if I am not a frequent rider I do believe that horses are good for the soul, so please, enjoy yourself. I shall keep Miss Karas company in the carriage."

She reached out and touched my arm. "Oh, thank you Mister Stirgil. That is so kind. I shall be very careful with her."

I was at a loss for words at that moment, so I merely nodded, and she strode off towards Peaches with a bounce in her step. In a few moments we were all following her back to the road, and we watched her hold the horse's face in her hands and peer into its eyes as though it were a child. She was saying something to it that we could not hear, and did not stop talking even as she put her foot into the stirrup and swung herself up on the beast's back. She waved to Irene Karas, who smiled and waved back.

"I don't know what you are talking about, Mister Stirgil, this is the sweetest girl I have ever met!" she called. She patted its neck and rearranged its mane slightly. "Yes you are, you are sweet like sugar candy!"

I settled myself into the carriage next to Miss Karas, ears buzzing and thankful to be out of the saddle. Young Lamb sat afore and chatted with Oliver about farmers' daughters. At the front of the train Helen Pulver squeezed her legs and flicked the reins, and Peaches set off in a walk. Sure enough, the woman had a grace to match the horse's, her back bounding easily like a sapling, no hint of stiffness or restraint. Her hat fell down and hung from the cord at her neck, and her hair bounced in the air as her backside bounced in the saddle. I felt the eyes of the dark one on me, however, and I tore myself away from the spectacle of the equestrian. "Enjoying your journey so far, Miss Karas?"

She ignored the question and studied my face. "She is very kind, you know." Her hair, too, had unloosened since first I saw her, and dark curls hung at her chin. "That is why animals like her. She is very quick to trust."

"Well, yes, those are good qualities I'm sure."

"Perhaps."

I was not quite sure what to say to that. Irene Karas's eyes were dark, very dark, and they were looking into mine. I found it hard to return her gaze. "And what about you, are you kind?"

She looked out across the fields. "I don't think I am *un*-kind, but that's not the same thing, is it?"

"I don't know."

"But I do have goodwill," she continued, "goodwill towards humanity, towards people as a whole. I would like to help make the world a better place for humanity. I think that is the best ideal one can have. Don't you agree?"

There was a noisy bubbling in my stomach and I felt an urge to belch. "Humanity? Don't know them. You'll have to introduce me some time." We passed a young negress carrying a basket on her head. Her face bore scars and one eye was milky-white blind.

Karas snorted. "What, don't know humanity?"

"No," I said. "I only know people."

I fell asleep not long after that, insensibility dropping down upon me like a gate. Out of that other murky world came dreams, dreams of endless theater anterooms, and a granite knocking that shook the walls. Then I saw that the ropy viridian curtains were vines and the divans were made of stone, their brocade patterns sprays of lichen and moss. Prehistoric trees stood high above me, columns for the black iron clouds that covered the world like a cathedral's ceiling. Terrible forms swirled in and out of those mists, so that I was afraid to look up at them, and I could only run from the thunder that shook the valley. Rising a crest I looked down and saw a great basin covered in green, and in the middle was a high, deserted ziggurat whose summit was stained with a crust of blood. Then, the jaguar!

I woke with a start, a cat's roar still in my ears, the thunder resolving into the knocking of the wheels against the stones in the road. Quite some time had passed, and Miss Karas was regarding me with an arch smile. "So our adventurer in dreamland has returned. What unknown country did you see? You are a very noisy sleeper, Mister Stirgil."

With difficulty I lifted myself into a more upright position and wiped my lips. "Did I cry out?"

"You did, when you weren't snoring loudly enough to frighten the horses."

I had forgotten myself, being still discombobulated from sleep, and I grabbed her hand that was next to me on the bench. "There was a cursed place, and a terrible sky, and blood. Everything was watching...."

"Yes, that will do," she muttered, and with a quick shrug she slipped out from under my grip.

Mister Lamb then turned to face me from the box, and his blue eyes shone through the shadows of the trees with excitement. "We are on the right track, Mister Stirgil! They came this way!"

"Who did?"

The Satanic Bridegroom

The young man gave me a puzzled look. "Why, Mister Seagrave and the captain, of course."

"Ah, those fellows. So, yes?"

"We made inquiries while you slept," said Miss Karas.

"We have made inquiries," repeated Lamb. "Two men fitting the description of our fugitives were seen riding a pair of mules on this very road."

"Where are we? Have we passed the road to Boom? Do we know which way they went?"

"Your foreman was to ride ahead and see if there was any news in Boom, but as luck would have it he came upon a family heading in the opposite direction well before that. They told him they had passed the two men yesterday farther up the highway."

Miss Pulver reined in Peaches and dropped back alongside the carriage. "We are on the right track, and we may have even gained some ground on them. However, it seems that we won't be able to catch up with them today. I should think it is about two in the afternoon. Do you know when it will be dark?"

"I'd say it will be about six o'clock when the sun goes down," offered Mister Lamb.

Oliver stirred on the box. "Aye, that's about right, six o'clock."

"Will we reach your camp by then, Mister Stirgil?" asked Karas.

"I should think so, or not long after, provided we press on and make good speed." I shivered once at the exciting thought that I would soon be there with Miss Helen Pulver.

The wheels ground on, bursting clods of earth and jolting against the stones. After a time Mister Lamb decided that he would roll a cigarette for himself, but the acrid smoke that billowed from his hedge trimmings sent Miss Karas into watery-eyed fits of coughing. She requested that she switch places with him, so as not to be downwind of the poison gas, and so Mister Lamb settled in next to me on the seat. I offered him one of my own cigars and lit one for myself; it was my own special blend, 66% Cuban tobacco and 34% dried buddings of hemp, of which I had my own private plantation some ways out of town. He gratefully accepted and began puffing like a factory smokestack, occasionally pausing to cough. "Aromatic stuff, this. Not much like what we grow back in Virginny."

"So you are an American too, I take it?"

"Yes sir. Norfolk, Virginia, born and bred."

"How amusing, my family originally comes from Norfolk as well, though a Norfolk situated somewhat more to the east than yours. Of course that was many years ago. I visited once, in my youth. They hardly knew my family's name any more. I dare say they all planted their behinds on our mahogany, though. What brought you down from your Norfolk to the Caribbean?"

"War and the Navy. I was stationed at Coco Sola."

"Ah, yes, of course. Thank you for keeping our sea safe from invasion."

"You are welcome. The fighting was rough, and the biscuits were rougher, but I am pleased to know that I have made a difference in the world."

"And I take it that you are no longer in the service?"

"That is correct, sir. I have been discharged."

"Ah, well, all things must pass. And what do you plan to do with your newfound burden of freedom?"

Mister Lamb gazed at Miss Pulver's rocking back and then took a slow pull on his cigar. "I am not certain. I...."

his eyes wandered to some flowers that speckled a bush by the way. He regarded the cigar. "This tobacco is rather potent, Mister Stirgil. I think I am becoming light-headed."

My own head was taking on a certain airy quality as well. I put my hand on his shoulder and whispered into his ear. "My own personal admixture, formulated to promote relaxation and bonhomie. Entirely harmless, I assure you. We have yet a ways to go and little to do. As a doctor of medicine I recommend that you enjoy it."

"*Are* you a doctor?" asked Lamb, taking another circumspect puff.

"Well, not in the strictest sense, but I take a great interest in physiology and psychology. You may consider me an enthusiastic amateur."

There was a snort from the box. "Next he'll be telling you about his pancreatic thalamus."

Regardless, young Lamb took my advice, slouching down in his seat and crossing his legs ostentatiously. He looked upwards at the deepening daylight as it shot the trees with color. When the wind blew, golden filigree worked the edges of the leaves. Then a bird burst upwards from the shadows, its wings catching the light from behind and turning it to a sunburst blaze.

"Phew! Did you see that?"

"I did. A firebird."

"Sweet."

"Indeed."

"There are fish of the deep that glow, liquid electric blues. Jellyfish and eels. Everything alive is shining, somehow, I think."

"Your poetic side is coming through again, Submariner Lamb," put in Miss Karas.

"Submariner?" I asked. "Is that a military rank? Like a sub-lieutenant?"

The young man grinned as he looked up at the clouds. "I am an undersailor, a spelunker of the sea. We travel *beneath*. Diving down with the fish, in a submarine."

"By God! Like Captain Nemo!"

Percival Lamb shot upright in his seat. "Exactly! Exactly that!" He leaned over conspiratorially. "I must confess that I am something of a fan of the writings of Mr. Verne." Then he stopped and thought for a moment. "Except I was not the captain. That was Adamski."

This new piece of information surprised me. "You served with this Adamski, the man who broke into my house? I see! I suppose now I understand better why you are here. Were you two on friendly terms? I mean, as friendly as one can be with a superior officer?"

Lamb's countenance took on a morbid cast. "I admired him greatly. He was a good man. We left the service within a few months of each other, and I was ready to follow wherever he led. But then there was that damned expedition, and Seagrave, and the cave. When we returned to Cuba he started drinking, drinking hard. And now...." He looked at me with hot, bloodshot eyes. "I think he has gone mad," he whispered.

I had very little idea of what he was talking about, except that Adamski was mad, which I also thought was very likely the case. Of course it was entirely possible that every person within a quarter-mile radius of where I sat was barking mad, with perhaps myself the maddest of all; however, it was best not to dwell on such things when smoking the special cigars. I put a calming hand on the boy's shoulder. "My friend, we will sort all that out in time,

The Satanic Bridegroom

I assure you. Are we not on our way to effect a rescue? With a little female persuasion and perhaps some rope everyone will be returned to where they belong. We cannot fail," I told him with a smile, "the sun is shining." The young man chuckled at this and relaxed once more into his seat.

Miss Karas looked back at us. "The sun is going down."

In time we passed the road to Boom and I once again took the lead on Peaches. There were fewer farms and travelers now, and trees crowded the highway. More and more the way seemed a gloomy tunnel in deepening darkness, and I worried that I would not be able to see the path to our camp. Finally in the distance I spotted the ragged canvas flag tied high in the trees, and I motioned the party to the hole in the brush to the west. The trail was only just barely wide enough to accommodate the carriage, and there were moments when one or both of the ladies were bounced off of their seats as a wheel rolled over a hummock. By the time we reached the shacks the dusk was deepening into night and the bats were whirring high among the eaves. The two bunkhouses stood off the ground on posts, and Beppo unlocked one and I the other. There were candles just inside the doorway to the foremen's quarters, and I lit them with a match. "The ladies will bunk in here," I announced to the group as they climbed down from horses and carriage, "the men in the larger barrack."

Miss Pulver had an adventurous look on her face as she bounded up the creaking steps. "Well, this is almost halfway cozy, Mister Stirgil," she said, as she took the candle from my hand and made the rounds. There were four wide bunks arranged in two tiers, plus a central table and a small stove. The far wall was adorned with an Oriental painted linen showing a sunburst mandala of tigers and birds and bare-breasted Indian maids riding elephants in a circle. Whorls disappeared into whorls, creating larger patterns that spiraled outward like radio waves, or so I fancied. Coarse pink-and-white-striped bedding lay on the bunks, and there were pink ribbons tied across the rafters as well, like a canopy. "Why, this is somewhat different than what I had expected."

"Now that the company does most of its trafficking by river, the camp is mostly used as a way station for our more far-flung social outings. If there are any females in tow, they bunk here in some semblance of comfort. You have to understand that the standards of luxury are somewhat different here in the British Honduras than they might be in your country, even among the upper echelon, as it were."

Now Miss Karas had entered as well, and immediately the minx spied a book that had tumbled under one of the bunks. "Well, at least we'll have something to read." Before I could react she picked it up and opened to one of the pages. She looked down upon it and after a half-second her eyes popped briefly and almost audibly, and then she quickly snapped the volume shut. She strode over and handed it to me. "Upper echelon," she said curtly. "So I see."

"Ah, yes, *A Newlywed's Primer*, with plates, 1865. Very instructive, I hear. I shall put it in the lost and found." Miss Karas began whispering in Miss Pulver's ear while I retreated to the night.

Later, after a supper of roasted chicken and pickled cassava shavings, the women returned to their shared boudoir and the four men and I sat around the table drinking whiskey and playing at cards. Submariner Lamb had taught the company the American pastime of poker, and Oliver and Arthur delighted in the game's sanction of lying and deceit. In time they began to enact elaborate arguments regarding the strengths of their hands over and above the betting, each claiming to have acquired combinations of unheard-of power and value in the annals of cardplay, with extra jacks magically entering the deck and then even somehow the greater arcana of the Tarot, leading to friendly arguments over whether the Tower ought to outrank the Hierophant or the other way around. In the end they would reveal their hands to show not even a pair, not even an ace high, and they would chortle and snicker and punch each other's shoulders, throwing money at each other like handfuls of hay. In the meantime I found myself appraising the scars of the place, carved curses, kicked tables, the charrings from overturned lanterns. The deep gouge by the doorway was from a man driven mad by a sudden onset of jealousy; he had picked up a hatchet and began swinging like one beset by devils, finally bursting forth to chase his bare-bottomed mistress into the trees. He brained her there, out in the ferns, and then returned home to hang himself like a good country squire. My foreman at the time buried her somewhere out across the highway and then left my employ. It was all right. It is well known that a ghost will never cross a road.

In time Submariner Lamb and I retired to adjoining bunks, shared another cigar, and listened to the night. Afterwards he retrieved from his belongings a paper pamphlet with the modest title of *Pine Cones* and began to read by the candlelight. Occasionally he would shiver, as though shaking off a spider. My body ached of time and miles, and soon I fell into the darkest sleep I have ever known.

V

When I awoke the following morning it felt as though I had not moved once during the night, and my muscles and bones were as stiff as the planks I had slept on. It was early, too early, and the daylight that streamed through the chinks in the walls had a washed-out, bluish cast. Everywhere dried-out husks of insects dangled from the webs of absent spiders. My throat was of an agonizing dryness, and the pain in my head so sharp that I was almost afraid to move. With a terrible creaking of the bunk I lifted myself upright and groaned my way to the door.

The sunlight was a calamity, a clangor, a terror unheard of that elbowed its way through the trees. I stepped around to the side of the bunkhouse, eyes half-closed, looking for something to drink, and nearly collided with Helen Pulver. She was crouched down at the water pump, wearing only jodhpurs and a camisole; her head was under the spigot, with the water running through her hair and coursing down her neck in runnels. Her eyes widened in surprise as she saw me and for a moment she was frozen there, her hands in her hair, looking at me sidewise, her mouth open. Then she crossed her arms over her breasts and stood up. With a dull clunk her head hit the spigot.

"Ow," she said.

For that one moment I could hardly tell her from some village girl caught in her prime, her fashionable American coiffure hanging down in soft, wet coils. "I'm sorry, did I startle you?" The words came out of my mouth with a sort of stunned thickness. "Let me see." She hesitated a moment, and then obediently pivoted, arms still crossed, her shoulder facing me, head turned away. I put my fingers in her hair and moved it from side to side, but I did not see any blood. "It seems all right," I said. The water beaded and rolled down her skin, and a smell like perfume wafted back up.

"Thank you," she said. Then she began walking back towards her bunkhouse, stepping carefully through the brush in her bare feet. "I hope we will be breaking camp early," she said without looking around. "It will make our task so much easier if we can catch them on the road."

"Without a doubt, Miss Pulver. I will rouse the men and arrange for breakfast."

Her body, what I had seen of it, had been even more entrancing than I had imagined, and the curve of her lip, so firm and perfect, had nearly unmanned me. I was lightheaded and shaking when I returned to the barrack, and for a few moments I waited to wake the others and instead merely sat on the edge of my bunk and thought.

We did indeed make our way out early, leaving the way station behind us. Miss Pulver and I did not speak to each other directly then, and her manner was quiet and guarded. Karas too seemed less talkative and more intense; perhaps the night in the woods had brought home to her the reality of the enterprise upon which she was engaged. And yet to me it still seemed a fantasy. We traveled up the road together, on horse or in carriage, each seeming firm of purpose, but there was a new note in the air between us; it seemed to me that at any moment one of us would suddenly halt the party and admit that it was all too absurd, that it had gone too far, that the game should be ended now, right now, before something happened that could not be undone. Here and there I glanced back at the others, and each was withdrawn into him- or herself; Karas with her chin up,

The Satanic Bridegroom

Pulver with hers down, but both with eyes that shone with defiance and seemed to look at nothing. The young sailor watched the trees with wariness, and my men all seemed to have a question on their lips. Even Oscar and Arthur were silent, and the only sounds were hooves, wheels, wind and birds.

For myself it did not matter. It was one new piece of madness among many. It would lead somewhere, and I knew that at the end of it I would find Helen Pulver in my grasp.

It was, perhaps, this very air of uncertainty that checked us when we spotted the Mayan standing by the highway. He was short and dark, as they all are, with a face that seemed at once dull in the way of a grown man but bright in the way of a child. He was dressed in a loose shirt of coarse cloth and trousers of deep blue with white piping that hung down only halfway between knee and ankle. He held a stick like a staff but did not lean on it, and he watched us approach with undisguised interest. We pulled up before him without discussion or even a shared glance. He looked us over, from one to the next, and then spoke the traditional greeting in thick, halting English. "You are I and I am you."

Beppo dismounted, walked forward and began speaking to the man in his own language. He asked a question and the Mayan replied, and after a time he made a sweeping motion of his hand from the north to the west.

"A woman from his village saw two men ride past last night. This morning his brother-in-law told him that the same two men came to his village and offered money for guides to bring them west."

"Did they say where they were going?" I asked. Beppo relayed the question and the Mayan shook his head.

"Perhaps he can take us to his brother-in-law's village, and we can follow them!" cried Miss Pulver.

"If we are correct about where they are headed, we can strike west into the forest here and perhaps catch up to them more quickly," offered Mister Lamb.

"But if we're wrong, we miss them," I said.

"Aye, that's true," said Lamb.

Beppo put another question to the little brown man, received a lengthy answer, and then turned back to the party. "It's more than a half a day's ride north to this other village."

We looked at each other, unsure of what to say or do. Then a gust of wind blew through the woods, seemingly from every direction at once, and Miss Pulver's hat was dislodged; it tipped forward off her head, bounced off her nose and fell to the road with a graceful plop. She jumped down off the carriage and retrieved it.

"I say we head west," said Miss Karas. There was still silence, however, and she added, "but of course the decision is Helen's."

Without warning, the Mayan man suddenly seemed to take an interest in something about Miss Pulver's person, and cautiously he walked to where she was standing with a quizzical look on his face. Though she was not a tall woman, still Helen stood well over the man, his eyes only at a level with her mouth. Carefully he reached towards her and took in his hand something that hung around her neck, a pendant that I had not noticed before; it must have been nestled inside her shirt and had only just now fallen out after she had jumped to the ground. It appeared to be a heavy, dull-looking cylindrical piece of dark stone, perhaps obsidian; at the top there was a thick, flat loop through which a lanyard had been threaded. The Mayan studied it carefully with a look of wonder on his face. Finally he said something sour-sounding to no one in particular and carefully returned it to her breast.

"What did he say?"

"Very old," I translated, for that much I had gathered.

"*Very* old," said Beppo.

Helen Pulver and Irene Karas looked to each other, then, and after a moment Helen turned to me. Her face seemed now clear of uncertainty. "We go west," she said.

The Mayan was now admiring Peaches, running his hand up along her ribs, and I asked him, as well as I could, where his own village lay. He looked at me in confusion for a long moment, then seemed to understand, and pointed off to the forest. Suddenly now I could see a trail snaking through the brush, hidden among the dappled shadows of the trees. It was odd, actually, that I hadn't noticed it before. "Beppo, tell him that we intend to travel west, and that we would like to hire two young men from his village as porters to accompany us."

Beppo had to think some time about how he should properly word this, and in stumbling speech with much vague hand-waving he made his plea to the Mayan. The small man's face grew steadily more consternated during the discourse; I could tell that he was attracted to the idea of money, but he was intelligent enough not to trust every gang of white men that appeared on the highway. Finally I simply dug into my pockets and pulled out all the coins I could find. I began tossing him the shillings as I extricated them, one after the other, so that he was hard pressed to keep up with the raining treasure. Finally he let fly a yelp when a coin slipped from his grasp and rolled under a bush, and I relented while he dove underneath in panic. After he retrieved it he bowed, pushed the money back into my hands, and gave a simple assent to Beppo.

That settled, I ordered Arthur and Oliver to unload our belongings from the carriage and the pack horse and set it all on the ground; Beppo, Lamb and I would carry it until we reached the village. The creoles were to take all the horses but one back to the camp and wait for us there. Oliver's horse would be brought with us to the village in case someone needed to be dispatched from there quickly; the Mayan assured us that his people would be able to care for it until we returned. In short order we said our goodbyes and walked into the forest, Pulver, Karas, Lamb, Beppo and myself, all following the Mayan man who led the horse and talked to himself in a quiet ongoing patter.

It was not difficult walking; the ground was level and only occasionally interrupted by the roots of trees that snaked across the way. The path was comfortably wide if we traveled single file, and while the foliage was thick it did not obstruct us. The two young women seemed confident and at ease, Miss Pulver offering me a broad smile when I turned to look back and Miss Karas one cocked eyebrow and a firmer squaring of shoulders. Even the horse seemed content, its tail flicking the insects away and occasionally knocking the hat from Percival Lamb's head.

After what I judged to be about a half a mile of travel there was a brightening in the trees and we came upon a wide clearing, a blank open space wrested from the jungle. At the center of this pause in the forest stood a clutch of stick dwellings with roofs of densely matted straw, and beyond that lay swaths of raw red earth daubed in varying degrees of verdure. In the first moment the place seemed oddly bare and quiet, but then with our arrival out in the open the people suddenly began to appear as if from nowhere, emerging from shacks or unbending from tasks to stare at us in gape-mouthed wonder or stony caution. The elder man waved his hand and called, however, signaling their ease, and they converged on our party with open faces or at least a forbearance of concern. The villagers were a variegated lot, some young and of pleasant aspect, others ancient and bent; one bowlegged, begoitered crone stared at us with rheumy eyes from her doorway, a polished forked cane in her hand. The habiliment of the people varied as well, with some wearing articles of proper clothing and others covered by little more than rags; there were even those among them that had painted faces, with bright orange smears on their cheeks and chins. One lithe young woman took a particular interest in Submariner Lamb and stared at him with careless intensity; she was, I supposed, not much more than sixteen years old, and was completely bare to the waist, her black hair hanging down in spraying locks like a waterfall. Despite the fact that she shared the broad features of her people her brown face had a startling beauty to it, as alluring and labyrinthine as any society debutante. While our host explained the situation to the people present she found numerous occasions to cross Lamb's path as she fetched water or bowls of food. Pulver and Karas were scandalized, of course, and for his part the young man tried to find items of interest to look at elsewhere, first the roof of a shack, now a well or a stray chicken. Finally the blushing seaman was reduced to playing hide-and-seek with the children to escape the siren.

Beppo too soon ran afoul of one of the town's inhabitants. While he stood attendant to the goings-on among the townsfolk, we watched a goat nimbly leap out of its enclosure by executing a flying bounce off the side of a donkey; it made its way some twenty feet away from the foreman, who had his back turned, and then, for no reason we could understand, it lowered its head and charged him. It was all too fast; we could barely raise our hands and formulate the warning on our lips before the man was face down in the center of town. The shock of the blow from behind had hit him like an earthquake, sending tectonic ripples across his ample flesh, and even when the dust had cleared his body still seemed to be jiggling like aspic. The Mayans all gasped and helped him to his feet, brushing his clothes and palpating his backside in search of trauma, though oddly enough the goat was not chastised or even shooed away but left free to nuzzle the poor man and rub its horns against his thigh like a cat in search of cream.

It was clear to all concerned that we ought to be sent on our way as quickly as possible, and so we were given two men to accompany us on our journey. The elder of the pair was Ixtab, a plump idler who wore next to nothing but who kept his face masked with blue-black paint. His companion was a reedy youth called Zotz who wore a pair of ragged white trousers with no shoes and whose hair fell over his eyes as though he had a black mop perched on top of his head. With many heaves and gruntings the pair managed to hoist the lion's share of our belongings on their backs, after which our host led us all to the western edge of the village. We walked into the jungle then, crossing the final line between the land of man and the trackless wild country, and when I looked back there was only the bare-breasted siren and the goat watching at the edge of the trees.

The Satanic Bridegroom

Already I was achy, hot, and itching. Within my head there was yet a sickly echo of pain that jolted with each step, thanks to the bottle of liquor that had made its appearance the night before. Each leaf that crossed my path seemed a terrific imposition, and to simply raise my arm and brush it aside was an effort that effected a tiny but recordable diminishing of my resources. And yet, there was something inside of me that was swelling and growing larger, a surging wave of some unknown expectancy. As the daylight of the Mayan village receded behind, I felt an energy flowing towards me, something from the forest that was primal and alive. Suddenly now the everyday pangs I felt for my chair, my book and my bottle of port seemed faint and far-gone, the walls that housed me superfluous, the voices and faces phantoms that held no sway. My mind was ricocheting from one thought to the next, loose and manic, but I knew that out here in the green it would center and focus, once and for all. I would be beyond good and evil. I would go native. I had taken my Webley-Fosbery from out of my pack and strapped it to my thigh, gunfighter-style. The last of the whiskey I poured away.

Lamb and Zotz had taken the lead, as young men will, and the two women walked some few paces behind. For a long time there was silence, and then something wrung itself from Helen Pulver's breast. "Ah, Mordecai, what have you done?"

"We'll find him," said Miss Karas gently.

"What's so absurd is that he never much cared for the out-of-doors, and here we are tramping through the jungle trying to find him."

"He was always so quiet, so bookish. I liked that about him."

"I as well." She gave a laugh. "Other men would have been quite happy to have a walk through the meadow with me back when we were sixteen. I practically had to drag Mordecai by the ear."

"Henry Thompson would have liked it, I should think."

Miss Pulver giggled. "Poor boy was nearly in tears."

"And Roger Clark."

"Oh, yes, Roger. And now he's gone, of course."

"What, Roger?"

"Yes, didn't you know? His number came up, and he was killed in France the year before last."

"Oh!" There was silence for a time.

"Mordecai was always so sweet and gentle."

"Yes, of course, Helen."

"That is, the real Mordecai, not that person in Santiago."

"Yes, of course."

"It was horrible, it was wrong, but he can't be blamed, can he?" Miss Pulver's voice had dropped, but I could still hear her words. "He wasn't in his right mind. He...." There was a slight choking noise. "That's why we must find him, Irene. We will find him, and we will bring him back to himself, and then they will see. Otherwise...."

"Otherwise he is a murderer," said Miss Karas flatly.

"Irene!" hissed Miss Pulver, and she grabbed her friend's arm. Then she turned her head quickly around to me, to see if I had heard. I should have dissembled at that moment, should have feigned ignorance, but it was all too quick, and something had changed, somehow. We had already taken a step beyond the threshold, a step past pretending that we did not understand. I simply returned her look. Murderer, innocent, it was all the same to me.

The Satanic Bridegroom

"We'll find your man," I said, though even as I did I had the tips of my fingers on the hilt of the gun.

Suddenly Miss Pulver collided with Zotz, and Miss Karas with Mister Lamb. The two men were frozen with their arms akimbo. Then there was a ratcheting sound from behind and Beppo pushed forward, shoving me aside. He thrust his rifle through a space in the confused knot of people and the gun exploded. In the split-second before the world became obscured by smoke I saw the reared head of a snake fly into a million wet pieces, spraying the underbrush like rain.

Beppo shivered and looked at me. "We almost walked right on it!"

Submariner Lamb was shaking. "Good Lord, what's it all about?" He had two flecks of red on his shirt and one on his face.

"You shot it!" exclaimed Miss Karas.

Beppo was as rigid as a post. "Yes, I did!"

"What was it, man?" I asked.

He turned to me, his eyes as wide as boiled eggs. "Tommy goff," he said.

"Couldn't we have just frightened it away?" asked Karas.

"That's the problem, Miss, they're not scared of nothing. They don't have to be. She was just about to show us why, and that would have gone very hard for us this far from a doctor."

The attitude of the two Mayans said as much again; despite the fact that the serpent had lost its head they approached it with great timidity. Ixtab nudged the corpse with his bare foot, and it did not move. That seemed to satisfy him; he hoisted the snake up and threw it over his shoulder.

As he passed to the back of the line he gave me a wide smile and tapped his hand to his mouth.

"Does he plan to … eat that?" asked Helen Pulver, still frozen in her tracks.

"I'm afraid so," I said. "And why not? It's fresh meat. We'd do well to have some ourselves."

Young Mister Lamb suddenly exploded into a guffaw. "That's jungle law for you!" He slapped Beppo hard on the shoulder. "Good shot, man! If it wasn't for you those two would be having *me* for dinner!"

Beppo returned a tight-jawed smile and slung the rifle across his back. "Don't worry, boy, they won't eat a white man." He blew his nose on his rag again. "Too much poison, even for those that would eat a bloody snake."

There could have been more to say then, but Zotz had already started off again into the trees. Lamb fell into step behind, shaking his head and chuckling. Miss Pulver and Miss Karas squeezed hands briefly, and then they moved on too, as did we all.

Back in the days when my father, brother and I would still occasionally tear free from our moorings and hike our way through the back country in search of timber to fell, I always found it interesting how our alliances would shift and recombine, in the same way that within a sweeping flock of birds the leader will change moment by moment, with currents separating off and cleaving together again like magic. Patterns of gait and fatigue, interest and mood would shuffle us hour by hour; now I would be with my father, discussing the logistics of bringing wood to river, and it would seem as though our friendship had been irrevocably bound together, two souls with the same mind. Then my pace might slacken, from too heavy a lunch, perhaps, and a word or a look would pass, a germ of annoyance, or the herringbone pattern on the back of his jacket would finally irritate my eyes, or my racketing cough would cause one more scowl of the whiskers, and without having made any clear decision as such my fast-walking father would be off in the fore with my brother, and I would have found better company in one of the porters or our old dog, Mateuse. Then a day later I would be with my brother, grumbling about our gruff forebear while he and his foreman had become inseparable chums. And so on.

So it was with us that day in the forest as well. Despite their tight bond, Miss Pulver began to have trouble keeping up with her friend Miss Karas; the latter had seemed to have become energized by our expedition, and she was practically bounding over every obstacle that stood in her path. Gone were the cross looks and sour grousings that I had become used to from that quarter; they had been gradually replaced by a clear-faced absorption in her own motion and inner drive. Now she checked her compass, now she examined a flowering vine, now she mounted a fallen tree for a better coign of vantage. At times she talked to no one in particular about terrain and meteorology and vegetable morphology, and on one or two occasions I thought I even spied a cockeyed smile on her lips. At first she gave her cousin gentle exhortations to keep the pace, but after a time these were given over and she simply forged on ahead.

In the late afternoon I helped Miss Pulver over a colossal ancient tree that had fallen across our way; so large it was that it seemed to stretch from one edge of the forest to the other, and it seemed more simple and expedient to surmount it rather than to wind around. I was able to climb

Joe Gola

up on top, and I held down a hand for her to join me. She took it and struggled up, trying to find purchase on the bark with her free hand and feet, but the long day of walking had sapped her energy. After a moment of watching her struggle Ixtab finally planted his hands on her backside and heaved her up like a sack of flour, eliciting a surprised cry of "Oh! Excuse me!" from the young woman. I let her down gently on the other side, and afterwards we fell into step together.

She was tired, I could see. Her face was flushed, and beads of perspiration had gathered at her temples. Her gait was less carefully graceful now as well, with her arms swinging more heavily at her sides and her back bobbing with a rhythmic sway. Still, though, her face had the same look of glowing determination, and still she was very, very beautiful.

"I admire your spirit, Miss Pulver."

She gave me a look which was neither encouraging nor unkind. "I suppose you think I am a blind, obstinate fool," she said.

"I would never dream of thinking such a thing."

"Oh yes you do. Of course you do. Why wouldn't you? But you don't understand. How could you? When you know someone for your entire life, and you come together and love each other, that means something, doesn't it? That's significant. That's kismet. You don't just ... give up on that person. I mean, haven't you ever had that kind of love with a woman?"

"I...." I searched for the right way to express my thoughts. "I love *all* women," I said. I regretted this immediately.

Helen snorted. "Oh yes, I know your type. How very magnanimous." She gave me a smirk.

192

The Satanic Bridegroom

"You think I'm insincere? Just because I can love many things instead of only one? Perhaps my love is equal to yours. Perhaps by loving many my love is multiplied."

"But what have you given up for that kind of love? How can you value that which was acquired so cheaply? Do you think that Mordecai was the only boy I ever knew? No, there were others. In fact there were some who thought that I could have done a lot better for myself." She snorted again. "What do people know! Mordecai would bring me flowers … why, I remember … I remember one January, yes, when I went out to play in the snow in my new Sunday shoes, I simply *had* to wear them, and by twilight I had nearly frozen my feet off. I was in tears … I couldn't even walk home. I had to hobble to Mordecai's, and I was too afraid to let his mother see, for she would have scolded me just as fiercely as my own, so I threw chips of ice at his window. He heard me and he snuck me into the house, up to his room, and then he held my feet, my damp stockings, until the feeling returned. We must have been that way for an hour. His friends told me he never looked at another girl when he was at the University, not a single one."

"I understand," I said.

"I understand many things too. I'm not entirely blind. I could have been like you. There were other boys, and I could have loved them all too. Yes, I have that capacity as well, Mister Stirgil. Perhaps that surprises you. But what would I have missed by not giving myself to only one, forgoing all others? Isn't that more meaningful? Isn't that *real* love?"

I did understand her, and perhaps there was even some part of me that agreed with her. Yes, I will confess that I did feel moved in that moment, and I had an urge to reach out and touch her face, though what that would accomplish I did not know.

Another man lived alongside this one, however. Still in my mind was the image of her as she knelt beneath the water pump, glasslike droplets on her skin, the elliptic curves of her body beneath the clinging shift, one arm raised as she wrung her wheat-gold hair. Her youth and beauty was like a perfume that intoxicated; it lingered in the air when she passed, and betimes as she stood before me I was ambushed and surprised by it, overcome with dizzy euphoria. It seemed to me as though she were a meal laid before me, ready to be devoured; the chef and maître d' were waiting expectantly beneath the chandeliers, as were the other diners, looking down from gilt-and-carmine balconies that leaned overhead like an avalanche. It blotted out all else, fears of censure or the law, even her love for this phantom of a bridegroom that was trapped inside a madman, beating the ribcage from within like a captive and crying through the smothering flesh for release. It mattered not. Our lives are a quick feasting and then an endless death. That is all.

My head ached with these thoughts as we made camp for the night. I watched across the fire as she prattled with Karas and Lamb about things silly and American: jass music and moving pictures, fountains of soda water and sprays of cowsmilk shaken to froth. Her teeth shone and her face was a golden glow in the firelight; she grinned broadly at Karas, demurely at Lamb. To me at times she looked too, and I received an odd, penetrating gaze that smoldered over a wry smile. The sparks that flew from the fire made her eyes flicker with pinpoints of light like two whorls of stars. Then Lamb made a joke, something I could not quite catch, and the two women burst into a hurricane of laughter, rocking back and forth on their bench of a fallen tree. As a reward she touched the top of his hand once, lightly, as it lay on his knee.

I sat on the ground between Ixtab and Zotz, sharing the snake and a last cigar. The Webley-Fosbery was beside me and for a jealous instant I imagined pointing it at the mariner's head and squeezing the trigger, smashing him with lightning. Then with a paranoiac chill the thought suddenly came: *they could surprise us in the night.* The darkness could be teeming with murderers; before my eyes I saw the midnight flash of haggard Adamski and catlike Seagrave, as I had seen from my bed those several nights ago: the wild, sunburned face of the captain, and then the shorter, darker shadow whose eyes were hidden. *Let them come.* My teeth ground together, the snake's tiny bones crunching and slashing my mouth, and then there was blood. I spit it into the fire. Let them come.

VI

I awoke to the sound of jungle birds, their cries almost deafening, folding in on each other with interleaving rhythms that coalesced to crescendos of intensity. For a moment I did not know who or where I was; the dark grey canvas of the tent around me was like being trapped in a womb, and I spent one terrifying moment trying to remember my name. It was akin to those dreams where one suddenly finds oneself on stage without knowing one's lines or even the plot of the play. Was there danger? I did not know. Finally I spied the flap of the door and I roused myself and burst forth into sunlight.

The forest brought everything back to me like a shock, like being struck by a wave at the shore. I knew now where I was and what I was doing, though it all seemed odd and hard to believe; the string of cause and effect, so inexorable before, was unraveling at its ends. Beppo was sitting on a nearby rock and eating a loaf of bread. He looked haggard and exhausted, his eyes dark and confused, his stomach sagging like a weight. I was little better off; my entire body ached and my skin felt raw, like a scraped hide stretched to dry. Nearby was a sack with more bread and hard cheese in wet cloth and some smoked meat. I grabbed some of each and gnawed on them as I stumbled through the jungle towards the women's camp.

We could not find a clearing wide enough for both tents, and so the two shelters were pitched some fifty yards from each other; the women enjoyed a relatively idyllic glade whereas Lamb, Beppo and myself made do with a smaller area crisscrossed by roots and other lumpy subterranean objects. We had offered the two Mayans a space under our

197

canvas but they preferred to construct a lean-to out in the forest and so attended to their affairs in their own way. As I neared the clearing I saw a flash of white through the trees and my heart made a brief hop at the thought of seeing Helen Pulver, but the figure instead resolved into the form of Irene Karas. She was standing in the center of the glade wearing short pants and a white cotton camisole; her arms were raised before her like two rails while she alternately pivoted at the waist and squatted. Through the thin white material I could view the brown tips of her breasts as they bounced up and down like frolicking rabbits in a snowy field. She halted when she saw me approach and put her hands on her hips.

"Mister Stirgil, are you all right? You look rather pale. You concern me."

I spoke through a mouthful of bread crumbs. "I will be fine soon enough. I … I just feel a bit groggy this morning."

"I would prescribe circulatory exercises upon waking. The brain needs blood, you know." She slapped at a mosquito on her bare shoulder and then scratched her armpit. "Do you think we will catch up with Mordecai today? How many miles have we walked?"

"I do not know, Miss Karas. This part of the country I do not know precisely, but we shall be reaching a pair of lakes soon, one after the other. We will skirt them to the south and then it will be a half a day's walk due west."

"Excellent," declared Karas. "I hope we are able to set out soon. I love to be moving, don't you? Yes, there is something invigorating about being in the wild." She flicked open a compass in the way that other women would a compact.

"Has north moved since last night?"

The Satanic Bridegroom

She snapped it closed again. "Don't be comical, Mister Stirgil."

Young Mister Lamb also appeared then in the clearing, and I thought I saw Miss Karas's shoulders set themselves back an inch and her chin tilt upward. "Good morning, all. How did everyone sleep?" He was infuriatingly jocular for the hour.

"Quite well, thank you," replied Karas. "I have been up since dawn practicing calisthenics. Do you know that I very nearly caught us a bird for breakfast? It was on a low branch and I threw a rock at it. I only missed its head by a hair."

"You want a slingshot," said Lamb. "Perhaps Mister Stirgil will lend us his suspenders."

The flap to the great conical tent then moved aside and Miss Pulver appeared with a blanket wrapped around her like an Indian squaw. Her thick golden hair had become disheveled in the night and had fallen over her eyes. "Yes, Mister Stirgil, will you lend us your suspenders so that we may hunt birds?" She yawned.

"I need those to hold my trousers up," I said, and retreated.

Karas and Lamb shared an interest in the natural world, and throughout the morning the two nattered together as they walked, pointing out flowers and frogs and birds and trees. They discussed biology and morphology at length, how it was that the animals sometimes happened to be suited just so to the conditions of their lives, whereas at other times they seemed to forget the laws of necessity and show an excessiveness of color or purposeless detail of design. How could something as impossibly inefficient as a butterfly survive? Was it God's will that such things be here, or was there some equally mysterious evolutionary cause-and-effect at work? Was there some lesson to be learned? The pinnacle of the pair's enthusiasm was their spotting of a small boa constrictor sunning itself high in a tree. While we watched the young woman dropped her shoulder pack and began climbing to take a better look. In two minutes she was some twenty feet up off the ground, one leg wrapped around the trunk, one hand clutching a branch. "Oh, Helen, the coloration is magnificent. You really should see this."

"Please come down," called Miss Pulver. "You're making everyone anxious."

"I am perfectly safe."

"If the bird whose head you missed with the stone spots you he's likely to peck at you and knock you down," I called.

"Oh, nonsense," muttered Karas. "I don't understand how some people can be so indifferent to the wonders of the...." Here she trailed off, and she appeared to be looking into the distance. To Miss Pulver's horror she then climbed several feet even higher, and still she strained her head upwards. "Mister Stirgil!" she called, "I see one of your lakes!"

We resumed our march, and in time we were greeted by an expanse of marshy water that was not terribly wide across but which stretched out as far as we could see to the north and south. Almost immediately we were beset by terrifying clouds of mosquitoes, and as tired as we were we found ourselves all but running through the forest in an attempt to get away from the parasites. We swatted them off each other's backs, where they endeavored to bite us through our clothing, and soon we had all gotten used to being unexpectedly assaulted by each other. Only Ixtab and

The Satanic Bridegroom

Zotz seemed unconcerned by the creatures, as they had daubed their exposed skin with mud from the shore. At first we chuckled about their homely appearance, but eventually Miss Karas put vanity aside and ran back to the water's edge to rub dirt on her face and forearms. Submariner Lamb followed suit, and then we all gave in; I helped Helen Pulver to cover her nape, and her eyes were of a startling whiteness as she looked up at me from a mask of dark earth. "We are becoming more savage by the moment," she jested, though there was a tremor of unease in her voice, and she spent an odd moment staring down at the backs of her hands, which were a rich, wet brown.

We continued on, silently, strange upright creatures stalking through the forest. There seemed little difference between us and the Mayans now, little difference between us and the insects and birds. At times I forgot who was leading who; the Mayans seemed to sense the mood as well, and I found myself falling in step with Ixtab, who began prattling to me about something or other; I could only understand occasional words, but my mind filled in the empty spaces with strange details that seemed to come from nowhere. I pieced together a story of another trek through the forest, but one of exodus, of a people fleeing in confusion, a diaspora brought about by madness, a return to the trees. They huddled in the rain for reasons they did not themselves understand, straining to remember the ties that held them together, running from doom. Cities were abandoned and taken over by ghosts, and even the meaning of the glyphs and pathways were forgotten. In my mind I saw great stone temples consumed by vines, howling empty in the wind, becoming haunted, returning to the gods, gods who circled through them as a presence, poised at any moment to return to solid flesh, a great basilisk lizard of legs and feathers, striking faster than the eye could see—a jerk, a maw that blotted out the sun, and then only teeth and tongue.

Near midday we reached the second lake, this time a lake proper. The scene was breathtaking; ferns and leaves crowded the water from the shore, creating striations of shade and shadow that offset the sunlit ripples skimming the surface like fire. There was warmth then, too, and gentle musical sounds from the trees. The mosquitoes had thinned out to their typical density, and so Helen knelt on the bank and washed her face and hands, the strange stone pendant dipping beneath the water as though it wished to drink.

Irene Karas stood not far away, also on the brink, the water touching the soles of her shoes. She looked out across the lake to the far side, her mind seemingly turned inward, her face placid like sunlight on soft water. Then she removed her hat and threw it to the side. She sat, unwound her puttees, and removed her shoes and short stockings. Standing again she unbuttoned her shirt, took it off, folded it once and threw it onto the hat. She had an odd striped look now, her neck and hands brown, the rest of her bright like ivory. Her trousers then she unbuttoned too, peeling them off one leg at a time, standing like a crane, revealing her pale firm legs. She was tall but well-proportioned, with wide but attractive hips, rounded thighs and strong calves. She removed her camisole, placed it more carefully on her other clothes, and then finally she slipped down her knickers, flicking them to the side with a kick, and she was completely bare. Tenuously she waded into the water, bouncing now and then as she navigated the uneven bottom, and then, when she had reached a depth that satisfied her, she dove in, round backside flashing once in the sun.

Helen watched her with a faraway look. At another time I supposed that she would be scandalized, reproaching her cousin for her impropriety and turning her face away in embarrassment. Now she seemed lost in her own thoughts, satisfied to roll up her sleeves and let the water run down her arms with their fine golden hairs.

Lamb watched as well. Slowly he brushed the dirt from his face, it crumbling and pouring like sand, only to be caught by the breeze and feathered into twinkling motes that disappeared in the sun.

In the mid-afternoon I had occasion to think back on my earlier travels through the country, asking myself, *was* there a river here then? Could I have forgotten such a thing? How did we cross, back in that time? Regardless, the fact was here before us now: a narrow but swift-flowing river blocked our path, no doubt some tributary of the Belize. At first the water appeared placid, and I was almost about to remove my shoes and wade through—it looked to be about neck-high at its deepest point—but young Mister Lamb pointed out the froth spewing over a rock some fifty feet away.

"We can't cross here, Mister Stirgil. Water like this will sweep you right downstream. It may not seem like much here where it's shallow, but once you go in over your waist you're not going to be able to keep yourself upright. It could sweep you right down onto those rocks." He cracked a dead branch off a nearby tree and pitched it into the center of the river. It moved away, smoothly but quickly.

Ixtab and Zotz were apparently in agreement, as they had turned to the right and started moving off upstream. We followed along. As we left the rocky shore for the shade of the trees I picked up a small rock and threw it as hard as I could. It plunked into the shallows on the opposite side.

"I don't recall you mentioning a river," said Miss Karas after a time.

I saw no point in dissembling. "I didn't recall the river."

Miss Pulver started. "You didn't ... *recall* the river? Are we lost? Have we made a wrong turn?"

"I don't believe so. We haven't turned at all. We're following the compass. Isn't that right, Miss Karas?"

"Yes, Helen, that's so. If Mister Stirgil is correct about the south shore of the two lakes being the landmarks from which to travel west, we are going in the right direction."

"Waterways can change over time, I should think," I offered with a shrug. "A river flows one way, and then it is blocked by silt or wrack and it changes to another. Maybe a number of smaller streams joined into one after a flood. I don't know. I don't think we should panic, however." This seemed to mollify the young woman somewhat, but she hurried off towards our guides nonetheless. She grabbed Zotz's elbow and he stopped, blinking at her pleasantly. Ixtab stopped as well.

"Aoxoa? Are we going the right way to Aoxoa? The valley?" she asked. She made a vague gesture with her hands as though she were feeling the bottom of a basin.

The two Mayans gave a short start of surprise. They looked at each other, and Ixtab repeated the word in a low tone. Then they looked back at Helen in wide-eyed silence.

The young woman was almost in tears with exasperation. "Yes, Aoxoa, that's where we're going. Didn't you know?" The two remained silent, watching her closely. She threw up her hands. "Oh, Mister Stirgil, what is going on?"

I spoke very quietly. "I did not tell them our destination, only that we wanted to travel west. It has been my impression that the place we are going does not have a good reputation among their people, and I did not want that to complicate matters."

The girl seemed stunned. She put both hands over her mouth and stared blankly into the jungle. Then she dropped them and gave a mirthless chuckle. "A bad reputation," she said. The two brown men looked at each other again, exchanging glances of which only they knew the meaning.

Just then there was a shout. "Here!" It was Lamb. I shouldered past the group and followed the sound of his voice to the edge of the river. A hundred yards away, almost out of sight around a curve, we saw what looked like brush in the water. We moved back into the woods and hurried north, and in a few minutes we had reached a great gaping hole in the forest where an enormous tree had become uprooted and fallen across the river. We moved around the sunburst of roots and followed the trunk down to the shore; the tree reached nearly four-fifths of the way across. Foam boiled around the parts of the tree that were submerged in the water.

Karas appeared behind us as we surveyed the scene. "Well, we can cross here, can't we?" She patted the fallen trunk, which here was at a level with her head but then angled down towards the water. "I would just need a leg up, or else get a bit wet."

"Well, I would go first," said Mister Lamb matter-of-factly. "We'll tie some ropes from the tents together, secure one end *here*,"—he pointed at the roots—"and the other end *there*,"—pointing at the far branches—"and then everyone will have something to hold on to to help keep their balance."

Miss Karas had her fists on her hips and was staring at him coldly. "And why should you be the first to go?"

Submariner Lamb looked to me, then back at Miss Karas, then back at me again. "Well, I should think it would be obvious. I'm a man. I'm stronger."

"What has that got to do with it? Nobody's asking you to lift the river. This merely requires some nimbleness and careful stepping, both of which I am perfectly capable."

"But what if you should fall into the water?" exploded Lamb.

"What if *you* should fall into the water?" retorted the young woman, whose face was now becoming a bright shade of red. "The female body is far more buoyant than that of a man. I shall tie the rope around my waist, and if I fall in you can use your remarkable strength to pull me out. It is as simple as that."

The young man threw up his hands and said something impolite to the forest; it was fairly clear that he preferred that any feats of daring be taken by his own person, and not one of the women. However, I was just then remembering how quickly she had shimmied up her tree earlier that day, and it seemed to me that she might well be the best candidate for the job.

We had in fact brought some supple twine ropes with us for the purpose of constructing our canvas shelters—and for bringing Miss Pulver's fiancé back to civilization by force, if necessary—and so we carefully tied two of these together and secured one end to a sturdy root that pointed to the sky like a finger. The other end we tied around Miss Karas, just beneath her arms. For a long moment she deliberated as to whether she should go shod or barefoot, and in the end she slipped out of her shoes and handed them to Helen for safekeeping. She and Lamb went down to the water's edge and he hoisted her on top of the dead trunk.

"Just crawl on your hands and knees, Irene," called Helen. "That will be safest."

Miss Karas was straddling the tree like a horse, her brows knit. She palpated the bark. "I don't think so," she replied. "It's very rough. I'm afraid I might flinch and lose my balance."

"Well, you can just scoot along on your behind, then."

Miss Karas turned red again. "Oh, really, Helen," she said, and then carefully drew in her legs and rose to a standing position, her arms reaching out into the air.

"Oh, dear Lord, Irene, please be careful," said her friend.

"That thought is foremost in my mind," Karas replied, and she began to move off. Her steps were slow and awkward at first, her arms at times wavering up and down like a stork landing in heavy weather, but then she fell into an easy rhythm: one foot would move forward and pat the bark, searching for a smooth and level patch, and, once found, she would carefully shift her weight and then bring her rear foot around. In this manner she was able to keep herself in slow, steady motion. Young Lamb carefully paid out the line behind her, making sure to give enough slack for her to move but not so much that the rope would dip into the water. In time the young woman was directly over the middle of the river, right where the current was swiftest. We heard her say something in her typical flat, detached tone, but the words were lost downstream. She moved gracefully along as we held our breaths.

At other times in my life I have observed that it only takes a split second for one to reverse one's own mind and declare a good idea to be a bad one, and in that split second one always has the thought that just *that* ought to be justification enough to be allowed to take back the move, like a queen pushed too far across the chessboard—just that instantaneous surge of humility and regret, and the solemn promise that one would never be rash and foolhardy in the future, no, not ever again. And always it is too late. Irene had just reached the point where the trunk of the tree was dipping deepest into the current, the water surging around it with a boiling spray, when the sodden bark on which she stood sloughed off like a peeling rind. We all gasped as her left leg lost balance and her right shot downwards along the slick wood. Her hands dropped to catch the trunk, but already she was spinning; we saw her face wide-eyed and rigid as she fell downward. Her right arm, outstretched, scraped against the bark from her shoulder to her wrist, and there was the sharp sound of tearing fabric. Helen Pulver screamed.

When I opened my eyes again Irene Karas was hanging from the tree. The cloth of her sleeve had gotten caught on the jagged stump of a branch, and we could see her hand twisting wildly as it tried to slip through and free. Her face was just at the water line, and with a rhythmic buffeting it repeatedly breached and submerged; she would be ducked under, the water coursing over her hair, and then with a thrash she would propel herself up again through the foam, her mouth a giant O as she gasped for air. Then she would be dragged under again. She looked like a salmon trying to make its way upstream, but for the struggling and the eyes full of terror.

Before any of us realized what was happening, Lamb was running down the trunk of the tree. He dropped and straddled it just as he reached the girl, and he threw himself forward. With his chest on the bark and his left arm wrapped around the other side, he grabbed her wrist and pulled, his neck and face knotted with strain. She rose out of the water a couple of inches, just enough to clear her mouth. Her black hair was wrapped over her eyes like a wet blindfold, and her free arm thrashed blindly as the current tried to drag her underneath.

Slowly Lamb inched himself forward along the tree, pulling the girl with him, desperately trying to keep her head above water. We could see her hand turning purple in his grip, and still she gulped in air, as though afraid it would be torn from her lungs at any moment. I only barely noticed the sudden stabbing pain in my arm where Helen Pulver was grasping it, digging her nails into my skin. As gently as I could, I wrenched her off of me and held her hands tightly. Beppo had charged into the water to pull up the slack in the rope, which we now realized could just as easily strangle the girl as save her.

With excruciating slowness, the man and woman moved towards the far shore, one straining, the other thrashing and helpless. Then they stopped. Lamb was panting, his right arm shaking, and in Karas's face we could see that she knew that she was going under. Though her eyes were wide, there was no terror in that moment then, only the knowing and the waiting. Every breath was a quick filling of the lungs in readiness for the plunge. But then, slowly, Lamb began moving forward again.

Joe Gola

In a few moments more they had reached the first branch at the top of the tree, and Karas wrapped her arm around it tightly. Carefully the boy let go of her wrist, and it fell and splashed like dead weight. They rested for a time then, her face hanging down, her lips and the tip of her nose just brushing the water, and then she began to move on. Hand over hand she pulled herself along the branch, and then we saw her shoulders rise as she began to stand on her own. Clumsily she waded up to the shallows, untying the rope wound tight around her ribs. When it came free her lungs heaved deeply in spasms, but still she paused to tie the loose end carefully around the branch. Then she sank to her knees, rolled over, and lay face up on the stones, breathing deeply. When Lamb had picked his way through the branches he rushed up and knelt over her, the two talking in close confidence. We could not see their faces.

Helen Pulver was on the ground now, hugging her knees to her chest and apparently praying. Beppo stood beside me.

"I'm not going, Mister Stirgil," he said.

I stared at him. "We need you," was all I could reply.

"I can't swim."

"But we'll have the rope. You can do it! The hard part is already done."

A dangerous edge came into his voice. "I am not going."

"For God's sake, man...."

Miss Pulver's voice burst out like the popping of a balloon. "Leave him alone! You can't make him!" Then, more quietly, she said, "I can't have that on my conscience."

"I'm sorry, Mister Stirgil."

210

The Satanic Bridegroom

It was of no use. I asked if he would remain here and wait for us to return; he agreed. We took stock of the remaining food—it was dwindling now, though none of us seemed to want to think about that just yet—and I gave him what little we could spare. He had his rifle and could spend his time hunting, presumably. I also gave him one of the tents; the rest of us would have to make do with the other. It only seemed right. As we divided our supplies I happened to look over to the opposite beach where Karas and Lamb were recovering. The young woman stood up, gave a quick shiver and a flick of her arms to throw off the water, and then climbed the rocks towards the trees. I could see a thin, straight trail of red through the tear in her sleeve. As she reached the tree line she turned her head once to Lamb, who was still sitting at the water's edge, arms crossed on knees, forehead on forearms, and said something. He looked up, and then after a moment he climbed to his feet and followed her into the shade.

I divided the equipment into three packs, one for myself to carry across and two for the Mayans. During the misadventure they had been as anxious as the rest of us for the safety of the two young people, and yet they seemed entirely blasé about the prospect of traversing the tree themselves. They merely nodded thoughtfully as they saw me repacking our gear, and occasionally threw in a suggestion by way of switching a pair of objects or resettling something in one of the canvas bags. Ixtab, at least, approved of Beppo's decision; when the man was out of earshot the Mayan nodded his head in his direction, waved his hands in a crossing motion and said, simply, "Too fat."

Zotz made a "splunk!" sound with his mouth and then waggled his hands and fingers together like a puppeteer to suggest something thrashing as it sank.

I decided that I would test the rope guide and that Miss Pulver would follow me, with Ixtab and Zotz bringing up the rear. With the Mayans' help I climbed up, and, as is always the way, what looked so simple and easy while on safe ground seemed anything but when one was poised to try it oneself. The trunk seemed absurdly high, and I found myself more anxious about slipping and falling upon the rocks on the shore than into the rushing water. Meanwhile the rope was of no help whatsoever; despite our best efforts it was still too slack, and it moved and wobbled erratically, ripple-like vibrations coursing back and forth with each jerky movement. It could only serve as a kind of last-ditch safety net.

My first steps felt endless; I hesitated long before settling on a foothold on the bark, and with every shift of weight my arms wavered wildly up and down. I had hardly gone anywhere at all and already my shoulders were aching, and I began to fear that I would run out of stamina long before I reached the other shore. The water moving in the periphery of my vision as I looked down at the tree made me dizzy, as though suddenly it were the tree that was in motion underneath me instead of the river, and several times this almost caused me to tilt too far to the right and plunge down. I was forced to keep my eyes fixed on the forest ahead, feeling my way with my feet. My left eye began to itch as sweat trickled down into its corner, but I dared not blink it away.

Remarkably, though, I did hit a kind of rhythm, and soon I was moving quickly down the length of the tree.

The Satanic Bridegroom

Forward motion made the balancing easier somehow, like a bicycle; it was only when I reached the spot where Karas's tread had shucked off the bark to reveal a smooth, slick patch that I found myself wavering again. My confidence fled almost completely, and for one second it seemed as though I would plunge down myself, but a wildfire burst within my breast and focused my mind to a pinpoint; I knew only trees, water and shore, and I pushed myself forward, almost at a run. I made ready to catch the branches that reached toward me like snaking arms, but at the last minute I did finally feel myself falling away, airless and out of control. I jumped, landing in the shallows, and my feet slipped and pitched me forward. My hands and knees plunged into the water and hit rock, but the river cushioned the fall. There was only a jolt and a scrape, and then all was still again. Though wet and shaking, I was across.

Miss Pulver was waving and yelling to me on the far side now. I smiled and waved back, motioning her to follow me across, but she pointed towards the woods and made an exaggerated, angry shrug to signal confusion. "*Where is Irene?*" I finally heard her say, anxiety straining her words. I waved to signal that I had understood and began climbing the steep shore in search of her friend.

After the brightness of the river the forest seemed like a cave, and for a long moment I could see nothing but a glowing darkness dappled with spangles of blinding reflection. It was cool here, too cool, and I shivered; my clothes were soaking wet. My knees ached dully from where they had hit the stones, and I could feel scrapes in the heels of my hands that were filled with grit. My shoulders were only slowly unknotting themselves from tight balls of tension.

I paused to assimilate all these sensations, and, once paused, felt an odd reluctance to start moving again; the momentary solitude was almost like stumbling upon some feast, and I could not tear myself away. As I stared blindly into the gloom my thoughts drifted off to a place where there was only me, only my own hunger and pains, only a sugary-sweet, halfhearted self-pity. With this, though, came also a kind of satisfaction, or even quiet exultation, for against all odds I was somehow alive and unhurt. There would be a fire, soon, and some little meal, and sleep and oblivion. If worst came to worst I could make it back, I knew—famished and physically beaten, perhaps, alone if need be, but alive—and all could return to the way it had been before. I closed my eyes and took a deep breath. For the first time I noticed how sweet the air was. It was like breathing life. All was quiet.

All was too quiet. I opened my eyes and looked about me; I could see through the gloom now, I could see the walls of ferns teeming over stones and the strange knife-like grasses that suckled at whatever sunlight scattered their way from the clearing of the river. Tenuously I took a few steps deeper. The leaves were soft and made little noise. Some impulse stopped me from calling out. The birds were here, as always, but silent. Larger, colorful ones I could just make out in the canopy high above, long tails of plumage hanging like some rainbow vine, and it was as though they were enjoying some other atmosphere, as though they belonged to some higher cosmology; if they flew off it would not be to ground but some level above, some floating platform in the ether, one with other trees of kaleidoscopic shape and color, where the rareness of the air would make every surface glitter like crystal. Lower down a wren-like thing held a seed pinned in its talon and pecked at it like a little taphammer. Peck peck. Peckity. Peckity peckity peck.

There was another rhythmic sound now too, something just beyond the ferns, a brushing or a rasping in the air. It was at once both homey and strange, and I seemed to recognize it without being quite able to say exactly what it was. On and on it went, not stopping, only shifting in speed and intensity. I walked forward slowly, heel-to-toe, and made my way around the brush. Then I saw.

Irene Karas was on top of Submariner Lamb, completely bare, moving upon him with a furious rhythm. One hand was braced on his chest and the other was at his throat. Though his face was turned away I could see a look of transfixion upon it. His hands were wrapped around her thighs just above the knee, moving with them as they surged. For a moment I was stunned, unable to move, and she turned to me. Her full lips were parted, her nares wide, and her chin tilted upwards as it rocked. Through the dark hair that had fallen over her face I could see her eyes; they were hard and glassy, looking inward as she held her body suspended on the brink of ecstasy. Then the eyes were looking at me. They contained a syrupy power, as though they were seeing through and into my own self. I felt a jolt. Her lips trembled, and I saw the white of her teeth.

Before I realized what had happened I was back in the forest, moving back to the shore, my face burning. Bursting into the blinding sunlight I was all but panting for breath. Across the water I could see Helen Pulver, hands wrung together, her eyes wide with fear and worry. Her face too was transported to some other place, some jungle country where jaguars roamed. I waved my arms in a weary way: *it's okay*. Was it?

She put her hand on her face and was still for a moment then. Slowly her shoulders lowered, and finally she looked up. Between us the water rushed without stopping, coursing over the stones, a great roaring of force. Inside it would be alive with fish, sleek river creatures poised in the current. Waiting in ambush they lay for whatever was foolish enough to let itself slacken and drift.

Helen tightened the straps of the small pack that we had rigged up for her and then she called over to Beppo, who was sitting on a rock and staring into the trees. With his help she climbed her way onto the fallen tree, her hands and forearms taut as she gripped the bark. Once on top she straddled it like a horseman and made her way in a sitting position, leaning forward, placing her hands on the bark, and then gripping the trunk with her calves and pushing her body. Then she drew up her legs and repeated the motion. The rope guide hung next to her limp and unneeded. She did not pause when she reached the deepest point where the water boiled and swirled, and in time she was on her feet and picking her way through the branches. Zotz and Ixtab were following in the same manner not far behind, but more quickly and talking all the while. As her feet splashed into the shallows I felt a reckless fool then; we all should have crossed that way. We had been behaving like clowns, or mad animals. In my mind I suddenly saw again Irene Karas's naked thighs gripping the young man's body, her belly tight, the clench of his jaw. And perhaps it was still going on, that abandon, life snatched from the jaws of death.

Suddenly Helen Pulver was all but on top of me; she held my arm in both her hands and pressed her face onto my shoulder. As she breathed her breasts crushed up against my side. There were flecks of mud in her hair and she smelled of perspiration. "What are we doing?"

My skin was on fire. "Don't worry," I said, and squeezed her shoulder with my other hand. It was soft.

"Something terrible is going to happen to us," she said.

I was still formulating a response in my mind when she gasped and abruptly stepped away from me. I followed her stare of amazement behind me to the trees; standing there were Miss Karas and Submariner Lamb, now fully clothed, but with them was a young Mayan man who looked back at us with an expression that was halfway between relief and terror.

In some few moments Ixtab and Zotz had finished crossing the river, and we now sat in a loose circle on the stones at the shore. We persuaded the new young man to join us with soft words and some stale bread, which he ate hungrily. His name was Balam, and he spoke English, though slowly and with effort. Zotz informed us that he was from a village to the north, with Ixtab supplying the detail that he was close friends with a relation of the young man, though that family relationship was a complex chain which involved several marriages and which took an inordinately long time to explain. Balam and Zotz seemed to greatly enjoy the retelling, however, and both nodded their heads in approval.

"Your village is very far away. What brings you here?" I asked.

Balam swallowed hard. "The two men said that they would pay me and Cocijo to bring them to Aoxoa. I did not want to do it, but they said they would give me much gold." Ixtab and Zotz glanced at each other.

217

"The two men, one was young, with long hair, one older, with grey hair?" I asked.

"Yes," said Balam.

"Why did you not want to go?" asked Helen Pulver.

Balam seemed to have some difficulty with the word 'why', but after a quick consultation with Ixtab he seemed to understand. "Our people know that is not a good place. We do not go there. A bad people lived there. That is all."

"Are they looking for gold?" asked Lamb. He pointed to his eyes and then bounced a cupped hand, as if he were weighing a purse.

Balam gave a confused look, and then thought for a moment. "They are looking for a god," he said.

Lamb frowned. "Perhaps he means an idol or some kind of statuary," he said to me.

"Yes, perhaps, some item of archaeological significance."

"Are they here? Do you know where they are?" pressed Helen.

Balam pointed to the forest to the west. "Not here. This way."

"Can you take us to them?" she asked, her voice edged with emotion.

Balam's face and posture betrayed a sudden distress. He seemed about to answer, then stopped, his hands rubbing his knees. "No! I will not!" finally burst forth from him.

Irene Karas threw up her hands. "Finally we meet someone able to help us and he refuses to do it." She turned on Balam with vexation. "Why not? Why can you not take us to him?"

Balam spent a long moment looking back and forth between us, his face knotted with anxiety, as if on the verge of

tears. "Those men … the one with long hair … his eyes.…"
He then spoke to Ixtab, relaying his thoughts in Mayan.
Ixtab seemed equally at a loss as to how to translate, but I
understood one of the words he used. Finally he could only
say, "he speaks of strange things. He is dangerous."

"That's ridiculous," said Miss Pulver, the words bursting forth hotly. Miss Karas and Mister Lamb stiffened.
Without moving their heads, their eyes flicked towards each
other and met.

"His god is old, an outcast." Balam searched for the
right word. "It is not one of our gods. It is from … underground."

"What of this Cocijo?"

Balam thought for a second and then gave a short, barely perceptible shrug. "He is from my village. He wanted to
leave, but.…"

"But?"

Again the shrug. "He is very poor."

There was a strained moment of silence then. The three
Mayans all seemed very uncomfortable, glancing at each
other and then away. Finally Helen Pulver spoke. "Can you
at least tell us how to reach them?"

Balam abruptly stood up. Then he began speaking directly to Ixtab and Zotz. His words sounded careful and
measured, yet forceful, like the taps of a hammer. With his
final words he pointed once at the chest of Ixtab and once at
Zotz. Then he began walking away.

Lamb started in surprise. "Should we … should we stop
him?"

It was too late. The young Mayan man was already hip-
deep in the water. He climbed up on the tree with ease, and
then simply walked along its back to the other side, his

hands swinging lazily at his sides, as though he were ambling across some golden meadow, returning at the end of the day. He never looked back, and he passed Beppo's stare without a glance or a word.

We moved on. There was little else to do. As the afternoon waned we found a little clearing where the grass was soft, and though there was still daylight left we stopped, all of the same mind that it was enough, the day was over. As we had left one of the tents with Beppo, the four of us were to share the other; Lamb and Karas seemed unperturbed at the prospect, but simply tied up a tarpaulin to divide the space into two halves. Zotz disappeared into the forest on a hunting expedition and returned some time later with the carcass of a large and very surprised-looking monkey and some fruit. He cleaned his kill and impaled it on a spit over the campfire. The two women looked at the animal with quiet horror as it cooked, but when the time came they took a share of the meat and chewed it grimly. At one point I found myself staring at a blackened miniature paw and thinking how strange it all was, how I ought to be throwing it away in disgust, and yet I did not. It was only afterwards that I realized that neither of the two Mayans had partaken of the meat. It seemed that the kill was only for us, but what that meant I did not know.

There was a strained silence in the camp. Irene Karas kept herself busy and appeared satisfied with her own company. Young Mister Lamb seemed to be avoiding everyone's gaze, and he occupied himself by building a hidden perimeter of dried sticks and twigs that would theoretically crackle and make noise if anyone tried to cross it in the dark. Ixtab was grimly bemused by this activity, and he aided Lamb in a comically inefficient fashion, spending long minutes searching the forest for just the right piece of wood, finally returning with a twig the size of a fountain pen and then placing it with exaggerated care in the grass. Helen Pulver simply stayed inside the tent, and it was somehow tacitly understood that she should be left to herself. I sat on the ground and tended to my blisters. When that pastime exhausted itself I hunted for the various insects that had wormed their way through my clothes and were biting my skin.

My thoughts about the woman were turbulent. My desire had been tempered by some other feeling now, something which ached in a sweet way that I could not define. I could see the profile of her face before my eyes, the curve of her cheek, the simple sureness of her hand as she smoothed back the hair that had freed itself from its rigid coiffure and which now fell in a riot of soft yellow. Once that night she met my eyes again across the fire, and again she gave me one kindly smile before turning away. Later, in the dark, I could sense her near me, on the other side of the fabric, and I felt a longing to reach my hand beneath and seek out hers. I longed to lay with her and blot out all that surrounded us, to taste her mouth, to smell her skin. Suddenly now, in the wilderness, my ordinary life seemed a vast emptiness, a living death. My home was a tomb, my bed a coffin. Only Helen seemed alive, shining from within. To lose her now would be to return into a hell of sleepless nights and bleach-bright days. My mind struggled to stay awake and make some sense of these things, but in the end my exhaustion gave way and two great hands reached up through the earth and pulled me down into oblivion.

VII

We awoke the next morning to find that Ixtab and Zotz had gone. Somehow no one was terribly surprised. For me there was no fear or panic in the discovery, only an odd sense of loss, as though we had been abandoned. Now there was only us four and no one else. Thankfully they had not taken any of our provisions, and we ate a carefully measured breakfast around the ashes of the fire. When we were finished we divided up our belongings into four equal packs and set out once again into the west.

Under cover of night a legion of clouds had marched from horizon to horizon, and today the forest was dark as we wound our way through the trees. The dazzling chiaroscuro of the days before had been replaced by an amorphous gloom, a color somewhere between the greens of a waiting snake and the hushed purple-blacks of a catamount. With our guides gone, the country now seemed dread and alien; I found myself reaching for my gun at every bird's call, and the fountain of conversation had finally run dry. Even the two women barely spoke to one another; Miss Karas formed the vanguard with her compass and tight-buttoned clothes while Miss Pulver remained in the rear with her slouch hat pulled low. She and I moved the hanging branches aside for each other and shooed away the insects that whirled over each other's heads. Once I gave her a swift slap on the shoulder to kill an enterprising mosquito that was oblivious to my threats and wavings; she tensed from the blow only a moment, then silently nodded, and kept on.

The trek had taken on some new significance for me, though what that significance was was unclear. This long time I had been straining my eyes forward, expecting at any

223

moment to spot the distant backs of the two fleeing men, but at some point my imagination had replaced those two with two others, had replaced them with myself and my father. It was as though the boy and the man had lost themselves out here in the trees all those years ago and I was to find and reclaim them. Perhaps I could put my arm around my younger self and correct his path, show him the right way to continue—some different way—any way. There had to be a way to start over. I could talk to my father, too, man-to-man; we could discuss women and the world, and for once I could truly take his measure. Perhaps I could finally take my own.

The jungle was empty, however—just a tunnel now, sucking us forward—and there was nothing to do but move on. My pace quickened as I felt our destination near, and I found myself watching Helen carefully out of the corner of my eye. What would she do when we found her man? What was her plan? She seemed at once both larger and smaller than before—more real, less an invention of girlishness and charm, but then at the same time diminutive and fragile.

"We'll be there soon, won't we?" she said to me as we sat next to each other on the ground during a break, our backs against a fallen tree. We were eating dry corn meal, as it might well have been noon. My pocket watch had stopped; I had forgotten to wind it. Karas and Lamb had both taken off their shoes and were comparing the holes in their stockings.

"We're very close, I think."

"Unless we simply go past it and no one notices," interjected Miss Karas, as she gave me a pointed look.

The Satanic Bridegroom

I scratched at what was the beginning of a beard. "I don't quite know how to explain why it's so," I said, "but it isn't the sort of place that one passes by without noticing."

"Is it a very deep valley?" asked Submariner Lamb.

"Quite the opposite," I replied. "It's shallow. One can hardly call it a valley at all."

Miss Karas snorted. "And how precisely are we to recognize your hardly-a-valley? Is there a sign? Will there be a welcome kiosk?"

I tried to send my mind back to that distant day in the past, to grasp again that feeling I had experienced. "It was something about the trees, and the quiet."

"I don't want to go back without Mordecai," Helen blurted out, addressing no one in particular. "If we miss him, we'll just keep going...." Her eyes were staring off into the trees. "We can just disappear." She took my hand for a moment without looking at me. "Wouldn't that be nice, Mister Stirgil? We can just disappear."

"Perhaps we have already disappeared," said Miss Karas in cold and carefully measured tones.

Slowly Helen Pulver's eyes tore themselves away from the forest and looked at her.

"Did you think to wire your family that you were tramping out into the wilderness of Central America? When you wired to say you were coming to British Honduras, did you mention to them that Mordecai had committed a crime and might possibly now be dangerous? Does anyone at all know where we are, besides the henchmen of this flim-flammer? Reckless girl! All this for little Mordecai Seagrave? And like a fool I followed you, Helen!" She tugged her shoes back on roughly. "Perhaps we have already disappeared," she repeated, and fell silent.

Helen dropped the piece of bread that she had been holding and stood up stiffly, her head carried high. She crossed the clearing to where Irene Karas sat until she was standing directly over her. Her fist raised up over her head and then came down quickly, hitting Miss Karas's forehead just in front of the temple. It was a hard blow, but it glanced off awkwardly, and I could tell that it had likely hurt Helen's hand more than it had hurt her friend.

Miss Karas was standing then, and with the swift and efficient stroke of a boxer she punched Helen in the face.

"Helen!" I shouted.

Young Lamb quickly grabbed Miss Karas's wrist and hauled her away from the scene. Her face was beet red, and her voice had lost its usual frigidity. "You can tell that little fool that I will flatten her if she does that again," she hissed.

Miss Pulver had gotten back to her feet and was now stumbling into the trees, a flow of bright red blood trickling out of her nose. "Helen," I called to her.

"Leave me alone, Mister Stirgil," she said thickly without turning.

"Helen, please, stop," I pleaded. "We can't run off willy-nilly, we could lose each other in the trees. This is serious." I reached out to grab her arm but she snatched it away and then shoved her shoulder back against me, pushing me hard. I stumbled over a vine and she bolted into a run.

"Helen, wait!" I clambered back to my feet and ran off after her, but she had somehow disappeared into the brush, vanishing like smoke. A rustling of dry leaves led me towards a glade, but this too was empty. My own breath was loud in my ears now and my feet aching, and yet a clock-wound tension within me drove me forward, a strange excitement that occluded thought. Forgetting my own safety I pushed my way through the green, first in one direction and then the next, until all of a sudden I very nearly tumbled on top of her. She had found a little stream and had knelt down beside it, carefully washing her face in the water.

"Helen!" I ran to her side; she paused, but did not respond, her eyes staring off into the trees. She was leaned forward upon her arms, her hands palm-down in the stream, the water slipping through her fingers with a gentle tumbling ripple. "Helen, please." I took her by the shoulders and pulled her up, lifting her to face me, more roughly than I had intended. She was wet, her cheeks shining, the clear water running down her jaw and into her collar. The fabric of her blouse was clutched in my fists, the front pulled taut across her chest. Her eyes stared into mine, defiant and shining with fire.

I pulled her to me and kissed her mouth, taking, like an animal. Her lips were soft but not yielding, and I tasted blood. Everything was warm and liquid, and behind my closed eyes I saw gunpowder flashes and flares of crimson.

Then her hands shoved me away with a strength I had not expected. She stared at me, her eyes wide, her breath only barely in control. "No, Mister Stirgil...." She swallowed and wiped the blood from her face with her hand. She looked past me, almost vacantly, her wrist raised against her lips. "I don't ... I ... I don't want that. We mustn't."

It was too late: the lamp-oil in my veins had burst into flame. I was beyond control. "I *must*," I said, and I grabbed her beneath her arms, pulling her to me. Her breasts crushed against my chest, warm and soft, and the breath that burned out from between my teeth fluttered the lashes of her wide, startled eyes. "I want you," I growled.

The young woman yelped and she lashed out with the heel of her hand. It caught me square on the chin, and for a moment my vision blurred. When I could see again, she was standing high on the bank with a rock in her hand. "Don't you do that," she said, trembling in anger.

The force had drained from me, and pinned beneath her stare I suddenly felt a terrible shame. "I'm sorry," was all I could say.

She stood frozen for a long moment, her breast heaving, her eyes twitching but not blinking. Her lips suddenly set tightly and she lofted the stone higher, as if she were about to throw; then she paused, and her face changed to a look of disgust. She let the rock fall to the ground. "Don't!"

"I'm sorry."

"You son of a bitch," she snarled. Then she turned and stalked off back the way we had come.

I knelt on the ground and tried to catch my breath. For a long stretch there was nothing; I could not say what passed through my mind. I was aware of pain and trees. The water ran purling through the green. The insects rang. A strange thought came and went: does a bullet feel ecstasy when the hammer falls? It passed unheeded, and then again there was nothing, only quiet, not even time. Finally, suddenly, inexplicably, a single word formed in my mind: *meat.*

Meat? The thought perplexed me for a moment, as it had seemed to come from nowhere, almost outside myself. Why had I thought that? I almost chuckled at the strangeness of it. Then suddenly I understood: I was smelling cooked meat. There was someone else here in the forest with us.

I stood up and drew my gun. Everything was silent except for the trickling of the stream and the wind brushing the trees. I turned my head this way and that, but the smell seemed to be everywhere; it was all around me, circling like a pack of dogs. Then something caught my eye, a clearing, and movement in the air. Slowly, carefully, I stepped over the water and edged towards the bright patch in the trees. The mud on my shoes softened the sound of my approach, but still I moved gingerly through the roots and leaves. Then, again, I saw movement: smoke, smoke rising into the air. A campfire!

My senses became taut, like elastic about to break. I felt a pain in my hand, and I realized that I was gripping the gun too tightly. I paused and took a slow, deliberate breath. *I will kill them*, I thought, pushing away my fear. *Come into my house, will you? Drag me out into the jungle on a fool's errand? Very nice. Except. You are a problem that I can solve. Do you understand that? I can solve the problem here and now.* The chaos and danger and desire and the sting of Helen's rebuff were hardening to anger. *I can solve the problem here and now because I am going to blow your heads off.*

With this thought I threw myself into the clearing, my mind tearing itself in twain with rage, but—there was no one. What had once been a rather unnecessarily large campfire had all but burned itself out to charcoal, and only one glowing eye of flame remained to send up its ghost of smoke. Scattered on the ground were the remnants of some recent feast, spat bits of gristle, bones cleaned white by teeth. Some of the cuts were only half-eaten, as though there had been more food than the party could quite handle. The diners had greedily gobbled the choicest bites and then tossed the rest aside for the scavengers. There was a tidy pile of ribs lying on the ground, covered in ants. My stomach growled.

There was no sign of any camping materials, however; no tents, tarps or bedding remained. All I could see besides the fire and the bones were a few rags of cloth that had been trampled in the dirt. Everything was still and dreary, and the hovering smoke felt oily on my skin. I exhaled.

My stomach growled again, and I found myself wondering what on earth it was that they had caught and killed. Whatever it was, it had been large. A jungle cat, perhaps? No, not likely; even the Mayans would have a tough job of that. Were there mountain cows that large here, so deep in the forest? That didn't seem quite right either. Then my eyes fell on something lying in the brush; I could see it only barely, but there was an awkward, gory look to it, and I immediately sensed that it was the rest of the carcass that had been tossed aside. I shuddered and looked away.

I stood staring off into the trees for some time, then, trying to think. They were close; likely they had had this meal sometime last night and had decamped this morning. We were probably only a half a day from each other now, maybe less. *We really could catch them*, I thought. The question was—could we take them? It was now only us four against the two of them, plus their one remaining porter. Would he aid them, I wondered, or would the fellow tear off at the first sign of trouble? Hard to say with those Mayans.

Suddenly my musings came to an abrupt halt, and I felt a horrific, icy chill run down my body. A thought was trying to force its way into my consciousness, and it stopped my breathing like a hand upon my throat. I looked down again at the bones, then at the bloody thing lying in the brush, then at the bones again. Finally I understood: *there was no remaining porter.* I screamed.

"Stirgil? What's wrong?"

I whirled around, gun raised, to find Lamb moving towards the clearing.

"Get back!"

He froze, staring at the pistol. "What's going on?" His eyes scanned what he could see of the scene. "Is this their camp?" he whispered, eyes widening. "Where are they?" he took a step forward.

"I said stay back, God damn it!" I threw myself at the young man. He had only time to raise his hands before I collided with him. He stumbled and fell hard upon the ground.

"For God's sake, what's wrong with you, man? Have you gone insane?"

I found myself raging at his blank stupidity but kept my voice under control. "Yes, it is their camp. Or was, rather. They're gone. I would judge by the state of the fire that they left this morning. But there's nothing to see, so just get up, turn around and walk back."

Lamb did not move. "You're insane. Give me that gun, Stirgil. You're going to hurt someone."

"Get up and get moving," I snarled.

Lamb thrust his open hand out at me. "Give me that gun, damn it!"

I steadied myself and spoke carefully. "Get moving or I'll give you the bullets."

The young man's face froze, his lip twitching once to the side, but finally he picked himself up and slowly rose to his feet. "You're insane," he repeated, and then he started stalking back the way he had come. I followed.

We were able to find the way to our own clearing easily enough, and through the trees I could see the two women standing apart from each other, waiting. When he finally caught Miss Karas's eye Lamb threw up his hands and yelled his diagnosis one more time. "He's insane!"

"Who's insane?" she asked.

"This madman," he spat out, jerking his thumb back at me.

She stared at the gun for a moment, and then looked back to Lamb. "You mean … more insane than before?"

"We're going back," I said.

Miss Pulver had been staring at the ground in silence but now her head snapped up to me. "Back? What do you mean?"

"I mean we're going back. To Belize. Pick up your things."

"What on earth are you talking about? Why would we do that?"

"This is over," I said. "Your man is gone, and that's the end of it." It was indeed the end, at least as far as I was concerned, but my voice was shaking.

Lamb began sputtering. "Crazy! Insane! There's a campsite right over there! The fire is still smoking! Do you understand what that means? We've found them! They're here! Seagrave and Adamski! They're really here!"

Miss Pulver's eyes widened and she clasped her hands together. "They were here? Oh my God! Mordecai! Irene, Mordecai was right here!"

Miss Karas was staring at me, however. "Good grief, he's gone all green."

"Forgive me … I think I am going to vomit," I said.

"Oh, dear Lord," spat Lamb with disgust. There was a change in his face, now, however; anger was being replaced by something that looked like unease.

Suddenly Helen Pulver was standing before me, and she slapped the gun aside with her hand. "You," she growled, and she shoved me in the chest, hard. "You pull yourself together, God damn it. I didn't come all the way out here just to turn around and go back. Go back yourself if you want to, you coward, you ... piece of trash."

My mind failed me as I stared at her face so hard with rage. The right side had swelled up where she had been struck, and the blood on her upper lip had turned to a brown smear. "I don't know what to say."

"Well, that's the best news we've had all trip," snorted Miss Karas.

"Get out of here," Helen hissed at me. "I don't ever want to see you again." She then strode across the clearing and yanked her pack off the ground. "Let's go, Irene."

"Oh. We're going now, then?" sniped Karas.

"Yes. Move your ass," said Pulver, and brushed past her.

"Oh!" said Miss Karas, but receiving no further reply she simply picked up her pack and followed.

Mister Lamb was staring at me, his look one of doubt and trepidation. "What did you see back there?" he asked, staring hard into my face.

I could see there was no getting out of giving him an answer. "They killed the other porter," I said in a low voice. Lamb's eyes widened. "I suppose...." I searched for the right lie. "I suppose he did something to displease them."

"My God," he said.

I grabbed his arm. "We have to protect Helen and Irene," I said. "They're in danger."

"Yes …" he muttered, and stared off into the trees. Then he seemed to collect himself. "Yes, I understand."

We moved quickly and quietly through the forest then, the four of us spread out at a shout's distance from each other. Karas, Pulver and Lamb had formed a kind of front line while I trailed along behind with my pistol in hand. Overhead the skies grew darker and more baleful, zephyrs whipping through the trees like ghosts. Anxiety surged through my chest whenever one of the other three was out of sight behind a bush or grove, and my steps would hasten in panic until all my companions were visible once again. Suddenly Lamb stopped, tense, and looked back to me. I hurried to catch up to him.

"What is it?" I asked. "Did you hear something?"

"No, that's just it … it's quiet."

He was right; there were no bird calls, no chattering of monkeys or buzz of insects; I realized now that there hadn't been for some time. Helen and Irene had stopped as well and were looking at us, puzzled.

The young man touched my elbow. "Didn't you say that you would know that you had reached the valley because of the quiet?"

"Yes, and the trees, I remember the trees were strange there.…" He and I looked about us, and sure enough, off towards the north, a particular tree suddenly caught my attention; it had an almost imperceptible tortuousness to it, as though it were writhing out of the ground in pain, and low, twisting branches reached out like waiting arms. As we edged closer and peered past it into the darkness beyond— the sky had deepened to an inky grey—we could see that the forest became denser there, with more low, gnarled trees growing thickly upon each other to make a kind of barrier or labyrinth. Suddenly in the distance I saw a streak of black moving low across the ground; it wove quickly through the brush and then was gone.

"Did you see that?" whispered Lamb.

"By God, I think I did," I said. My skin was prickling all over.

"What was it?" he hissed.

"Some kind of animal, I expect."

"But did you notice?"

"Did I notice what?"

"It made no sound. It was running over dry leaves. It should have made a sound."

The two women came up beside us then, and I tried to erase whatever look of alarm was surely upon my face.

"What is it?" asked Helen.

"I think we are here." I pointed to the north. "Aoxoa."

For a long moment the two stared into it, and then they looked back at Lamb and me. "We should be cautious," said Helen.

"I agree."

"Do we know what it is we're looking for?" asked Miss Karas.

"Not me," I said.

"It might be wise to stay close together from this point forward," said Mister Lamb.

"Yes," said Miss Karas. "We may take them by surprise, and we don't know what frame of mind they might be in."

"Yes, that is good thinking," said Helen. "Well ... I guess ... we should go on then?" In answer a single droplet of rain pecked the brim of her slouch hat. "Oh!"

Lamb took the lead and started moving off to the north. Overhead a growl of thunder moved across the sky. I looked at the trees as we passed and felt a sense of nameless unease; they had a bilious, menacing character to them, and even though the way had become difficult from tangles of roots and knifelike brush I was loath to reach out and steady myself against their trunks. It was noticeably darker in this part of the wood as well; low branches and vines hung woven together like a canopy, and through it we could only see glimpses of the thick, purple clouds that had blotted out the sun.

Miss Karas suddenly tumbled to the ground. "Oh, my knee! God damn these roots to hell!"

"Don't blaspheme, Irene," said Helen quietly, as if only to herself. "Not here...."

"Why not here?" whispered her friend crossly as she picked herself up and rolled a pant leg to examine her knee.

"I don't know," murmured Helen. "I'm not sure why I said that."

"But it *is* like it's listening, isn't it?" interjected Mister Lamb. There was no answer given to this question, and we began moving on again. "Huh, what a funny-looking bird."

I looked up to see a black mass in the trees not far above; it was surprisingly large, larger even than a vulture. It did not shy away as we passed beneath it, but only swayed slightly on its perch, seeming for a moment like the silhouette of a corpse hanging from a gibbet. Helen grabbed my arm and only let it go again when the thing was well behind us. I looked back over my shoulder; it had not moved, though what might have been the head had seemingly turned to follow us with its eyes. "If we weren't in the process of sneaking I would shoot that filthy thing out of its filthy tree," I whispered to the young woman. As though it had heard, the bird spasmed and emitted a guttural sound like a chuckle.

"Put your pistol in its holster," said Miss Pulver flatly.

"And what if your friends react badly to our appearance?" I asked.

"Let's not kill my fiancé unless it's absolutely necessary," she snapped back.

"The ground is sloping downward," interrupted Lamb. "Can you feel it?" Indeed it was. We moved along in silence after that, our ears and eyes pushing at the boundaries of the sensible, but it seemed that we were alone. The air around was gravid with rain, charged with the electricity of a coming storm. At some other time this would have pleased me, this chemical sense of the world going about its business; I might have imagined to myself titanic expanses of rock slumbering beneath us like a giant, or the motherly rocking of the tides, a rhythmic licking of the shore. Above me would rise the mountains, and I would picture myself there, alone in some hovel, ascetic, close to the gods, a friend to the lightning as it struck down to Earth from some higher invisible Olympus. Then I would gaze upon the valley below, and a new picture would form; now I was simple man of the lowlands, a friend to my neighbor, a straw hat upon my head as I led the cattle to pasture. I could be a farmer, a plump wife by my side, a soft scented honey hill to climb on the winter nights, and climb and climb and climb, until the flood was in the valley and the corn began to grow. Such would be my thoughts on some other day's rain, but not today. We had strayed too far, like Orpheus or Odysseus, and there were no mountain hovels or valley farms but only this strange descent into Aoxoa. I looked at my friends. Irene Karas had become leaner since that day we first met, more distant, and our undersea sailor was drifting, carried by the unnamed currents of some other world. Helen Pulver was bloodstained and drawn, her former girlishness replaced by anxiety. She was beautiful yet, but her eyes had become hard and opaque, like the heavy black pendant which hung from her neck and even now tapped at her breastbone like a stone hand beating at a door. When the rain finally came, pelting down hard and painful, the thought came to me that for all our hardship we may have had only gained entry to the obsidian gates of Hell.

"Do you see that, through the trees?"

My eyes followed where Miss Karas was pointing, looking for sign of the two men, but there was no color or movement anywhere, only the forest and the rain. "I don't see a thing," I whispered.

"It's a rise, like a hillock, or a barrow. Don't you see?" She took my elbow and steered me forward through the trees, pointing. Then, finally, I saw: at the very edge of vision I could make out the scrub and brush suddenly rising, as if the ground had somehow folded back on itself. It was oddly dizzying, and for a moment I felt as though I were looking at the bottom of a ravine from a height. Our faces turned upwards as we took in the size of the thing, and with surprise we saw that the summit was at a level with the tops of the trees. In breadth it appeared to be two or three times as wide as it was high, and of a strangely steep and regular aspect. Here and there deep-grey stones protruded through the grass and brush like shattered bones piercing skin.

"What an odd geological formation," spoke Submariner Lamb. "What do you call that, Mister Stirgil?"

The Satanic Bridegroom

I could only shake my head. "I don't call it anything, for on my life I don't know what it is."

"Surely it can't be a natural formation, Percy," said Irene. "It's practically cornered. Look." She pointed to the right, and indeed we could see that it was almost as regular as a barn.

The trees began to thin out as we drew closer, and the rain beat down with more force. The world had settled upon the idea of soaking us steadily and thoroughly, and my clothes began to weigh down my frame like the sodden rags on a scarecrow. When we finally emerged at the foot of the hill the sound of falling water was deafening and the muddy ground sucked our feet into itself like a mouth. Lamb pointed around the side to the northeast, indicating that he meant to circumnavigate the strange, high hill; I nodded and we all followed. Sure enough, the thing appeared to have a roughly rectangular shape, and we could now see that the stones were arranged in vaguely horizontal tiers, as of a terrace.

"It's some kind of barrow, isn't it?" said Lamb. "Or...?"

The mound loomed over us like a monster; we could not quite take in the summit because of the rain falling into our eyes, and I had the strange feeling of being a mouse running upon the floor, not looking up for fear of what might be pouncing from above. It came into my head that the apex was some kind of unholy place—not a quiet peak upon which to be closer to God and Heaven, but some forbidden scene of outrage that was all the more hateful for being inescapable, like a cursed light in the sky. No ordinary man could say what took place there, and the ones who carried out their dread tasks on that mount wore masks of terrifying aspect. If one tore those masks away it would reveal faces whose eyes had been seared from their sockets, the mouths ruined, open holes. I grabbed Irene Karas's arm. She looked back at me, surprised.

"What is it?"

"I don't know...." I couldn't find the words that would make it all sensible.

The woman looked at me in her odd way, blankly, like a lizard. Then, much to my surprise, she linked my elbow with hers. Before us Lamb crept forward as though a hunter, and deerlike behind him followed Helen Pulver, her head twitching this way and that as she scanned the slope and the jungle for any sign of her lost love. But there was nothing; it was only ourselves and the deafening falling rain. Irene's touch was warm; I nearly shivered with thankfulness for it. "I suppose this is some holy place for the Mayans," she said. "The eye of the forest or some such thing."

"Not the Mayans," I said. "I don't know ... someone else." I thought for a moment. "It *is* watching us, though, isn't it?"

Her young mouth twisted. "Mounds of dirt don't watch things, Mister Stirgil." Then, as if on cue, a shrub high up on the slope directly over us shook, as though it were being throttled by an unseen hand; no doubt some animal had been spooked and had bolted to its hole. Irene did not flinch, but her eyes began taking in our surroundings with more care.

"Look at you two," said Miss Pulver, arching an eyebrow over her shoulder. "Bosom chums, now." By way of answer Irene stretched out her free hand towards her, palm down; Helen stopped, the rain running down her hat brim in swift rivers. When we reached her she took the proffered hand and fell into step alongside us.

"I wouldn't want to be left out of the Best Friends' Society," she said to the forest in a wry tone.

We were just rounding the fourth corner of the thing to return to where we had started when suddenly Mister Lamb stopped, his eyes directed up the slope. The side here more irregular than the rest, with block-like stones half-tumbled and scrubby trees taking root on the uneven ground. One section looked as though it had suffered some kind of geological collapse, and we could see a cavity within the gash in the rocks and brush.

"What is it, a hole of some sort, Percy? Perhaps some of us could get dry for a moment," said Irene.

"I don't know what it is," said Lamb, and immediately he began climbing the slope.

"Come along, Mister Stirgil," said Miss Karas, and we all followed the young man up the hill. It was difficult going in the rain, and more than once I found myself slipping down onto my hands and knees. Gradually the opening came into view, and as it did I felt myself shivering once again. It was narrow but high, about four and a half feet from top to bottom, and within it was surprisingly dark. Angular stones were thrust from the earth around it like a palisade.

Lamb was leaning forward and peering into the blackness. "I can't see a thing," he said in a hushed voice, "but there seems to be a space within." Carefully he twisted his shoulders and sidled inside.

"Be careful, Percival," said Miss Pulver. She was hunched over in the rain, her hands gripping themselves tightly.

Once inside, the young man removed his pack and fell to a crouch. He withdrew a lamp, and after carefully wiping

241

his hands on a cloth retrieved a box of matches as well. In a moment he had produced a weak glow, and in its sparse illumination I could see vague hints of the terrain within: an even floor, as though carved from stone, and walls receding away in parallel.

"A tunnel!" cried Irene, and she pushed her way into the hole.

"Wait! Look!" Lamb was holding the lantern low by the floor, his other arm back in a warning gesture. Miss Karas paused, and then the two gathered to stare at what he had discovered. Miss Pulver shook her arms once to slough off the rain and joined them.

I paused to take one last look around, and it occurred to me that it would be unpleasant to be trapped in such a place from without. We were halfway up the barrow, at a level with the thickest part of the forest's canopy, and the ground lay far below. There was no movement or life, only the swaying of the leaves in the rain. We were alone, beyond all, beyond everything except for that presence from the past which I could feel watching us from the top of the hill like a ghost. I glanced upwards again; there was only the grass and a roiling sky. A flash of light burst from within the clouds, outlining thick, ominous arms writhing across the firmament, and a crack of thunder echoed back and forth over the valley below. I hurried inside.

In the darkness the three young people were squatting over some invisible object and peering off into the space beyond. I looked down; the floor was in fact stone, regular and smooth as if worn down by time. There was also a thin, even layer of fine dirt covering all, and in that dirt there were bootprints.

The Satanic Bridegroom

Submariner Lamb looked back at me, pointed at the prints, held up two fingers, and then pointed into the darkness beyond. His meaning was obvious. I nodded.

I could see now in the orange gloom that the space was indeed a tunnel, the walls and ceiling cut from large slabs of stone. Odd patterns were carved on every surface in bas relief, the style reminiscent of the blocky geometries of the Mayans, but also incorporating seemingly chaotic curves and angles, like licks of petrified flame. On one block at breast level I could make out a story writ in the stone, human figures in procession with monstrous birds and beasts in attendance, their long, spiderlike legs making crooked posts for the men to weave through. The focal point of their pilgrimage was a mystery, however, for some unseen hand had gouged the stone there, the censor's chisel leaving only a ragged hole in the rock, as though the tiny humans were being sucked into an obliterating chaos under the swirling whirlpool sky.

The others were standing now, Karas and the young man stooping slightly to keep their hats from brushing the low ceiling. Miss Pulver had begun wringing her hands again, and was straining towards the blackness. For a moment her breast hitched, as though she were about to call out, but Lamb grabbed her arm in warning. He put his finger to his lips and made a staying motion with his hand: caution. Then he turned and held his lamp out toward the void. The tunnel was empty, merely receding away. He looked back again, met each of our eyes once, and then began walking forward.

I understood everything now; this was no hill or barrow but a temple, one of the ancient ziggurats that had been lying silent in the jungle for long centuries, abandoned by their makers who knows when. So long had this one stood that the lichen and moss and wind and water had crumbled rock into soil, and grasses and shrubs had taken root. Perhaps it had been a relic even to the Mayans in their golden age. Now Seagrave and Adamski had come here— why? To plunder its secrets, dreaming that there would be gold left unpried from masks, statuary and totems left snugly in alcoves, as if the brown men here in the West had never learned how to rob, as if they two were the first to hit upon the all-too-human idea of plunder?

The floor began to slope downward, and we turned one corner and then another, leaving the watery blue light of the surface far behind. There was nothing to see now save for the footprints and the carvings, and the bouncing glow of the lantern made both shift and move in the gloom. The wall decorations became stranger as we advanced; the carved men gradually becoming more stylized and primitive, almost animal-like; they were seen communing with great chasms in the ground beneath their feet, and the hurling of one of their number screaming into the abyss was a common motif. Chaos reigned everywhere, with great scenes of strife and murder. The artists seemed to be particularly preoccupied with the flowing of blood, for each knife-wound or head split by stone brought forth a foaming river depicted with great beauty and care. Featureless plains were littered with corpses whose life-fluid had merged into boiling seas, their women naked and wailing on the shore, the children drowned and still at the bottom. This was not the most horrific tale the carvings had to tell, however, for I saw also a giant bas-relief three feet high which was entirely comprised of a great pile of corpses lying thick upon each other, the slack faces and limbs rendered with obsessive

The Satanic Bridegroom

precision. Horrifically, the chests and skulls of those on the bottom were shown crushed and distended by the weight of the bodies above, while the freshest specimens at top were stiff and bloated with corruption. The sight of this thing gave me a terrible jolt, as though I had been spat upon, as though some knife had cut me from behind. For one moment I felt as though something were tearing at my mind, trying to yank a part of it away from me, but I clenched my fists tight and kept moving forward.

We turned a double corner then, and suddenly a new, remarkable scene met our eyes: before us was a large square hall, perfectly regular and some forty feet to a side. Crumbled stone braziers flanked the space in symmetrical lines, and in one of these an upended torch was now burning itself out, casting a wan yellow light through the serpents of hanging smoke. Facing us from the rear was the great stone face of a god, a cyclopean carving on a slab, its wide eyes blank and staring like platters, the mouth a grimace with mossy teeth and a rolling, choking tongue. It seemed to stare through us into some other place, like a catatonic peering beyond the veil into some phantom landscape, a banquet of bones.

Sitting on the floor in the center of the room was a ragged-looking young man with long, dark hair that fell to his shoulders. In the reflected glow of the fire we could see that he had dropped himself on top of a pile of baggage, elbows on knees, and from the two glints of light in his eyes I could see that he was regarding us with a fixed, unblinking stare.

"Mordecai!" Miss Pulver all but screamed. "Oh, Mordecai!" She rushed towards him, but then drew up short, frozen. All was still for a moment. Lamb's lantern had fallen on the young man, and we could now see that the long, low bundle he was casually resting upon was not some pile of chattel but instead the body of a man, face down. Seagrave was sitting upon him like a couch or a fallen log.

"Good Lord," croaked Lamb. He pointed his hand at the figure, his long arm throwing a shadow upon the wall. "Who is that?"

Seagrave looked down at the form, then back up at Lamb. "You know who it is."

"Captain Adamski," said Lamb.

Seagrave stared at Lamb, and then shrugged. His eyes drifted off to the right, where a fist-sized rock was lying on the ground.

"Have you gone mad?" asked Lamb in a low voice. It was, perhaps, a rhetorical question. Then, in an oddly measured tone: "I should kill you right now."

Seagrave only sneered at first, but then his face abruptly darkened and he leapt to his feet, his arms tense at his sides. The body on the ground did not move.

"Hold," I barked. I had drawn my pistol and was point-ing it at Seagrave's chest.

To my surprise, the young man did not flinch or back away, but instead lunged for the weapon. I was so startled that I failed to shoot, but instead reflexively snatched the gun up out of his reach. His momentum brought him forwards, arms out to grapple, and with all the strength I could muster in that awkward moment I brought the butt of the pistol down onto his skull. The young man crashed into me and it was as though my lungs had been knocked out of my body; I tumbled to the ground gasping. Seagrave fell on the floor beside me, and I jerked the gun away from him in a panic, but then I saw his glassy, blinking eyes and his arms flailing on the floor as he vainly tried to right himself. He was stunned.

"Tie him up!" barked Miss Karas. "Helen, help Mister Stirgil, quickly!" I saw the shadow of Miss Pulver flutter to my side and felt a warm hand on my shoulder.

"Are you all right? Did you lose your pistol?" cried Helen. "Oh, you have it. Is anything broken?" Meanwhile my attacker was flat on his back, and Submariner Lamb had grasped both of his wrists in his hands and held them pinned against the ground. In the dim light I thought I could see the captive's eyes simultaneously moving in different directions, as though they belonged to two different heads. Miss Karas was busy rummaging through a rucksack, and she soon produced a ball of leathern cords that had been used for the tying down of tarps and the like. Lamb rolled the still-dazed Seagrave onto his stomach and tied the prisoner's hands together behind his back while Karas bound his ankles in the same way. Then Lamb picked him up from beneath his arms and dragged him to the wall, where he propped him into a sitting position. Helen retrieved the lantern and went to her man, examining his scalp where he had been struck. "Mordecai, can you hear me?" There was no answer, however, and still Seagrave's eyes had a glazed look, like a sleepwalker.

"Are you quite comfortable down there, Mister Stirgil?" Irene Karas was standing over me. "Would you like a pillow for your head?"

"Harpy," I said, grasping her hand.

"Sybarite," she replied, pulling me to my feet. She beat the dust from my trousers with the flat of her hand. Her skin was still wet from rain and perspiration, and in the torchlight her face shone like a glass mask.

Having finally gotten my breath I noticed that there were different, competing smells in the air; at the fore were the smoke from the fire and a pleasant, earthy aroma, as of a flowerbed in July. Underneath that, however, there was something else, something sour and acrid which I could not place, like a caustic mixed with offal, or a snake's venom. It would disappear at times, as though blown away on a breeze, and then just as I was about to forget that it had ever existed it would return sharp and fast, like a slap to the face. The only sounds now were the crackling of the torch, some soft words murmured by Helen to Seagrave, and a faint bubbling trickle that echoed throughout the room. Then a dull thud of thunder came down to us from above, making us all start save for the semi-conscious prisoner and the body face-down on the floor. The flame flickered and threw shadows across the room.

Miss Karas was now squatting before her pack and brushing the rain from her dark, tousled hair. "It must be getting on towards twilight," she said without looking up. "Perhaps we should make camp here."

"Do you think that's safe?" I asked.

She performed one of her typical haughty snorts. "Whatever this place is, it looks like it's been sound for a thousand years. It seems unlikely that it would decide to collapse today."

That wasn't precisely what I had meant, but then I wasn't sure what I had meant myself, and so I let it pass. Instead I walked towards the far end of the room to look at the great stone face that hung on the wall. Halfway across I froze in my tracks and gasped when I thought I saw the thing leer at me—the lip subtly flickering into a sickly grin—but I realized that the movement I had seen was nothing but a little runnel of water that was seeping down the face of it from the ceiling. The stone was a deep green, with subterranean veins of black and sunbursts of translucent chartreuse, and where not chipped by time it was as smooth as oil. Overall the thing had a blocky, geometric quality to it, but at the same time there were subtle, perverse asymmetries that gave it personality. At once the eyes stared both blankly and pointedly, as a god might, or a devil. Green, stringy roots had descended from fine cracks in the ceiling to create a scraggly wig of hair for it, and water oozed down like saliva.

"I think I shall call him Harold," I said, but even as I spoke I felt my courage falter, and the jest dropped lifeless to the floor. I could almost feel the weight of the thing bearing down on top of me, and I backed away quickly.

Lamb was kneeling over the body, his face in shadow. His head moved slightly as I approached, and he confirmed its identity. "Adamski."

"Your friend," I said. "I'm sorry."

"His skull is broken," he said quietly, so that Helen could not hear. "That one killed him."

"But he had been acting oddly, no?" I whispered. "Perhaps he went mad. Perhaps it was self-defense."

There was a pause. "Perhaps."

"But, of course, perhaps not."

"Someone went mad, in any case," said the sailor.

"We're going to have a job of it bringing the body back to civilization," I said, but Lamb seemed not to hear. He reached out and put his hand on the thing's shoulder.

"It's getting cool." He looked up at me, and for some reason I felt a compulsion to touch it myself. I squatted beside Lamb and put my hand out. He was right; the flesh was heavy and slack, almost chilly to the touch. "We may have to sleep here," said the young man.

"Yes, Irene suggested the same."

"We can't leave him here." He was looking at me hard. "I … I don't think I'll be able to bear it, him lying here." His eyes flicked to the corners of the room. "It could attract … rats."

"Well, yes, but … where can we put him? There aren't any other rooms, you see. In the tunnel?"

"No, that doesn't seem right. We have to bring him to the surface and bury him."

"And leave the two women here with Seagrave?" I whispered. "And with no lantern? What if the fire goes out? Or do we try to fumble our way back up in the dark?"

"Yes, yes, I see your point, Stirgil, but we can't keep him *here*."

There seemed to be no way out of the impasse, but then my mind suddenly jumped back to something I had seen during our descent. "There was a fissure in the wall of the tunnel, remember? Not far back? Just at the place where some stones had tumbled out onto the floor? There was a space there, a space in the wall. We could put him there."

Lamb did not answer, but only stared off into the darkness. When his voice came it was hard like a knife. "It's disrespectful. It's God-damned disrespectful. Stuff him in a hole in the wall?"

"Pull yourself together. There's no good answer, and as you said yourself we have to do *something*."

Again Lamb was silent and still, but then he abruptly rose and positioned himself by Adamski's head. "Take his feet." I quickly did as commanded and without further discussion we turned the corpse over and lifted it off the ground. We both grunted with the effort; it was absurdly heavy, flesh stuffed with flesh. The torch flared and I could see tears on the boy's face.

We met Karas just without the entrance; for some reason she was returning from above, the lantern in her hand. She gasped and put a hand to her mouth, but soon steadied herself. "Bring the light," I said through clenched teeth.

"But Helen's alone!"

"Seagrave is tied up and has been practically knocked stupid," growled Lamb. "Bring the damned light so we can see!"

She hesitated, but then began following. "Where do you think you're taking him?"

"Just be quiet, please," snapped the young man. I could see Miss Karas's jaw set and her eyes narrow, but she made no reply.

About thirty yards and two bends up the corridor we came to the place where the wall had partly collapsed. I was right: there was a large fissure with an empty space behind it. We let down our load and Lamb took the light from Miss Karas. He shined it into the hole; there was not much room, but perhaps just enough.

"We could stand him on end, perhaps?" I suggested.

"Don't be ridiculous," spat Karas.

Lamb covered his face with his hand and exhaled slowly. "No, let's try it. Just … quickly, please." He handed the lantern back to Irene and once again put his hands beneath Adamski's arms. I wrapped my own around the chest and tried to think of some other thing, something other than the corpse. Whiskey … women … Baudelaire—

Quand, les deux yeux fermés, en un soir chaud d'automne,
Je respire l'odeur de ton sein chaleureux,

Joe Gola

Je vois se dérouler des rivages heureux
Qu'éblouissent les feux d'un soleil monotone

With an animal grunting we pulled the body upwards, and then with a Herculean effort we heaved it into the space. The now-misshapen head suddenly lolled itself onto Lamb's shoulder, and for a moment it seemed as though it would tumble back out upon us. The young man shuddered, said something low and guttural, and then gave a great final shove. We heard a crumbling sound and several small stones fell from above, bouncing off the captain's head and shoulders, but the body was stuck fast; we had wedged it into the crack. It was upright, with the knees bent, and its mouth was now hanging ajar. I stared as I caught my breath, the image burning itself into my mind, but then Karas whipped the light away and started back down the tunnel. We said nothing else, but only followed.

Helen was still sitting cross-legged on the floor next to Mordecai when we returned, the firelight gilding her hair. Propped against the wall, the young man once again looked like a fallen mannequin; he had come to his senses, but his eyes twitched and moved oddly, as though he were hearing words that were difficult to understand. Helen held her hand on his knee, and after a moment I saw her reach out and stroke his cheek. Submariner Lamb came to her side and asked if he had spoken yet; she turned her head only slightly and said something curt. He returned back to where Miss Karas and I stood, shaking his head.

"Best to leave them be," I advised. Lamb shrugged and began digging in his pack, eventually removing a bedroll and a greasepaper package of the pokenoboy fruit that the agile Miss Karas had collected from the canopy on one of

252

her climbs. He lay down upon the bedding and began biting into the thick skin with bared teeth. In a moment his friend sat down beside him, shoulders slumped, staring out past him at nothing. He held out one of the little spheres and she took it without looking, groping with her hand to encircle his and then plucking the fruit free.

I began to prepare my own sleeping arrangements as well, and as I worked I took the opportunity to study the man by the wall. He was dark-haired and wiry, as I remembered from that lightning flash one long week ago, but now the patches of beard had grown thicker, curling about his chin and the angle of his jaw. His hair hung down in long, greasy strands, almost touching his shoulders, and his clothes were stained dark from sweat. And yet, for all of that, I had to admit: he was a handsome lad. His features were fine but masculine, and for all his current confusion his face still had a sharp intelligence to it.

"What were you looking for?" I heard Helen ask.

This question seemed to reach the man, and he stilled his head and licked his lips. "The god," he croaked, eyes half-lidded.

Helen had almost jumped at the sound of his voice. "What god? You mean, a statue? That one?" She pointed to the great green face on the far wall. "Are you looking for … treasure?"

Seagrave's eyes opened at this, and like two black seals swimming to the gelid sea surface they finally focused on the woman before him. A flicker of a wry grin twitched at his mouth. "The god. The one who speaks."

"The god who speaks? What does that mean?" Helen's voice was soft, a mother talking to a child.

Irene leaned towards Percival Lamb. "This is the first I've ever heard *him* talk about God," she muttered. The echoing stone walls carried her voice, however, and Seagrave snapped to attention.

"Not your Bible's god, you cow," he snarled.

"Mordecai!" admonished Helen.

Miss Karas recoiled. She glanced at Lamb, and then me, and moved closer to Percival's side, knees and elbows touching.

"What kind of god is that, anyway?" continued the bound man. "Silent? Hidden? Where … up in the sky? Like a puffy cloud?" He snorted and kicked his heels. "No, not that god. Not old Puffy."

"Well, what kind of god, then?" asked Helen.

Seagrave paused and slouched back against the wall, his eyes drifting off to some dark corner. "A real god," he said, "one who moves, a force, here, powerful. Not a servant to man, or a father, but something else, something … *outside*." His eyes searched the room before him for a moment, and then he sat forward, his words coming faster and hotter, flecks of spittle flashing in the firelight. "There is something beyond everything here, a door that will transform the world. They walked the earth in ancient days, on Mount Moriah, Mount Sinai, Mount Olympus, Babylon, Nineveh … and here! These temples, these ziggurats, they're places of power … dynamos … power … they're houses for … these … *other* gods." He began to trip over his words now, his thoughts seeming to become more unglued as he spoke. "And … and this one is alive! A god here, on Earth, in this place, trapped, but ready to be set free! Do you understand what that means?" He sank back and his eyes half-closed again, the shadow of his lashes fluttering in the gloom. He all but whispered now. "It spoke to me in the darkness under the water … it told me about this place. I can't find it, but it speaks to me still. I can … hear it.…"

Helen Pulver did not move, but only sat rock-still and looked at him. Finally we heard her speak again, her voice faltering. "What does this god say to you?"

Seagrave opened his eyes and looked at her, and suddenly there was something like fear on his face, as though he were remembering something terrifying, some midnight horror of the mind. "No! No!"

"'No' what?" asked Helen, her voice rising with anxiety. She leaned forward and put her hand on his arm.

The young man froze for a moment, twitched, and then his face changed back to a scowl. He shrugged her hand off his arm viciously and strained against the cords that bound his wrists. "Untie me, you fool!"

Helen was on her feet now, but her shoulders were steady, her breathing slow and even. "We need to bring you home, Mordecai. You're not well. We're going to help you."

He stared at her for a long moment, as though she were a stupid child. "Home? What do you mean?"

"Home. To America."

"Why? What for?" He looked back and forth between us, as if desperately trying to understand. "Why?"

"Because I love you," said Helen Pulver. "You're unwell. You need to get better. We were to be married. Do you … remember?"

There was a short, puzzled pause, and then the young man exploded into a shock of laughter. Helen's body flinched in one great spasm, as though her very soul had been struck, but she said nothing. "You love me, then?" Mordecai Seagrave grinned, his drawn, whiskered face contorting into a pale jester's mask. "Forever? Shall we celebrate our unbreakable bond? Shall we be together, then, forever? As one?"

"Mordecai...." The sound was as soft as the dropping of a leaf, as the falling of snow.

"*I do*," said Seagrave, and then he lunged forward, hurling himself sideways at her feet, and sunk his teeth into her ankle. Helen Pulver's eyes and mouth gaped wide with surprise, and a scream of horror and pain burst forth. The three of us leapt to her rescue, but she had already dropped into a crouch and was beating at the man's head and face with the heel of her hand. A furious blow landed on his ear and he recoiled; his teeth were red with blood.

As we gathered about them the pair had become still; Helen was down on all fours, panting, her eyes still wide with shock, and Seagrave was staring at her with what seemed like amazement. He was not looking at her face, however, but rather her breast; the odd stone pendant had fallen out of her blouse and was now hanging down and swinging like a pendulum. His eyes followed it back and forth as if hypnotized.

Then Helen raised her arm and slapped his face, hard. Seagrave recoiled from the blow.

This time, I thought, he would surely kill her somehow, even with hands and feet tied; I lunged forward and planted my two hands onto his shoulders, pinning them to the floor. To my surprise, however, he did not resist, but simply let himself fall back. Then he blinked and looked at me.

"If you do something like that again I will shoot you in the head," I said.

The young man lay limp and panting, and slowly his muscles relaxed against the stone floor. There was no struggle; he had given up. "Yes," he said, simply, in between slowing breaths. "I understand."

I leaned in closer. "Do you understand that I will be doing so not merely out of obligation, but also for my own pleasure?" I whispered.

Seagrave smiled warmly, the slanted firelight casting shadows across his grinning face. He licked the blood from his teeth. "I do."

Later we fashioned a makeshift rope out of the strips of burlap, and we used this to tie the cords that bound the man's hands to one of the great stone braziers that ran the length of the room. He offered no resistance, but instead allowed himself to be dragged by me and Lamb with a closed-eyed deference. Helen had rolled down her stocking, and on her ankle there were two bloody lines curved into the shape of teethmarks. He had bit her quite hard—very hard—but he seemed not to have critically damaged any muscles or sinews; there was only the insult to the flesh. Great round tears had rolled out of her eyes as we bound the wound, her shoulders shaking, but she made no noise other than a quiet whimpering. She stood for a moment afterwards and was able to put her weight on it, but we helped her to a bedroll, and she lay down quietly with her face to the wall. She wanted no food, only some water, and we left the young woman to herself. Outside the thunder crashed with a racking boom that made the floor leap like a pulsebeat. The air was dead and heavy. We had to stop.

VIII

I had meant only to rest, to close my eyes. Surely there could be no sleep, between the madman tied in the corner and the great stone face on the wall with the water trickling down—the sound almost like whispered speech, little giggling words I could not hear. The room was heavy with murder, with doom ... between us and the surface a corpse stared from the wall, and who knew what else, lizards, jaguars prowling, a cockatrice with venomed wings. And then I was in the jungle again, in the terrible light of day. Something coursed through the brush, fast, dark and hungry, and now the armlike branches clung to me, reaching for me when my head was turned, winding through my button-holes. The force was drawing closer, each moment speeding faster, something terrible falling from above. The black birds filled the trees like great rotting fruit, blotting out the sun, heavy and reeking of death. I ran down, my heart pounding, and then in a flood of sunlight the great temple was before me, looming and angular, squatting and alive. I was exposed, and there was only the black wound of the entrance in its side to run to. A screeching sound slashed through the air. Terrified, I raced up the hill and plunged into the hole, charging through one passage and the next, the light growing dimmer and the angles becoming stranger. Down and down I went. My legs grew heavy, as though I were wading through treacle, and in a panic I tried to wedge myself around a corner, but it was too tight; my chest was trapped, my head pinned, and I could see only blackness. Then there was breathing, and something curled up my leg....

I started awake. Dim firelight flickered, reddening the ceiling that pressed down from above. I turned and a shadow loomed before me, and then the liquid flash of a knife. I gasped. The shadow hung poised over the still form of Helen Pulver, but its eyes were locked into mine, the guttering light making the whites spark and swim like fiery bleach. I opened my mouth to shout, but a heel came down upon my head, followed by a blast of pinprick stars. I struggled to open my eyes through the pain, to surface from the midnight sea that engulfed me, and when my vision finally returned I saw Seagrave at the side wall, a fresh torch burning at his feet. The stale, smoky air had put us all to sleep, but somehow he had wriggled free from his bonds. He had Helen's strange stone pendant in his hands, the cut lanyard still threaded through the hole, and he seemed to be trying to twist it one way and then the other, as though to uncork it like a bottle.

"Seagrave ... what?" My voice was slurred and thick, like syrup. I heard a stirring from my comrades beside me.

The young man paid no attention but only redoubled his efforts with the pendant. His jaw trembled as he gave one final, ferocious twist, and with a *crack!* the thing split into two. Gingerly he eased the pieces apart; in the flickering light I could just see that there were geometric bumps and striations upon the end of the shaft of the half with the loop. Seagrave stared at the thing for a moment, mesmerized, his eyes wide and his mouth agape, but then he broke from his reverie and reached down to snap up his torch.

Cautiously I raised myself up onto my elbows, fearful of making too sudden a move and drawing his attention. The spell of nausea and dizziness from the kick to the head was receding, and it was now replaced by transfixed wonder

260

The Satanic Bridegroom

as to what the young man might be about. He was crouched at the wall, his torch raised and his nose almost touching the stone as he searched a particularly disgusting relief depicting stylized pygmy hunters slaying a skeletal, wide-horned animal. "Yes," he suddenly murmured, "yes, now. Yes!" He put his fingertips into a depression in the design and stood frozen, head cocked, as if listening to a whisper through the wall. I listened too, but there was only the crackle of the fire and the water dripping down the face of the green stone god. He dropped his light once again, and then with a swift movement he thrust the pendant into the little hole and twisted hard, at the same time shoving his shoulder up against the wall. A key!

For a moment nothing happened, but then I heard a low grinding, like the turning of a millstone deep beneath our feet. The strange underplanet sounds seemed to encourage the young man, and he redoubled his efforts, his entire body taut and shaking, his shoulder all but crushed against the rock. Then, as I watched astounded, the panel suddenly shifted, pivoting inwards, inch by inch, and in a half a minute's time a square of black emptiness like the gullet of a beast had been revealed. There was a rushing of air with the breach, and for a moment the torch blazed brighter; it threw Seagrave's shadow up high against the wall, a giant hunchback looming over the world.

"Seagrave, wait, stop!" It was Percival Lamb, one hand stretched out in warning.

Mordecai grabbed the light, slipped through, and was gone, sucked up greedily through the wall.

Helen Pulver and Irene Karas were standing now too; the three of them shared a look, briefly—a moment—and then as one they charged towards the hole, Lamb grabbing the lantern from the floor as he passed. Before I could speak they had slipped through into the darkness, one by one, three more morsels gobbled inside. Then there was only the patter of feet receding quickly into silence.

I was stuck frozen for a moment, bewildered and at odds with myself. Briefly I had the notion to leave all four of them to the devil and be done with it, to return to home and safety, but instead I bolted to the brazier, grabbed the last guttering stub of a torch, and ran to the wall. I peered through the doorway, straining every sense, but all was black as ink; there was only a hushed, deadly stillness, as of an unseen presence holding its breath. A single cobweb fluttered down through the air on the far side and vanished.

One last sane impulse yanked at me, and I turned back to my belongings. The pistol was still there, buried at the bottom of my pack. Then I ran to the hole and stepped through.

The tunnel beyond was dank and chill, and as my eyes adjusted to the gloom I began to make out that the walls were different here from those up above; the stones were less carefully cut, less precisely fit together, and yet the surfaces were rounded and smooth as though polished. It pitched downwards like a sluice, hypnotic and dangerous. Ghosts were everywhere, or so it seemed, screaming silently, dragged ever earthward. Somehow I knew that this had been a place of disaster once, of terror beyond all, of torture and fright in the sunless underground gulf. Unheeding I followed the distant echoes of shouts, running as fast as I dared, my torchlight strangely powerless against the black. Soon my heart was beating hard in my chest and my head was buzzing noisily; the passage jinked down a series of cramped turns and the air became more sour and unpleasant by the step. The space was narrowing as well, the walls and ceiling moving in, and claustrophobic panic rose within me like a shriek.

"*Stop!*"

I had just turned a corner and now skidded to a halt, my mind shocked to stupefaction. The tunnel had ended abruptly, and through an arch of irregular angles I could see a wide, empty cavern opening out beyond, a great vaulted room of jagged rock with no bottom, rough walls falling downwards into blackness, tomblike and terrifying. A cut stone floor or platform extended into this void some thirty feet, but then it too dropped off at its edges so that it formed a narrow knifelike outcropping over a great yawning pit. Just beyond the doorway stood Lamb, Karas and Pulver, still panting for breath, and at the very edge of the promontory stood Seagrave, his torch borne high and his hand outstretched in warning. His face was wild and his eyes were crazed; it looked as though his head were about to boil.

"Stay where you are!" he barked at us, his teeth bared.

Helen took a step forward, her hands held together before her in supplication. Two muddy tracks of tears cut through the dust on her face. "Mordecai, please, come back. It's not safe there." Her voice was cracked and pleading.

The young man was no longer listening, however, but was instead peering down into the darkness below, spinning one way and then another. "It's here! It's *here*! I know it! I can *feel* it!"

Karas leaned towards Lamb and spoke quietly. "I don't think we can reason with him," she said. "We just need to calm him down before he hurts himself."

"What *is* this place?" muttered Lamb.

"There must have been some kind of collapse," said Karas. "God only knows how far down it goes. It could probably happen again at any moment."

These last words sent a visible jolt through Helen. Her hands snapped apart and flew into two fists at her sides. "Mordecai! Get back here! Get back here this moment or I will come out there and drag you back myself!"

Seagrave stopped whirling about and looked at her. Carefully he straightened himself, and his eyes pierced the distance between them, his face as cold as the bottom of the sea. "No, you will not," he said, his voice echoing strangely.

"You're sick," said Helen. "You need help. Come back to us and we can help you. Remember...."

Mordecai waved a peremptory hand at her. "Still you don't understand! Something is coming, now, something beyond everything we know. 'Remember?' What is there to remember? Man's history is an insignificant sputter, a spark in the blaze. What we have fathomed of our world is but a sliver of a slice of a mote! Just imagine what courses down beneath us unseen, what slides overhead in the sunless gulfs above, there behind the stars! Underground the titans sleep, intelligences from another age, gods that were here from the darkest reaches of memory. They speak to us, betimes, through madmen and dreams. And one of them has called ... me...." Just then a single bright spark leapt off the end of his torch and floated down over the edge like a flare. Mesmerized, I watched it descend into the blackness below and shuddered. Instead of curving to form a basin, I could see in its glow that the walls only fell away to expose a yawning depth, a horrific limitless pit. At the final edge of vision, however, I thought I saw a reflection, some rolling shimmer that seemed to reach up and snuff out the flame.

The Satanic Bridegroom

Helen Pulver was only an arm's length from him now, her hand held out as though a lifeline to a man hanging from a precipice. "Come," she said.

Mordecai Seagrave's voice blasted out like an explosion. "Leave me alone! Leave me alone or I will drag you to Hell!" He threw his torch to the stones at his feet and lunged for her neck; he grabbed her and then shook her so hard that her head snapped back and forth like a reed in a hurricane. Then he threw her to the ground, snatched up his light, and jumped over the edge.

"Mordecai!" we shouted, and Karas, Lamb and I raced as one to where he had disappeared. He had not plummeted into empty air, however; instead we saw that he was only some yards below us, picking his way through tall, spiky boulders that littered a steep and rocky slope. Irene ran back to Helen, but the young woman was already on her feet, coughing and holding her throat. In the meantime Lamb had descended in pursuit, his lantern bobbing in the black. "Come quick, I've found a way!"

The moments that followed were ghostly and unreal, like the scene of a dream. We clambered down a pitched tumble of glassy black rocks as tall as a man, a forest of towering angles thrust high from the earth. Mordecai was faster than we, recklessly leaping from one perch to the next, but the span between us was not great. At one point he landed badly and rolled sprawling across a great tipped slab, his torch a pinwheel blaze; afterwards he was slow in rising and moved awkwardly, as though the wind had been knocked from him. Amongst ourselves we raced without word, but our heavy panting was like a conversation in and of itself, a communication of exertion. Lamb kept one eye on Seagrave and the other on Karas, though she was as nimble as any; Helen stayed close to me, following my trail exactly, and at times she was near enough that I could hear the hysterical hitches in her breathing, something between laughter and a sob.

Then it happened: I was sliding down the face of a crag and expecting my feet to catch on a lip of rock below when with a piercing stab of horror I realized that there was only empty space beneath me—I was falling. I fought back a scream as the air accelerated past and I became one with the void, but then the giant teeth-like rocks lunged up to meet me and I crashed and tumbled, bouncing from one landing to the next until rolling to a stop. Miraculously, I was unharmed; I had only dropped some six or eight feet in the end, and the angle of the ground had broken my fall. However, the terror of the plunge still clutched at my chest like a stone hand and would not let go.

In the light of my fallen torch I saw a wide-eyed Helen Pulver hurrying to meet me, skirting the drop-off that had caused my descent and shimmying down the grade that had sent me spinning. When she reached my side she fell to her knees and took my face in her hands, panting for breath. "Alexander, are you all right?"

It was the first time that she had used my given name; I was not aware that she had known it. "Yes, I'm all right now," I said.

She collapsed for a moment upon me, cradling my head between her forearm and cheek, a hand in my hair. For one moment we stayed that way, her breath heavy on my neck, her curls falling over my eyes in soft tickling coils. Her skin was caked in grit and her breath smelled like fear.

"Helen...."

"Yes?"

"He must be stopped … I think we have to kill him."

She raised her head sharply. "What? No! What are you talking about?"

"Mordecai is a murderer."

She recoiled, sitting up sharply and trying to get away, but I grabbed her by the arms and held her tight. "He killed that man Adamski, and together they killed the second porter in the forest."

"He's sick!" She tried to twist out of my grasp, but her eyes yet stared into mine.

"He killed someone in Cuba too, didn't he?"

The struggle stopped, and in the firelight I could see her face frozen stock still, staring into mine, mouth trembling.

"*Didn't he?*"

"Yes." The word was barely a whisper.

"He's a madman. He's dangerous. More people could die. We have to finish this!"

"No! Please!"

"He could kill again!"

"No! It's murder!"

"They killed the porter *and ate him*!"

"No!" she shrieked, trying to wrench her arms away. "Leave us alone! Leave us alone!" Her face was contorted with defiance and despair, and she twisted her body like an animal caught in a trap. She lunged her mouth at my left hand as if to kiss it, and I felt her teeth close down upon my wrist. She bit me, my flesh singing, bone against bone. The pain was oddly sweet. With my other hand I grabbed a fistful of her hair and pulled her off. Her eyes stared into mine.

Percival Lamb's voice rang out in the dark. "There's nowhere left to run, Mordecai."

Together we jumped to our feet. Some yards below us the grade had flattened out to a gentle slope, and Mordecai, Lamb and Karas stood at the edge of what looked like an endless underground sea. The long-haired fugitive held his torch in one hand and his knife in the other, waving both at the other two to hold them at bay. His feet were just touching the edge of the iridescent oily water that licked at the shore; in the firelight it had an almost pinkish hue, and it moved oddly, as though it were viscid in some places but not in others.

"Please, Mordecai," said Irene, her hand held out to him. "It's over."

Seagrave seemed not to hear; he was hunched as if in pain, and his head snapped this way and that in search of something.

"There's nothing here!" she shouted.

"No! No! It's here! I can feel it!" His eyes were wide from panic or mania. "It can't be ... it can't be *nothing*!" He took another step backwards, one foot splashing into the oily lake. He lunged at the air between him and Lamb with the torch, sparks falling like dying stars, but his face was turned to the dark. "Where are you? I came! You reached out to me, in Atlantis, and I came! The valley in the dark! The obsidian city! Antitetragrammaton!" In the firelight the ripples on the lake circulated a recursive radius of waves.

"He's insane," said Irene.

Seagrave threw the torch onto the stones near his feet and then carefully drew himself upright. His chest swelled, and he bellowed, "*I am your priest! I command you to rise!*" With a powerful sweep of his left arm he stabbed the forearm of his right, impaling it and sending the point of the knife through the skin on the other side, the spray of blood like fireworks in the light.

"Mordecai, no!" Helen had somehow made it down to the edge of the shore, and now she broke into a run.

"*Jesus, stop!*" I cried. The woman skidded to a halt at my shout, and Lamb and Karas gaped up at me. I could only point. The words would not come. Seagrave was frozen, staring into the dark as though hypnotized, red blood coursing down his arm.

The water of the lake had moved; out of the corner of my eye I had seen a sudden, subtle rise that had spanned many yards, except it was not as if something had passed beneath the surface but rather it was a billowing or coursing of the surface itself, as though a giant muscle had suddenly flexed, defying gravity in a way that had been abruptly dizzying. Then the water rolled again, this time from many directions, separate but all charging towards the same object. I could feel a low, deep vibration rumbling in my feet.

"Earthquake!" gasped Karas, backing away in panic. "Earthquake!"

The water of the lake suddenly burst upwards around Seagrave, as though something enormous were breaching, except it was only the water itself, hanging in the air. It pounced upon him like a giant, agile slug and enveloped his undamaged outstretched arm. Then it fell back, dragging him downward.

In a moment Helen Pulver was at his side, her feet splashing in the water. She grabbed his blood-soaked hand and began heaving in the opposite direction, pulling at him with all her weight. It was a strange, ghastly tug-of-war, and at its center was Seagrave, who seemed oddly confused, his eyes wide and staring. He looked at Helen, then at the strange, pinkish-gray mass that had swallowed his arm, then at the others on the shore, and seemed to understand nothing. Then his face transformed into a mask of terror.

"Helen!" I cried. "*Run!*"

It was too late. Fingers of the liquid were already squirming across her ankles, feeling their way like inchworms along her stockings. Just then Mordecai's hand, slick with blood, slipped out of her grasp; she stumbled in the opposite direction and fell headlong into the lake. There was no splash, but only a seasick churning of the fluid around; immediately she tried to extricate herself, but thin, eely tendrils began slipping around her wrists, almost like a caress. "Oh, help, help!" she shouted.

"Helen!" shouted Lamb, and he charged towards her.

More twisting coils of ooze were moving upon her now, writhing and thickening. Each time she tried to stand her feet slipped out from under her and she was pulled back down onto her hands and knees. A tendril as thick as a snake squirmed up her forearm, searching. "Oh no! No no!" she yelled. "It's biting! *Irene, it's biting!*"

In a moment Lamb was there; he attacked the foulness with a fury, tearing the bonds from her skin and kicking blindly at the water around her. The ooze snapped like elastic and dropped back down into the muck, and with a final heave he pulled her to her feet and all but threw her onto the shore. Then he turned to Mordecai.

Twisting in the lampglow that held back the dark, Mordecai Seagrave had been transformed into a freakish statue of horror. The jelly had all but overcome him, as a great undulating blob had somehow lurched up from the surface of the lake and now covered the entire left half of his body.

Strands had even attached themselves to the side of his face, which was stunned and gaping with mute surprise. Heedless, Lamb crashed into the amorphous mass like a charging bull, slashing at it with a knife that he had drawn from his belt, and from my distance I could just make out that the glistening stuff was not quite like a homogenous jelly after all, but rather that there were wriggling insect insides, all basted in a twitching treacly sludge. It recoiled for a moment, but then abruptly surged upwards, towering over Lamb like a wall. Its surface mottled itself with a billion pockmarks that resolved into twitching black holes, orifices like eyes and ragged sucking mouths, and then it fell upon him, a crashing mountain from above. It lifted him into the air, and with a horrible, terrible, ghastly *crack* he was bent backwards at the waist, the crown of his head touching his ankles, eyes staring upwards in shock. Then he was sucked inward and was gone. I heard a last muffled, strangled shriek, and then nothing.

There was silence for a moment, and then screaming came from everywhere at once, and I believe I began firing my gun. The last sight I saw before I bolted was Mordecai's face and wounded arm descending into the surface of the lake, the mass around him quivering and surging as though feasting. He was screaming nonsensical words as he sank, a language unknown—*"Fah tai'iginen! Kewah! Mortoru kalaia iesain!"* Then the pinkish-gray fluid poured into his mouth and there were only two staring eyes, until they too were gone.

By this time I too was on the beach, the lantern in my hand. "Out, out, out!" I screamed. Karas had managed to grab the wrist of the dazed, wild-eyed Pulver, I grabbed Karas's wrist, and together we ran as one for the wall of stone. At my feet I could see with growing horror that rivulets of oily liquid were somehow flowing upwards through the sand. Fear shot through me. "Faster faster faster!" I bellowed, barely knowing myself, barely knowing where I was. Up the punishing slope we climbed, hand over hand, the sharp, shining stones cutting our knees and elbows. Helen Pulver's eyes were wide and glassy, like a madwoman, and she seemed to struggle upwards without knowing what she was about. She was making a hysterical, horrifying sound, halfway between a shriek and a whimper. Once, near the summit, I dared to turn the lantern to the rear and look back, and I could see fingers of liquid creeping over the fissures in the rocks below us, and in fact *the whole surface of the lake* had surged out of its basin and was slowly flowing up the slope in a giant mass, as if it were one great organism, bulbous and squirming, the entire face of it split by tiny, writhing holes. I never looked behind me again. When we reached the promontory of the great open cavern I gripped one of Helen's arms and Karas grabbed the other and we ran. I could see now that Helen had been smeared with mucous from the thing, and her eyes were rolling and wild. We all but dragged her through the doorway and up the sloping passage, and in our haste she would occasionally bounce off the stone walls like a broken kite. The floor trembled beneath our feet and we heard a single tearing word in the air, a cry unknown, archaic and evil. We all but collided with the dead end of a blank wall, the fear rocketing upward through my body like a geyser, until I spied the low doorway to the room with the grinning stone face. We scuttled through, panting. Karas and I let go of our charge and bolted for our packs while Helen stood in the center of the room and howled and clawed at the slime

The Satanic Bridegroom

on her face. The trickling noise was strangely louder now, and it sounded as though the mask of the god were laughing deep with menace. We grabbed Helen again and bolted upwards, through the winding passages with the horrible reliefs, past the ghastly crack in the wall at which I dared not glance, and then finally through the distant ragged hole we saw the faint blue glow of the British Honduras sky.

Karas and I all but fell down the hill, panting; the freshness of the air was a shock, and it burned my lungs like fire. A fine rain pelted at us as cold as metal, and I felt a maelstrom's dizziness that sent every part of my body spinning, my hands and legs seeming to float away from where they were joined in a terrifying corkscrew rush. I looked up from the ground to see Helen once again trying to scrape the foulness from her body, her face wild and unreachable. As we watched, she tore off her blouse, and then her shoes and trousers, and without any warning she dropped to the ground and began rolling in the mud, all the while making crazed, animal sounds. Irene and I watched in horror as she writhed, her eyes and mouth wide, her feet kicking in frenzy.

My pen pauses. Outside the window of this room the sun beats down upon the jungle, the long night over, the dew blazing upon the leaves, burned by sky. Birdcalls fly and return. The native woman putters below, perhaps kneeling, washing her long black hair, lifting it in great ample handfuls, a harvest of warm enveloping night. The child within her stirs too, perhaps, stretching and kicking and reminding the world that he wants to be born. Everything is new, but I am empty; the terrible story out of me now, I feel as if the pith of me has fallen away, leaving only something hollow and toylike remaining. That void within frightens me; it feels like the finger of Death.

Helen Pulver never came back to her senses. In time we were able to calm her and dress her, and she allowed us to lead her away from the place, but she said nothing, nor even seemed to know our names. At times she was pliable and could be led by the hand like a child, but then at unexpected moments a terror would come over her and she would panic and bolt into the trees. At night we had to tie her down; Irene Karas cried the first time, then she too fell mostly silent, her face as blank as stone.

Of the journey home I remember little, except that it was hard; there was no food beyond what we could scavenge from the trees, and now one of our party had to be led like a sheep. Karas and I barely knew in which direction we headed; we knew only to move forward and nothing else. I remember once stumbling down into a little rocky streambed, bouncing bodily off a gnarled tree and hitting the rocks below; I cut my face and my arms, and the blood ran down into my teeth. Karas picked me up without a word, and despite the grit in my shoes we walked on. Helen became fascinated by the injury and even went so far as to try to touch or poke the wound on my forehead; I had to slap her hands away.

One night I was awoken by Helen Pulver pulling at her bonds; she said nothing, but only whimpered and struggled over and over again until her wrists and ankles were raw. I wept, then, shocked at the change inside me; once I had loved her—yes, I will say it—a kind of love I had not known since I was young, when my mother was alive and hope was still new. Now there was only an urgent repulsion, a repulsion which caused me shame and grief and yet which overrode all, as though I were lying beside a corpse. The woman had gone mad, but it was not the madness that unnerved me, it was instead as though she had been irrevocably stained, and my very bones were revolting against her. I think Karas felt this too and could not endure it; she spent many hours crying, until something inside her broke and she would begin laughing instead, laughing in a way that gave me terrors.

Somehow we found our river crossing, and there on the other side was Beppo and his pipe, scruffy pelts drying on the rocks beside him. He nearly bolted when he saw us, as though he were being attacked by ghosts, and by the time we had crossed the great tree he was speechless in fright. We fell on what little food he had like wolves, Helen too, and then all but collapsed onto the rocks to sleep.

Beppo led us home. I clung to him like a child to a father, or a drowning man to a last bobbing cask, all but weeping with gratitude, until I realized with growing horror that my house and grounds would be an unknown country to me now, as trackless and alien as the bottom of the sea. We returned, and the people I met twisted away like phantoms; I could not read their faces, their words were like the barkings of dogs, and they shunned me like a stranger in the reeds.

Afterword

According to public record, "Irene Karas" completed a graduate degree in comparative zoology in 1925 and subsequently traveled to Papua New Guinea as a researcher attached to a scientific team to catalogue new species. She vanished from her camp in the mountains on October 9th of that year, and despite an extensive search was never seen again. An inquest was undertaken to determine whether there had been an act of foul play or criminal negligence, but it was ruled that the senior members of the team were in no way accountable, for it had appeared that she had left the camp of her own free will.

"Helen Pulver" returned to the United States as an invalid and was immediately institutionalized in a sanitarium, where she remained for the rest of her life. She died from cardiac arrest in 1953, her heart possibly having been weakened by the accidental ingestion of a small quantity of rat poison in 1938.

An attendant—then young, now elderly and under care herself—recalls the woman who was Helen Pulver quite well, and speaks of her with affection. Though severely dislocated from reality and at times panicked or disruptive, she describes Helen as being a kind and gentle soul who made little real trouble and was agreeable about her medication. Her favorite pastime, she recalls, had been the writing and illustrating of children's books, though the books that Helen Pulver produced were not likely to have ever been given to an actual child by anyone in their right mind. They were eerie, grotesque and strange, with great quantities of scribbled black crowding the edges and far corners. The recurring theme was that of a young maid to be married, except that the groom was always unknown, always hidden behind doors or in strange swaths of darkness, or else he would simply be a giant outsized shape, so large that its form spilled beyond the limits of the colored paper page and could not be apprehended. In a horse-drawn carriage she would come, with white gown and bouquet, the sun shining through a bower or upon some lonely blonde meadow lined with elves. A jolly, inhuman celebrant with round florid cheeks and crickets' legs for arms would perform the service, joining the two, the small, childlike woman with the massive black shape. As clouds rolled in from the north, the pair made their vows, their final pact, and the rabbits and faeries fled, the summer garden now a blasted plain. The final page was the same every time—maddeningly, horribly so—always drawn in a fast, ragged hand, as though it had forced its way from her mind, that last image only the woman's face, the veil torn in two from top to bottom, her eyes freakish and wide, her mouth nothing but a giant, screaming O.

CPSIA information can be obtained at www.ICGtesting.com
Printed in the USA
LVOW06s0719250814

400704LV00002B/77/P